Praise for THE ORPHAN ARMY

"Fast, frightful, and fantastic—a faerie story like no other."
—Dan Abnett, writer of the *Guardians of the Galaxy* comic for Marvel

"There's a surprise on every page and
full-throttle action from beginning to end."
—D.J. MacHale, *New York Times* bestselling
author of the Pendragon series and the SYLO Chronicles

"A sequel can't come too soon for readers who will be eager
to see what this unlikely team can accomplish."
—*BCCB*

"The secret to becoming a hero is hidden
between the pages of this unforgettable adventure."
—Kami Garcia, #1 *New York Times* bestselling coauthor of *Beautiful Creatures*

"An electrifying thriller that builds to a climax
as gripping as it is thoughtful and satisfying."
—A. J. Hartley, *New York Times* bestselling author
of the Darwen Arkwright series and *Steeplejack*

"Jonathan Maberry is a magician, a writer of
great talent and versatility. From spooky fun to
cinematic action to heartfelt character, he can do it a
—Christopher Golden, *New York Times* bestselling author
of *Snowblind* and coauthor of *Cemetery Girl*

"The Nightsiders is heart-pounding action and a well-paced
thriller from one of the masters of sci-fi and fantasy!"
—Melissa de la Cruz, #1 bestselling author of
The Isle of the Lost: A Descendants Novel

"Only one word sums up this barrier-breaking, multi-faceted book in its entirety: 'fantastic.'"
—Steve Hockensmith, coauthor of *Nick and Tesla's High-Voltage Danger Lab* and *Pride and Prejudice and Zombies: Dawn of the Dreadfuls*

"The Nightsiders will terrify, thrill, and delight with the frantic turn of every page."
—Thomas E. Sniegoski, *New York Times* bestselling author of the Fallen series and *Stupid, Stupid Rat-Tails*

"Nightsiders is a thrilling mashup of sci-fi, adventure, and supernatural fantasy with a heart. Nothing less than the survival of mankind is at stake, and the most powerful weapon against a nightmare is a dream."
—Tonya Hurley, *New York Times* bestselling author of the ghostgirl series and the Blessed trilogy

"Nightsiders is a smart, action-packed adventure, perfect for anyone who has ever wanted to fight alongside magical monsters against alien invaders. And really, who hasn't wanted to do that?"
—Kendare Blake, author of *Anna Dressed in Blood*

"Jonathan Maberry is a master of fast, scary, and awesome. *The Orphan Army* will submerge you in its world, and you won't want to come up for air."
—Adam Gidwitz, bestselling author of the A Tale Dark and Grimm series and *Star Wars: The Empire Strikes Back So You Want To Be A Jedi?*

The Orphan Army

THE NIGHTSIDERS

BOOK 1

JONATHAN MABERRY

Simon & Schuster Books for Young Readers

New York   London   Toronto   Sydney   New Delhi

SIMON & SCHUSTER BOOKS FOR YOUNG READERS
An imprint of Simon & Schuster Children's Publishing Division
1230 Avenue of the Americas, New York, New York 10020
This book is a work of fiction. Any references to historical events, real people,
or real places are used fictitiously. Other names, characters, places, and events
are products of the author's imagination, and any resemblance to actual
events or places or persons, living or dead, is entirely coincidental.
Text copyright © 2015 by Jonathan Maberry
Cover illustration copyright © 2016 by Owen Freeman
All rights reserved, including the right of reproduction
in whole or in part in any form.
SIMON & SCHUSTER BOOKS FOR YOUNG READERS
is a trademark of Simon & Schuster, Inc.
For information about special discounts for bulk purchases, please contact
Simon & Schuster Special Sales at 1-866-506-1949
or business@simonandschuster.com.
The Simon & Schuster Speakers Bureau can bring authors to
your live event. For more information or to book an event, contact
the Simon & Schuster Speakers Bureau at 1-866-248-3049 or visit
our website at www.simonspeakers.com.
Also available in a Simon & Schuster Books for Young Readers hardcover edition
Interior design by Laurent Linn
Cover design by Krista Vossen
The text for this book was set in Minister.
Manufactured in the United States of America
0916 OFF
2 4 6 8 10 9 7 5 3
The Library of Congress has cataloged the hardcover edition as follows:
Maberry, Jonathan.
The orphan army / Jonathan Maberry.
pages cm. — (The Nightsiders ; [1])
Summary: In the future, bug-like aliens are taking over Earth and young Milo
Silk learns through dreams and strange encounters that there are other, ancient
monsters on the planet that are also threatened by the aliens, and that he may be
the hero destined to lead his friends in saving the universe.
ISBN 978-1-4814-1575-0 (hardcover) — ISBN 978-1-4814-1576-7 (pbk) —
ISBN 978-1-4814-1577-4 (eBook)
[1. Science fiction. 2. Supernatural—Fiction. 3. Monsters—Fiction.
4. Extraterrestrial beings—Fiction. 5. Heroes—Fiction. 6. Magic—Fiction.]
I. Title.
PZ7.M11164Orp 2015
[Fic]—dc23
2014014576

To the memory of two great writers who, long ago,
took the time to offer advice and encouragement
to a thirteen-year-old aspiring writer:
Ray Bradbury and Richard Matheson.
They were the mechanics of dreams, the architects
of the impossible.
Happy journeys through the limitless forever.

And, as always, to Sara Jo.

FROM MILO'S DREAM DIARY

I had another dream about the witch last night.

The Witch of the World.

I still don't know what that means.

In the dream the Bugs were looking for something, and they were knocking down trees and breaking open mountains to find it.

We were all running from them.

The shocktroopers were dropping from the landing ships and firing their pulse rifles at us. They're taller than most people—seven feet or more. Like praying mantises. Worse than that. Huge and ugly, with long legs and two sets of arms. They jumped down to the ground, ready to kill. Some stood on two legs and fired four pulse guns; others ran on four legs, as fast as dogs, and dragged people down.

I saw Shark get hit. And Lizabeth and a few of the other kids.

My mom and dad were there too. Running from the
Bugs.

I couldn't see Dad's face, though. I never see his face
anymore in the dreams.

I wish I could.

The Witch of the World kept whispering to me, and I
could hear her even though it was really loud with
the explosions.

She does that. Whispers.

I never see her.

I only hear her voice in my head.

She said something really weird, too. After the Bugs
attacked the camp and we were all running from
the fires, she said that I needed to fight back.

I told her that was stupid. I'm a kid. I can't even win
at grunt-and-grapple games in gym class.

She said that wasn't what she meant. She said that I
needed to find a weapon.

I told her that I had a weapon. My slingshot.

She laughed at me. She said that's not what she meant.

She said, "A hero does not need those kinds of
weapons. A hero is a weapon."

I told her that I didn't want to be a hero. I couldn't be
a hero. I'm just a kid.

She said, "Only a fool asks to be a hero. A real hero

rises when all others fall. Whether he wants to or not."

Before I could ask her what she meant, there was a big explosion and I woke up. For a while I couldn't tell if the explosion was in the dream or not.

I didn't get back to sleep.

Part
One

Six Years from Next Monday . . .

"We could never learn to be brave and patient,
if there were only joy in the world."
—HELEN KELLER

Chapter 1

Milo Silk wasn't afraid of the monsters under his bed.

He didn't have a bed for monsters to hide under.

Milo had a sleeping bag, and that was usually spread out on rocky ground up on Mount Driskill or on moist, buggy dirt in the swamplands along the Louisiana bayou. Sometimes he slept in a net hammock that dangled between a fuel truck and a tank with a crooked cannon.

Besides, all of the monsters were way above him in their spaceships.

It was a Tuesday when everything went bad.

Not that things weren't bad to begin with. At least that's what all of the adults always said. Big old bad world.

But every single one of them wanted things to be the way they were before bad became worse.

Milo and his friends learned about it in school. And school was a patch of ground or a fallen log or a muddy beach under a camouflaged canopy. In the bad *old* days, there were schools with desks and chairs. Now school was wherever the teacher said school was.

All because of the aliens.

All because of the Swarm that had come down like locusts from the stars.

They came in a fleet of hive ships, each one many miles long and made from a thousand kinds of scrap metal. The plates did not look bolted together but instead looked fused, or melted. Or grown. As if they had been chewed into metallic pulp and then spat out to be woven into a spaceship, the way a wasp builds a nest from chewed plant matter. Each vast machine even looked like an insect nest. They filled the skies and blotted out the sun. Impossibly old, still cold from their journey between the stars. Thoroughly ugly, completely alien and utterly dangerous.

The Dissosterin destroyed most of Earth's major cities in their first assault, and with every passing day, they were ruining more of the planet and wiping out more people. So, sure, things were already way over in the "bad" category. Horrible bad. Scary bad. But in a weird way Milo didn't really understand how bad it was. He knew that he didn't know. It was something that was happening to other people somewhere else. He never saw a burning city. He never saw a dead person.

He just heard about that sort of stuff. He once saw a massive hive ship in the far distance, hovering like a storm cloud over New Orleans. A few times he saw Bug drop-ships pass overhead, or the smaller hunter-killer machines buzzing at treetop level. Small robotic insects that came in a hundred frightening shapes. All of them deadly. But none of them were ever close enough for him to get a good look. Or for the Bugs to see him.

The ships he did see were all wrecks. Drop-ships and transports, a couple of the big mining ships that had been brought down by portable rocket launchers.

He saw them much closer in his dreams, though. Each night he dreamed of the hunter-killers coming in swarms.

He dreamed of the small, fast drop-ships deploying the Dissosterin shocktroopers. Many times he would come awake gasping and terrified from a dream to freeze there, clutching his thin blanket, listening for the sounds of war. Or he'd awake in the morning after a long, bad night and be afraid to open his eyes for fear of seeing the camp in smoking ruins and all his friends lying dead.

But those were only dreams. They weren't real.

In many ways, the whole war was so far away from him that it wasn't totally real.

Until that Tuesday.

This is the story of what happened on a very bad Tuesday.

Chapter 4

And what happened after.

The tree Milo hid behind was called devil's walkingstick. All thorns and spikes, but it offered good cover. There was a whole row of them growing wild along the muddy slope leading up from the bayou. Most of them were hidden in the mists that moved like armies of ghosts across the flat, still swamp waters.

Milo had his slingshot out, a sharp stone fitted into the leather pad. Eyes open, ears alert, breath almost still in his chest.

On the other side of the row, somewhere in the dense swampy woods, something moved. Not the squadrons of mosquitoes that filled the air day and night. Not the legions of ants that crawled over everything.

Something else.

Something he was positive shouldn't be here.

Milo was sure it wasn't anyone from his training pod. The other kids were following different trails, each trying to find what he'd already found. So, it wasn't them.

That left a lot of things it could be.

Most of them were dangerous.

Not all of them were from Earth.

That was the problem with the world. That was life since the invasion. It was life since the hive ships arrived.

He crouched there. Still and quiet, as he'd been taught. Listening to the forest. Watching the movement of each mossy branch, each stalk of marsh grass, each leaf. Letting the natural world whisper to him so that he could hear the sounds of what was unnatural.

The shadow moved.

Too far away to see it clearly beyond the tendrils of Spanish moss that hung from the trees. Too deep inside the shadowy woods to tell anything about it. He licked his lips. The slingshot was good for target practice, and he could take down a squirrel or a rabbit for the stewpot, but whatever was out there looked bigger. There were still a few black bears left in the woods here along Bayou Teche. A rare eastern cougar, too. And some of the older scouts said they'd seen coyotes. A slingshot was no good at all for anything that big.

He had some better stuff in his pockets. Flash-bang poppers, cutwires, and one ultrasonic screecher, but if he used them and it turned out to be a lost deer or a confused raccoon, he'd be doing kitchen duty until he was a hundred years old. Tech was rare these days, and it was never—*ever*—to be used except in real emergencies.

"Come on . . . ," he murmured, his voice so quiet it made no real sound. A dozen yards away, bream popped the surface of the bayou, eating water skaters and luckless flies. Cicadas kept up a continuous buzz in the trees. A great egret stalked through the shallows, lifting its stick-thin legs to place each step with great delicacy.

Milo edged along the row of thorny plants, trying to get a better look.

There was a clearing in the woods that hadn't been there the last time Milo's pod had scouted this part of the wetlands. On the northeast side of the clearing stood the shattered remains of a small stand of holly trees. Only uneven stumps still stood upright. The rest of the trees had been destroyed and partially burned. Beyond the stumps Milo could see the impact zone. It was about three hundred feet across at its widest and roughly circular. Every growing thing inside had been destroyed. The stink of ash filled the moist morning air.

Milo had been to enough crash sites to be able to read the scene. Something had come in low and hot—maybe a helicopter from the Earth Alliance, or more likely a Bug drop-ship. It had broken up in the air and the pieces had torn through the trees along the bayou. Most of them apparently missed the water, clipped the small grove of hollies, then crashed. None of the pieces he could see looked very large. Smaller than an oil drum. Which meant that the machine was blown to pieces. It must have started out pretty big, though, because there was a lot of debris and a lot of damage to the forest.

Like all of the kids in his pod, Milo had studied photos, drawings, and models of dozens of different kinds of craft. He knew all of the EA stuff backward and forward and could sketch from memory most of the enemy ships. The big city-sized hive ships, the skyscraper-tall harvesters, and the mobile diggers that walked across the face of the world on titanic metal legs, the smaller manned scout and pursuit ships, and all of the robotic hunter-killer drones.

The most common were the drop-ships. These were thirty feet across, round, shaped like hubcaps, with a spherical pilot's compartment in the center. All along the curved edges were smaller platforms on which the tall, gangly Dissosterin shocktroopers stood. The 'troopers could either detach their mini-platforms from the drop-ship and come down under power, or they could attach steel lines and rappel down. These ships were fast and hard to hit, but they weren't heavily armed, and a well-aimed shoulder-mounted rocket launcher could destroy one.

Milo thought that the debris in this field might be one of those. That was good news because the EA technicians had been trying to build a drop-ship from parts scavenged from crashes all over the south. Milo had overheard his mom talking about it a couple of times. The drop-ships were incredibly easy to operate, and the lowest-level Bug drones could fly them. A human pilot who was helping rebuild one said that a five-year-old kid could fly one.

The next stage of that project was sketchier, but Milo's

friend Shark said he heard some of the soldiers talking about guys volunteering to crew the drop-ship and pilot it up to the hive ship along with a cargo of ten tons of high explosives.

The plan was maybe five good scavenge jobs away from being workable, which meant that every crash was a potential step toward hitting the Bugs back like they'd never been hit before.

Milo also knew that the EA scientists wanted to get their hands on a living Bug—whether a drone or a shock-trooper. So far they hadn't been able to, and from the mangled state of this wreckage, Milo couldn't believe that anyone or anything had survived.

And yet . . .

The whatever-it-was in the forest moved again. Eighty feet away, behind a wall of wild rhododendron that was tangled up with bright orange trumpet creepers. Milo still couldn't see it. Not really. Just a hint of something dark and big. Definitely big. Much bigger than a raccoon. Maybe as big as a deer.

The color troubled him. Was it a downed pilot in a camouflaged flight suit? Or one of the seven-foot-tall four-armed alien shocktroopers in their distinctive black-green Dissosterin shell armor?

Or something worse?

A *Stinger*, maybe. Or one of the other mutants the aliens were breeding in their hive ships.

Just thinking about the possibility of it being a Stinger made Milo's mouth go completely dry. The stone he'd fitted into his slingshot felt ridiculously small and stupid. If that *was* a Stinger, the stone would do about as much damage as blowing a kiss.

Stingers were monster dogs bred by the Dissosterin. Once upon a time they had been ordinary mastiffs and wolfhounds. Then the aliens did something to them. The camp science teacher, Mr. Rawlins, called it "transgenic manipulation," which he explained meant that the dogs were altered at the genetic level. Parts of different kinds of animals were combined through weird science. The Stingers had the massive bulk of a two-hundred-pound canine, but their bodies were covered with tough insect armor. Worst of all, they had enormous scorpion tails arching over their backs.

Milo had never seen one, but he'd seen pictures, and the creatures in those pictures came stalking through Milo's nightmares. He knew kids who had lost parents, aunts, and uncles to Stingers.

He licked his dry lips and studied the crash site. As he saw it, the scene in the burned clearing said everything that ever needed to be said about the world. Something came from the skies and either broke or burned everything that was beautiful and thriving. Leaving ash and wreckage.

And *things*.

Sweat trickled down the side of his face.

This was their second year in swamp country. Last year it had been only a little above the normal midfifties to low sixties of March; but this year the swamp was hot and so humid you could almost swim in the air. Ever since the Bugs arrived and began their strip mining, the whole planet had been getting hotter.

Wait. Something moved.

There was a *crack* as a heavy foot stepped down on a branch.

It was a small sound, but everything in the woods instantly froze. Birds and bugs and Milo Silk all held their breath.

There was another soft, furtive sound.

Whatever was out there was sneaking through the woods. And it was coming straight for him.

Chapter 6

Milo raised the slingshot, ready to fire.

As he did, the day seemed to change around him. There had been patches of heavy storm clouds in the sky all morning, and now they moved to cover the sun. The brightness of morning was instantly transformed into a twilight gloom. Green and yellow turned to purple and gray. Everything clear became hazy and unreal. Details became instantly vague and elusive.

Milo peered into these new shadows, trying to make shapes out of the shapeless walls that had been shrubs and flowers moments ago. The spaces between and beneath the bushes were almost totally black.

He narrowed his eyes and peered into the darkness. The trick to finding Dissosterin in any low-light situation was to look for a faint green glow. Each of them had a small green jewel embedded in their chests. These "lifelights" were somehow tied to the actual life force of the Bugs and their mutant creations. Soldiers in camp spent so much time working on their marksmanship because if you blew out the lifelight, you stopped a Bug.

Shocktrooper, Stinger, or one of their robot hunter-killer devices—they all had the same lifelights.

Milo searched for even a hint of that ghostly emerald glow, but he didn't see anything like that.

However, as he peered into the darkness . . . something peered back at him.

Milo's heart froze in his chest.

He blinked, trying to get a better look.

There it was.

Eyes.

Two large eyes stared at him from the shadows beneath the rhododendron.

Strange eyes. A blue that was almost silver. His friend Lizabeth had light blue eyes that the adults called arctic blue, and for a moment, Milo thought that he was seeing his friend. She was out here too, somewhere in these woods along with the rest of their school pod. Twelve kids and a team leader spread over a few square miles of terrain.

The eyes stared at him.

He almost fired.

He did not.

Instead he lowered the slingshot and eased the tension on the band. Not entirely, but mostly.

Those eyes . . .

They seemed like girl eyes to him—though he had no idea why he thought that. It was a feeling. Girl eyes the color of a winter moon.

"Lizabeth . . . ?"

Even as he spoke her name, Milo knew it wasn't her. Pale as her eyes were, these were paler still.

And . . . different.

Strange.

"Who's there?" he asked.

The eyes stared at him, unmoving, unblinking. They were low, down at waist level, like someone crouching to hide.

Or . . . a dog?

Was that all this was? A dog?

If so, it was a stray. There were a couple dozen dogs back in camp and some wild strays that followed every time camp was moved to a new location, but Milo knew them all. None of them had eyes like this. And even Captain Allen's old husky had eyes of a different color—one brown and one a darker blue.

Was this a wild dog or a runaway?

It wasn't a Stinger; he knew that much for sure. The mutant scorpion dogs all had red eyes. Demon eyes, according to Lizabeth.

"It's okay," said Milo, rising from cover and taking a tentative half step. "It's okay, girl. . . ."

The dog—if it was a dog—did not come out of the shadows.

Milo shifted the slingshot to one hand and used the other to fish in his jeans pocket for a piece of jerky. He always carried a few pieces to chew on. Then he carefully eased between two of the devil's walkingstick trees and moved cautiously to the edge of the clearing. He held the jerky out as he took another careful step. And another.

The eyes watched him with what appeared to be great interest, but the dog didn't come out of the shadows.

"Here, girl. . . . Come on, girl. . . . Good girl . . . ," Milo soothed. "It's okay. . . ."

The look in those eyes was not openly hostile. He'd seen how a dog looks when it's ready to pounce. This wasn't like that at all. These eyes were intelligent, but they were not at all friendly.

No sir.

Even so, Milo took another step. The animal fascinated him. If it was a stray, then maybe he could tame it and bring it back to camp. His best friend, Shark, had a dog, a Jack Russell. Milo's dog had died during the invasion, back when he was six. He hadn't had any pet since then, and five years is a long time not to have something to love and cuddle and play with.

The eyes blinked once, very slowly.

Milo paused. "It's okay. . . . I won't hurt you."

He took another step.

The eyes blinked once more, but this time they did not open. Milo stopped and stared as hard as he could into the darkness, trying to make out the dog shape.

The eyes did not open again.

After a few more seconds, Milo realized that the dog must have turned away during that second blink.

He moved over to the spot, but when he got there, the shadows were empty. He unclipped his rechargeable flashlight and shone the light over the ground.

Nothing.

Not even paw prints.

The soft ground was completely unmarked. He pressed his fingers lightly against the dirt and withdrew them. They left a very clear mark.

So, why hadn't the dog?

"Weird," Milo said to the gloom, and he stood there wondering if he'd seen what he thought he'd seen. A dog with eyes that big would have to be pretty large. The size of a shepherd, or bigger. And yet it hadn't left a single print.

He tucked the slingshot into his belt and swept the flashlight beam slowly around the burned clearing. From that angle, he could see inside the grove of shattered holly trees. As he steadied the light, he realized that the trees were not there by accident. There were plenty of holly trees in swamp country, but these weren't growing in a random pattern. They'd clearly been planted to hide something, and now that something was revealed.

It was a mound of stones. Orderly and tall. Four sloping sides with a wide base and a narrow top that probably stood at least twelve or thirteen feet high. Or they had before the crashing vehicle clipped off the top. Now the top few feet of the structure lay in a sprawl of cracked and burned stones.

Milo stared at it in wonder. It was something so odd, so out of place that it caught him totally off guard.

The ruined structure was . . . a *pyramid*.

Stuck into the cracks between the stones were flowers—all withered now from the heat of the crash—sprigs of herbs, small pieces of old jewelry, and tiny carvings of animals made from various kinds of stone and crystal. There were wolves and bears, owls and snakes. And some animals Milo couldn't identify. Strange things that looked like centaurs and mermaids and gargoyles.

All of it was covered in a thin layer of soot.

"So weird," Milo said again. But it was more than that. Looking at the pyramid touched some feelings that were buried so deeply in his head that he couldn't identify them, couldn't begin to catalog them. They raised goose bumps all up and down his arms. The hair on the back of his neck stood up.

Get out of here, he thought, giving himself an order, knowing that flight was the best thing. Their training protocols for any situation offering even the possibility of danger was simple: *Run, run, run.*

Yet he lingered, the flashlight playing over the remains of the pyramid.

When he finally switched off the beam, the darkness

rushed back to fill all of the lighted places. In that darkness, the pyramid became nearly invisible.

It doesn't want to be seen.

The thought came into his head from left field, and Milo grunted aloud at the strangeness of it.

He thought about the dog eyes—if it was a dog.

They had watched him from right here, right beside this pyramid.

The storm clouds, already dark, thickened to blackness.

Milo began to doubt that he'd seen the dog. There had been no footprints after all. He tried to tell himself that he'd imagined it. That he hadn't seen any weird eyes. That what he saw wasn't what he thought. Conflicting and confusing suggestions warred with his memories. And in his instincts.

He *had* seen something.

The dark, however, had taken it away and left no trace.

The dark does that. Milo knew that for sure.

And Milo didn't like the dark.

It was dark that night when Dad went missing.

The dark scared Milo.

A lot.

It was too easy to lose things in the dark.

Chapter 7

The eyes and the shadow that owned them were gone. That's what Milo thought. The forest felt somehow different. Still strange, but not as threatening. It didn't have the kind of vibe he imagined would be there if one of the Bugs were here. Or one of their mutant creatures.

"You read too many crazy books," he told himself, then repeated what his teachers told him all the time. "Do your job. Investigate, locate, identify, scavenge."

That was the key to survival in this broken world. Find the tech—ours or theirs—and bring it back, so the soldiers and scientists could repair it or adapt it to help in the war.

Milo crouched by the edge of the crash site and studied the debris. That was another thing he'd been taught: Observe first, touch second.

He wondered what it would be like to scavenge a hive ship. That would be fascinating, and there would probably be a lot of useful tech aboard. There were seven of them around the world.

Thunder rumbled far to the east.

At least Milo hoped it was thunder.

In his dreams—and Milo dreamed too much and too vividly—that sound was always a bad thing. It was never a coming storm. Not in any natural sense. In his dreams the rumble was low and mean and heavy, and it brought with it a lumbering hive ship. The ship would stop above the camp and hang in the sky like a weapon that refused to fall but instead remained poised to strike. Then it would release the thousands of hunter-killer drones that clung to its keel, and when they had done their damage, then the shocktroopers would come down on the saucer-shaped drop-ships, firing weapons with each of their four segmented arms.

Those were not nice dreams.

Milo hated his dreams.

Mostly.

He'd seen a crash site in the dream he'd had last night. It was why he'd veered off from his pod and come this way. At first he was delighted to be the one to find the wreck. Now, as the thunder rumbled behind the trees, he wasn't so sure.

But now he saw flashes of lightning far above the darkness. They veined the clouds with red.

It was only a storm.

Rain and wind, but not here. Far away.

He relaxed by one micro degree.

Then he heard a sound behind him.

No, that wasn't right. It was more of a *feeling* that there was something behind him. He paused, because in moments like that it's hard to know whether you should whip around to confront whatever's there, or turn slowly so as not to provoke something that's just idling.

The woods were too creepy and he was too scared, so he leaped to one side, twisted around in midair, and landed in a crouch with his slingshot raised and his mouth opened to yell out for help.

Milo froze right where he was. In that position.

There was no lurking Stinger there ready to kill him.

Nor was there a black bear, an eastern cougar, or even an old swamp alligator.

No, the thing that stood there in the woods behind him . . .

. . . was a girl.

Chapter 8

The girl was a stranger.

And she was strange.

Small, slim, about his age. Eleven. Maybe twelve. With lots of long pale hair that looked almost gray. Or silver. The ends of her hair danced as if there were a breeze that blew past her but went around Milo.

She stood in a slanting shaft of sunlight that cut through the thickening clouds. The girl wore a simple cotton dress without pattern or fancy stitchery, but it didn't look homemade. It looked old, like some of the faded linen Milo had seen in houses his pod had scavenged. Antique cloth, edged with milky white ribbon. Around her waist she wore a simple brown belt of braided leather set with a plain, square wooden buckle. Her legs and feet were bare. Around her neck she wore a chain of copper links that supported a black onyx pendant inlaid with a crescent moon made from carved bone.

Milo took in these details, cataloging them the way all scavengers are taught. See everything, observe it, store it.

However, the thing that riveted Milo and kept him standing there, arm raised, mouth open, was her eyes.

They were girl eyes in a girl face, but they were the exact pale arctic color of the animal eyes he'd seen staring at him from the shadows.

Exactly the same.

Which he knew was impossible.

That hadn't been a girl back there a few minutes ago. No way on earth.

And yet this girl's eyes were the same color, and they studied him with the same frosty intensity that bordered on hostility.

Milo realized that his mouth was still hanging open. He closed it, swallowed, then said, "Hey . . . are you okay? I mean, are you lost?"

The girl looked at him but said nothing. They stood twenty feet apart. A damp breeze blew flower petals and torn pieces of leaves between them.

"What's your name?" asked Milo. "Where are you from?"

Those eyes seemed to drill right through him. It was not the friendliest of expressions.

"Look," said Milo, "I won't hurt you. I—"

"You, boy . . . ," she said. "You shouldn't be here."

Her voice was as strange as her eyes. Soft, with a touch of bayou country French accent. Refined and remote.

"Who are you?" he asked.

Her eyes narrowed quickly into suspicious slits. "And what would you do with my name, boy? Would you conjure with it?"

She had a girl's voice but she spoke like an adult.

Even her inflection seemed older than her years. Milo had encountered something like that once before, with a kid who had been traveling with a pack of refugees who were all adults. The kid hadn't been around anyone his own age since the invasion, and because times were so hard, he'd never had the chance to act his age.

"I have no idea what that means," said Milo, half smiling.

His smile was not returned. Instead the girl lifted her chin and looked down her nose at him.

"Then tell me *your* name, boy," she demanded.

"First, stop calling me 'boy.' My name's Milo. Milo Silk. I'm with the Third Louisiana Volunteers. My mom's the commanding officer and—"

"You're stupid to say that much."

"I . . . um . . . why?"

She looked at him as if he really was stupid. "Because the more people know about you, the more power they have. Everyone knows that."

"I don't."

"That's why I said you were stupid, boy."

Being called "boy" was wearing thin on him even with the strangeness of the encounter. The way the girl spoke, the straight way she stood with her head high and chin raised, it was like she thought he was a spitty place on the ground. Like he was not only younger—which he wasn't—but somehow "less" than she was.

"Not really sure how that works," he said, his smile

totally forced now. "The Bugs can't understand English. Actually, they can't understand any Earth language." He paused but couldn't help adding, "Everyone knows *that*."

She glared at him. "Of course I know that."

"So," he said, "you're not going to tell me your name?"

Instead of answering that, she snapped, "You're not supposed to be here. This place isn't for you."

"I know that," he said, and his words seemed to surprise both of them. With a jolt, he realized that he *did* know it. There was nothing about this place that felt welcoming to him. No, that wasn't quite right, and Milo searched his feelings to put a better definition on it. This place wasn't *for* him. It was meant for . . .

For what? For whom?

He had no answer for those questions.

The girl seemed surprised by his response. She had begun to say something and stopped, lips parted, a frown line between her brows. After a moment, she said, "Well, good, then."

She seemed to be expecting him to leave. *Fat chance*, he thought. If she was part of some rogue group of scavengers, then Milo didn't want to lose this crash site. No way. Besides, as annoying and strange as the girl was, he felt bad for her. If she really was with a rogue group, then they would be living very rough. Unless you traveled with a large group that had doctors, teachers, storytellers, and the rest, it was hard to ever be happy. Being happy was one of the things that kept the human race alive despite the hardships and loss. His mom had told him that once, and it stuck in Milo's mind. He and his friends had a lot of schoolwork—in the field and sit-down—and more than they wanted as far as chores went, but there was always time for playing, hanging out, doing normal kid stuff. Or, as normal as stuff was since the invasion.

This girl, though, didn't look like she ever spent a summer afternoon playing make-the-rules-up-as-you-go goofball, or plotting evil master plans for breaking into the food cart to steal some pies, or catching frogs among the reeds down on the riverbank.

"I didn't know this place was even here," he said. "My pod is out on a scavenger hunt. We were told there was a wreck and we came to find it."

"Pod?" she asked, clearly confused. "Were you grown from a seed, boy? Are you an elemental?"

"Um . . . no?" he said, and mentally added *"weirdo."* "I'm talking about my training pod. You know, twelve kids and a pod-leader? That's how everyone does it."

She shook her head. "You don't make any sense."

"Neither do you."

She looked him up and down. "Is that your aspect?"

"My what?"

"Never mind."

"You know, you don't make much sense, either. People ever tell you that?"

When she didn't answer, Milo pointed to the blackened clearing where the wreckage lay amid tangles of withered grass. "Did you see it come down?"

She didn't answer. Instead she wrapped her arms around her chest as if there were a cold wind.

"Did you—?" Milo pressed.

"You should not be here," she said, repeating her earlier comment but this time spacing her words out in a clear warning.

"I know. We already agreed on that. Why do you keep saying it?"

She took a couple steps to the left, moving toward the very edge of the debris field to where the broken pyramid stood. At first her eyes seemed dreamy and distant and there was the smallest hint of a smile on her lips. Like someone about to see an old friend. Milo turned with her, and he saw the exact moment when she spotted the pyramid.

She froze as if she'd hit a wall. Her eyes flared so wide he could see the whites all around the irises. Her pale skin went dead white, and a small cry burst from her throat.

"Oh no . . . ," she breathed. "Spirits of Night . . . how? *Noooo!*"

"That?" Milo pointed. "That wasn't me. It was like that when I got here. I swear."

Tears filled the girl's eyes and began pouring down her cheeks as the first heavy sobs broke in her chest.

"What is it?" asked Milo, taking a tentative step toward her. "Are you all right?"

The girl wheeled on him, eyes blazing with sudden heat, lips pulling back from her white teeth. Her hands came up, fingers curled like claws. For a moment Milo was certain she was going to attack him.

"What . . . have . . . you . . . *done*?" she snarled, and in that moment, she did not sound like a girl. Or even a girl trying to talk like an adult.

For just a moment her voice was much lower. Rougher. Infinitely stranger.

Milo took several stumbling backward steps, all the way to the edge of the woods, ready to turn and flee. He was immediately and completely terrified.

Of a girl?

Yes.

Of this girl.

"I didn't do anything," he protested, holding his hands up, palms out. "Believe me, I didn't do anything."

The girl continued to glare at him. Then she whirled and rushed to the pyramid, brushing the stones with her fingertips, searching it with her eyes, looking at the fallen pieces. Then she screamed.

She screamed so loud the birds leaped from the surrounding trees and fled into the eastern sky.

The girl staggered back from the pyramid.

"It's gone!" she wailed. "Shadows save us all, it's *gone*!"

"What's gone?" asked Milo. He wanted to go over to her but didn't dare. She was visibly trembling, and he was afraid that if he moved at all, she'd spook and bolt.

"The Heart! Sacred Spirits of Night, the *Heart of Darkness* is gone."

"What's that?"

Once more she faced him, teeth bared like an animal, fists balled, eyes burning like molten silver. "What have you *done*?"

The movement was so powerful, so threatening, that Milo stumbled backward and tore the slingshot from his belt.

"I told you," he yelled. "I didn't do—"

"Oakenayl!" she said sharply. "Bind him."

That fast Milo was grabbed from behind.

Powerful hands clamped around his ankles and knees, wrists and elbows, and a thick, bony arm wrapped around his throat and squeezed. The speed and force of the attack was terrifying. He couldn't move, couldn't breathe. He tried to scream, but the arm around his throat squeezed tighter and cut off all breath, all sound.

He felt someone lean close, felt lips as hard and rough as tree bark brush against his ear as a voice spoke in a dangerous whisper. "Try anything, boy, and I'll crush you like a bug."

The voice sounded like a boy's, but the strength of that grip was greater than anything Milo had ever experienced. Even the biggest soldiers in the camp could not be this strong. The breath on his cheek was as cold as dirt and smelled of soil and moss.

The girl hurried over to Milo, eyes blazing, her teeth

still bared. She knotted her fingers in his hair and gave his head a violent shake.

"Where is it?" she snarled in a voice that was no longer that of a little girl. This was a guttural voice that was like the growl of a hungry animal.

Milo's mouth worked, but he could not force a single word out.

"Tell me!" she demanded.

Milo squirmed and tried to kick and elbow whoever was holding him. There had to be more than one person because there was an arm around his throat and hands were pinning his arms and legs. He couldn't punch or kick or use any of the survival skills he'd been taught.

He was totally helpless.

The girl cupped his chin in her other hand, thumbnail pressing into one cheek, fingernails digging into the other so hard his gums hurt. She stood on her toes and bent close so that their faces were less than an inch apart.

"I will eat your heart and leave your bones for the crows," she said.

In a world of horror and monsters, this was the most frightening thing anyone had ever said to him. It was like something out of nightmares. It was the kind of thing a monster would say.

Chapter 9

Milo tried to speak. He really tried. But he could not. He couldn't even breathe. The world began to smear and blur around him. Black flowers of pain seemed to blossom in his eyes as he drifted on the edges of consciousness.

The girl stared into his eyes.

Deep.

So deep.

Into the very center of him.

"Why did you take the Heart of Darkness?" she asked again and again, hammering him with questions and accusations. "Where is it? *How* did you break the enchantments? What did you do with it?"

Then it seemed to occur to her that he was trying to answer but couldn't.

Annoyance flickered on her face. "Oakenayl, let him speak."

The stricture around his throat eased, though only slightly. Milo spat out the stale breath in his lungs and gulped in fresh air.

"Let . . . me . . . go . . . ," he gasped weakly.

"Tell me," repeated the girl. "What did you do to the Heart of Darkness?"

"It wasn't me," insisted Milo. "I didn't take *anything*."

"I can make him talk," whispered Oakenayl. "Let me pull off an arm or two. He'll tell us."

The girl chewed her lip like she was considering it.

Actually considering it.

Milo's knees began to tremble, and if he hadn't been held so firmly he would have collapsed.

"I didn't do it!" he cried. "Whatever it was, I didn't do it. It wasn't me."

"This boy is lying," said Oakenayl. "His kind always lie. It's all they ever do."

"I'm not lying—and stop calling me *boy*! I don't even know what you're talking about. What's this Heart thing? I didn't touch it. I just got here. . . ."

The girl studied his eyes. Her gaze flicked back and forth to the unseen face of Oakenayl.

"He's lying," insisted the brute who held Milo. "Don't let him cast a spell of doubt on you."

"I'm not lying," Milo seethed. "If you don't believe me, check my pockets. I don't have anything of yours. Go on—check."

The girl did check. First she upended his pouch and let all the stones drop to the damp ground. She gasped when his lucky black stone fell out, but after picking it up and peering at it, she growled in annoyance and let it fall. Then she removed everything from Milo's pockets, glanced briefly at them, and dropped each one on the ground. His slingshot, his knife—a Swiss Army knife that had everything from a spork to a pair of wire cutters—his compass, and a first-aid kit. The girl looked at it without interest and let it fall. She dug deeper into his pockets and found various bits of tech; a few pieces of beef jerky; a signal flare; his microtool kit, which he used to dismantle scavenged tech; a plastic photo holder with a picture of his parents and a five-year-old Milo taken a month before the Swarm arrived; and a spool of string.

As she searched, Oakenayl continually and quietly began tightening his hold again. The girl apparently did not notice this, which was clearly what Oakenayl intended. He was slowly choking Milo again, shutting off the air once more.

The girl removed the last item from Milo's pockets—a tiny metal tube in which was a coiled fishing line and hook—tossed it away, and flicked her eyes back to lock on Milo's. He saw expressions come and go on her face. First hatred and intense anger, then growing uncertainty as each item she found proved to be something other than what she expected to find. Then doubt. Finally, the lights in her eyes faded into the dullness of confusion and despair. That was an emotion Milo knew very well. One that he saw in the eyes of refugees when they first came to the EA camp.

One that he saw in the eyes of soldiers who came back from patrol with too many of their comrades missing.

She staggered backward from him as if pushed. Her heel caught on a broken rock and the girl fell. Tears sprang into her eyes and rolled down her flushed cheeks.

"It's not here," she gasped. "Not here . . ."

Her voice trailed off as she dropped the last item.

"Then he's hidden it," said Oakenayl.

"No. There was no time for that. Whoever he is, he did not do this."

"Then he knows who did," insisted her companion. "I will make him tell us."

The powerful arm around Milo's throat tightened even more. The world began turning dark. He managed to force out one strangled wordless croak before Oakenayl cut off the last of his air.

That croak, though, was enough.

The girl suddenly looked at him as if she'd never seen him before. It took several seconds for the blunt shock in her eyes to come into focus with what was happening.

"Oakenayl," she said, waving her hand. "Let the boy go."

"I'll let him go when he tells us where it is."

"It wasn't him. He is not the one we need to kill. Let him go." She was sobbing as she said it.

For a moment the hands and arms restraining Milo tightened, and Milo thought he was really going to die. Right there and then.

"You live this time, boy," whispered Oakenayl. "What a shame."

Then suddenly he was free.

Staggering forward. Unbound and unfettered.

Falling to hands and knees.

Hanging his head like a dog.

Coughing, choking, gagging.

Gulping and gasping in air. Filling his lungs with life. Feeling the blackness recede, seeing the dark flowers fade like sparks.

He was free, but far from safe.

Chapter 10

The girl sniffed back her tears and straightened, regaining some of her composure—or at least pretending to. She wiped her cheeks and took a deep breath, held it, and sighed it out. Milo could see this from where he lay, but he was too hurt and dazed to even look over his shoulder at the people who'd grabbed him.

"Oakenayl," said the girl, "find Mook and Halflight and tell them what's happened. Tell the other orphans, too. Tell them the witch was right."

The witch.

Witch?

The word "witch" seemed to ignite inside Milo's head.

How many times had he dreamed of a witch? The Witch of the World. She'd spoken to him so often in his dreams, and he'd written down every word in his dream diary. Now, hearing this mysterious girl mention a witch made a freak moment even freakier.

The girl looked like she was going to faint. "Tell . . . tell the others that the prophecy was right. The shadows are falling. Go now."

"I can't leave you alone with this boy," insisted Oak-enayl.

"Why? You think I can't handle one human boy?" said the girl, a new sharpness in her voice.

"I didn't mean—"

"Please, go tell the others to search the forest and all up and down the bayou. We need to find who *really* did this. Maybe there's still time."

"I don't like it."

"Please . . . *go!*"

She spoke like a grown-up, but the panic in her voice made her suddenly sound very young. Like a little kid. There was so much fear there that Milo could taste it. Bitter and wrong.

"Go," she said one last time.

There was no answer except a rustling of leaves. This time Milo looked over his shoulder to see who had been holding him. Hating whoever Oakenayl was and whoever was helping him—all those crushing hands and arms.

He stared.

And saw no one. There was nothing there except an oak tree wrapped in vines. No people. No brutes with powerful arms.

His panting mouth formed a soundless "Oh" of surprise.

They were gone.

Gone so fast.

Gone without sound.

He turned back to the girl, who was getting to her feet. Tears still ran from her eyes, and her lips trembled with fear and shock.

"Who—what . . . ?" He wheezed as he sat back on his heels. "What was that . . . all about . . . ? Who *are* you? Who are the orphans? What's going on?"

She angrily wiped at the tears. "The shrine is defiled. The Heart of Darkness has been stolen."

"What the heck is a Heart of Darkness?"

She glared at him with eyes that looked both frightened and a little crazy. It was so intense that it scared Milo. He'd heard lots of stories about crazy people out in the wilderness of what was once America. People driven insane by loss of family or loss of world. Was that what he was seeing? Milo wished Barnaby, the pod-leader, was here. Even though Barnaby was only a few years older, he knew a lot about the world. Especially about refugees and rogues.

"I thought you were a sorcerer," she said in a soft and distant voice, "but you're only a boy. You're only one of *them*."

"Them?" he asked, rubbing his bruised throat. "Them *who*?"

"You're probably happy the Heart is missing, aren't you?" she continued as if he hadn't spoken. "Now your kind can finish what you started."

"Finish what?"

Her lip curled into a sneer. "Without the Heart, you can finish killing us all."

"Whoa! Wait. What are you *talking* about? I'm not a Bug. I—"

She cut him off. "Your kind was killing us long before the Bugs got here, boy."

"Stop calling me 'boy.'"

"It was you who drove us into the shadows. It was you who pushed us to the edge of nothingness. It's because of you that there aren't many of us left."

She spat on the ground between them.

"That's total garbage," Milo fired back. Despite his fear, he was getting tired of this crazy girl and her wild accusations. "I never killed anyone. Never. And the people in my camp? All we're doing is fighting the Bugs to try to *save* this planet."

"You want to save it for *you*," she countered. "Not for us."

"Who's 'us'? Can you even *try* to make sense?"

She came over to where he knelt and stood looking down at him. "If you could," she said, "you'd kill me right here and now."

"That," said Milo, "is the stupidest thing anyone's ever said to me."

"It's true."

"No, it's not. Why would I want to kill you?"

"Because that's what your kind do."

"What's with the 'your kind' stuff? Am I supposed to know what that means?"

Something flickered in her eyes. Maybe it was doubt. Milo didn't know her well enough to tell.

When she didn't answer, Milo got slowly to his feet. The girl backed up a few steps, and he didn't try to close the distance.

"Look," he said with as much patience as he could manage, "I don't know who you are or who you think I am. But I'm just a boy—as you keep pointing out. Milo Silk. That's all I am. I don't kill people, and I don't want to kill people. I don't want to kill anyone. I don't hate anything that much. Except for the Bugs. Not too crazy about them."

She sniffed. "And why do you hate them? Because they're monsters?"

"Aside from the fact they destroyed a lot of the world? Gee, let me think," said Milo sourly. "How about I hate them because they took my dad? He was a good guy. He was a teacher. Before the invasion, he taught music. Even after the invasion, he taught people how to play music and sing so we wouldn't all go crazy. The Bugs took him, and now he's gone. So, yeah, I freaking hate them for that. Does that work for you?"

The girl's expression changed again. After a pause she said, "I never knew my father. The Bugs took my mother and grandmother and all of my aunts. Everyone I love."

"That's what I mean," said Milo. "I may not be an orphan—and I'm sorry you are—but everyone's fighting the Bugs. If you think someone's stolen something, I kind of think that's where you should start looking."

"How would they even know what it is?" she asked. "They have insect minds."

"How would I know? Maybe if you told me what this Heart of Darkness thing is, I could help you figure it out."

Hostility seemed to drain slowly from her expression. It left her looking tired and, for the first time, like a kid, rather than a kid trying to pretend to be an adult.

"It's not safe here," she said quietly.

He snorted. "Well, yeah, nowhere's safe. That whole alien invasion thing."

"No," she insisted. "This *place* isn't safe, boy. You need to leave."

"Why?"

There was a sound far off on his right, and they both turned in that direction. It was impossible to tell if it was a falling branch, a running deer, his pod-mates, or trouble. The girl raised her head and sniffed the air like a bloodhound taking a scent. Then she immediately began backing toward the wall of burned shrubs, putting distance between herself and Milo as well as from the broken pyramid. There was sudden panic in her stiff posture and in each word she spoke. "You need to leave now."

There was another sound, and Milo turned to see a rabbit cut through the grass. When Milo turned back to the girl, she was gone.

Absolutely and completely gone.

Like she'd never been there at all.

Milo looked for footprints and found none. He sighed in frustration and confusion, and quickly bent to retrieve his items, muttering to himself about crazy girls, homicidal rogues, and the general craziness of the world. The last thing he picked up was his slingshot. As he straightened, he wondered if the dog whose eyes he'd glimpsed earlier belonged to the girl.

As if in answer to his thought, he heard a soft sound behind him, and once more he turned, ready to fight or run.

And once more he froze in place.

Standing on the other side of the clearing, right where he'd stood a moment before, was an animal. Big and gray, with eyes the color of a winter moon.

It was not a stray dog.

It wasn't a Stinger or a gator or a bear.

And it wasn't a little girl.

The thing that stared at him with those cold eyes was a wolf.

Milo's mouth went dry and his heart nearly froze in his chest.

The wolf was only twenty feet away.

He could get a stone out of his pouch, load it into the slingshot, aim, and fire. But could he do it fast enough or hard enough to stun the wolf before it could close the twenty-foot gap between them?

Not one chance in ten billion.

Milo was absolutely certain that if he tried, the wolf would kill him. No question about it. This wasn't a contest he could ever hope to win.

The wolf, seeming to sense his thoughts, wrinkled its muzzle to show him all of its razor-sharp teeth. There were a lot of teeth in that savage mouth.

The wolf took a single step toward him. Slow and careful.

"No!" said Milo.

The animal paused, and those pale eyes narrowed for a moment as it cocked its head to listen to what the wind had to say. Milo turned too, hearing it now. Off to the northeast of where they stood, there was the sudden sound of voices and footfalls. No rabbits or falling branches this time. It was the unmistakable sound of people moving through the forest. Milo had no idea if that was the girl returning, or that brute Oakenayl, or if it was his friends—Shark, Lizabeth, Barnaby, and the rest of the pod.

He turned back to the wolf.

But it was gone.

The woods were empty, and there was no trace at all that it had ever been there. Not a print, not a bent strand of grass.

Beyond that spot, the burned clearing waited to be explored, the wreckage waited to be examined, which was why Milo and his pod were here.

However, all he could do was stand in the place where the girl had been and stare at the spot where the wolf had stood, trying to understand what had just happened.

He was not, however, able to understand a single thing.

FROM MILO'S DREAM DIARY

I had the dream about the party again.

It was different this time. Not sure what that's about. It was the same for a long time. Now there's new stuff happening.

It started the same way. With lots and lots of food.

Shark and I were sitting at a big picnic table. There was so much food. More than we ever have at one time. More than we have in the whole camp, even in the storage carts. Months' worth of food. Roasted turkeys and boiled hams, grilled ribs and pots of boiled crabs. Shark had a steak so rare it almost mooed when he cut it. A mountain of mashed potatoes and an even bigger one of yams. Every kind of vegetable. I couldn't even name all of them. Bowls of gravy and a foot-long tray of bread stuffing that was baked crisp along the top, the way Grandma used to make it.

I miss Grandma. I hope it was quick for her when the bombs fell.

She would have liked the party. It was crazy, 'cause
   I kept being hungry and kept being able to shovel
   more food down. So good. And we threw scraps to
   Killer, too, who was hiding under Shark's chair.

The dream always starts happy like that.

We heard a sound in the sky. Like thunder. We all knew
   it wasn't, but nobody said anything. We were too
   busy eating.

I remember Dad was there too.

He's always so tall in my dreams. Taller than I think
   he really was, but I don't remember. I was smaller
   when he got lost. He was talking to Mom, not
   looking at me. But it felt good to have him there.

Is he still out there somewhere? Is he still alive?

I hope so. I prayed about it for a long time, but he's
   still gone.

Are prayers ever answered? I don't know.

A lot of people must have prayed when the invasion
   started. The Bugs are still here, so I really just
   don't know.

Anyway, that's when tonight's dream changed from the
   one I had most nights.

Someone said, "Do you want this?"

And I turned to see an old lady sitting right next to
   me. She had to be like a million years old. She had

so many wrinkles I couldn't even see her eyes. Dressed all in gray clothes covered in dead flowers and spiderwebs all over them. Really creepy.

She had a bread plate in her hands, but instead of rolls and corn bread, it was filled with these little crystal eggs. I think they were eggs. They were all the same size, about an inch and a half. The size of crow eggs, but these looked like they were made from crystals. Smooth and sparkly. And it looked like they had little lights inside them. Not electric lights. I couldn't see any bulbs. But they glowed.

I started to take one, but the old lady said, "Be careful. I think they're ready to hatch."

That's when I realized who she was. It was the same voice I heard when I dream about the Witch of the World. It was _her_!

I started to pull away, but then she said, "Go on. Take one. They won't bite. Not yet."

And I took one. It was really weird. The egg was warm and soft. It looked like crystal, but it felt like skin. It made me sick to my stomach to touch it.

The egg got brighter all of a sudden. Then it seemed to shut off and go dark. Not completely dark, though, because when I looked real close I could still see a little spark. But even that was creepy, because the spark moved. Wiggled, like a maggot.

The witch said, "Now you've done it."

All the other eggs on the plate did the same thing. They all started getting dark.

"They'll hate you for this," said the witch. "That's the only emotion they have left. They'll hate you and they'll never stop looking for you. They'll tear up mountains to find you."

"What's going on?" I said. "Why is this happening?"

"The world is broken," she said. "The people of the sun—your people, my child—hammered in the first cracks. Now the Swarm has come from behind the stars to kill what is already dying."

I told her I didn't know what that meant. And I told her that it wasn't true, because even though I didn't understand her, I didn't want what she said to be true.

"The truth is the truth," she said. Then she reached out and touched me. Her hand was cold and damp, like she was dead. So creepy. She said, "The world does not want to die."

That really scared me. "It can't die!" I said.

"It can. But it wants to fight back. It needs an army, child. It needs champions."

"Like who? My mom is a good fighter."

"The world needs a hero." And the way she said it, I knew she meant me, which is stupid. I told her how stupid that was.

The witch squeezed my arm. "You are a dreamer, child of the sun, but it is time to wake up and take a stand. Will you fight to save the world?"

"Yes," I said, but just saying that scared me silly. I didn't know what I was saying.

Then she said, "The world is always half in shadows and half in the sunlight. That's what makes a world. If there were only shadows, the world would die in the cold. If there was only sunlight, it would burn up. It needs both sunlight and shadow to survive. Do you understand?"

I said no, I didn't.

She asked, "Would you walk in the shadows if it meant saving the world?"

I turned away to find Mom and Dad, to tell them about this crazy old lady. But even though I kept yelling at them, they didn't hear me.

When I turned back to the witch, she was gone.

That's when everyone at the table seemed to all hear the thunder at the same time. Except that we all knew it wasn't thunder.

We all looked up and saw that there was a dark rain

cloud up there. Then the rain cloud broke open and something came out of it.

Something big and dark.

A hive ship.

It wasn't alone, though. There were a hundred drop-ships and one red one. That's weird because the Bug ships aren't any color. Just metal colored. This one was dark red and it scares me more than anything. Even more than the hive ships. That one flew right toward us.

Then all the ships began shooting and everything caught fire.

Chapter 12

Hey, loser," said a voice, and Milo jumped three feet in the air.

He landed, whirled, and glared as a big chunk of the shadows detached itself from the gloom between the storm-darkened trees. It resolved into a shape that was short and almost as wide as it was tall. Except for height, everything about Shark was big. Big hands, big feet, big belly, big neck, and a head that looked like a big bucket. Skin the color of dark chocolate, intensely brown eyes flecked with gold, and hair that—after he lost a bet last week—was tied into neat little cornrows.

William Sharkey. Shark to everyone.

A second, much smaller shadow followed at his heels. Killer. A tiny Jack Russell terrier Shark's aunt Jenny had brought back from a patrol. It was about the size of a good meat loaf and seemed to think that all humans existed to either feed him or pet him. In Milo's experience, most humans tended to accept this as the way things should be.

"Yo," called Shark, grinning broadly enough to show a lot of teeth. "Wow. What's your damage?"

Milo cleared his throat. "Oh. Hey."

Shark ambled up, hands shoved into his pockets. He glanced at Milo's face. "Geez, what's wrong with you, dude? You look like you seen a ghost."

Milo pointed to the clearing. "What's wrong? Didn't you see it?"

"See what?" Shark was the same age as Milo. Almost twelve. Though unlike Milo, Shark already had the beginnings of black smudging on his upper lip. He had armpit hair, too. A lot of it. As the camp cook, Mr. Mustapha, once said, "Shark didn't hit puberty. Puberty ran that boy down with a truck."

"The wolf!" exclaimed Milo. "And the girl?"

"What wolf? What girl?" Shark began to smile, waiting for this to turn into a joke. When it didn't, he said, "You serious?"

Milo explained what happened. Not all of it, though. He told him the bare facts—finding the crash, seeing the eyes, meeting the girl, being grabbed, then seeing the wolf. For reasons he couldn't even explain to himself, he didn't go into all the details. He found himself deliberately holding some things back and didn't know why.

He told Shark about Oakenayl and the orphans and all of that, but he didn't mention the witch. Not yet, even though the girl's words rang in his head.

Tell them the witch was right. That's what she'd said. He tried to tell himself that there was no way she could possibly have meant the Witch of the World, that strange old crone who'd been haunting his dreams.

Though . . . more than once things from his dreams had appeared in the waking world. This was one thing he did *not* want intruding into real life. A witch? Seriously. No.

It all sounded too bizarre, too crazy, and he knew Shark—who was very smart and very sharp—would ask a lot of questions that Milo simply could not answer. The whole story would go into his dream diary. That's where he always stored away the absolute truth.

Even the abbreviated version of the story was strange enough, though. As Shark listened, his face became more serious. When Milo was done with his story, Shark grunted.

"Okay, that's really, really weird."

"I know."

"You never saw who grabbed you? This Oakenwhat-ever jerk?"

"Oakenayl, and . . . no. Or whoever was with him. Had to be a bunch of them."

"And that Heart of Darkness stuff? That make any sense to you?"

"Absolutely none."

"That's . . . nuts."

"I know."

They stood there for a moment in silence, neither of them knowing how to talk about it.

"You sure the girl wasn't from camp?" asked Shark. "There's two new rogue families that just came in from—"

"She's not from camp. I never saw her before."

"She cute?" asked Shark, who was starting to take some interest in girls as girls rather than as other kids.

Milo, who didn't much care about any of that, simply shrugged.

"Is she or isn't she?"

"I guess. For a freak. But that doesn't matter, Shark. She's out here all alone, and she's totally loony-bird crazy. Not to mention there's a freaking wolf out there."

Shark gave him a sideways look. "And you're sure it was a wolf?"

"I think so."

"Could it have been a husky? Or a malamute? Maybe an Akita? They look like wolves."

"It was a wolf."

Shark laughed. "In Louisiana?"

"Yeah."

"No way, dude. There aren't any wolves around here."

"Yeah, well, there weren't Stingers or alien invasion fleets either," retorted Milo, "until there were."

"Oh, so you're saying it's an alien wolf? Did it have a green lifelight?"

"No. And I'm not saying it was a Bug."

"Then what are you saying?"

"I'm saying I don't know *what* it was."

"I never heard anyone in camp talk about wolves," mused Shark. "None of the guys on patrol ever said anything. Barnaby never said anything."

"Maybe it just got here," said Milo. "I really don't think it's Dissosterin at all. Maybe it came from somewhere else?"

"Where?" asked Shark. "Mars? Jupiter? Uranus?"

He deliberately mispronounced the last one.

"No, blockhead. I mean somewhere else in America. You heard about the fires and the attacks up north? People are clearing out of whole areas. Maybe animals are, too."

Shark thought about it and gave a shrug of agreement. He wore a cut-off denim vest over a sweat-soaked T-shirt with OLE MISS printed on it in faded letters. His jeans were as heavily patched as Milo's, and their sneakers had been looted from the same destroyed shopping mall. He was carrying a chunk of twisted metal that was smoke-stained and pitted. He dropped it unceremoniously on the ground.

"Okay. So maybe it *was* a wolf. So what? Why are you obsessing on it? Why's that more important than someone nearly choking you to death?"

"It wasn't that bad," lied Milo. He wasn't sure why he lied, but he passed it off as if it were nothing of any real consequence. "Just a couple of refugees out in the woods. They didn't hurt me. I'm okay."

Shark gave him a shrewd glance. "You don't look okay."

"I am."

"You don't sound okay, either."

"Will you let it drop? I'm fine."

Shark held his hands up. "Okay, okay. Don't bite my head off—*boy*."

"Shark . . . ," warned Milo.

His friend chuckled, then added, "Seriously, dude, I think you should tell Barnaby."

Milo shrugged. "If I do that, then we're going to spend the rest of the day looking for that girl, and we're not going to get any salvage done."

"So?"

"So, that's not why we came out here."

Shark snorted. "Oh, suddenly you're Mr. Salvage, and getting jumped in the woods by a pack of weirdos is nothing?"

"I'll tell my mom about it when we get back, okay?"

Shark sighed but didn't press him on it. However, he continued to search Milo's face with skeptical eyes.

Milo avoided his gaze by squatting down to scratch Killer's neck. "Hey, boy, catch any Bugs lately?"

Killer gave his hand a thorough licking.

Shark walked over to the far side of the clearing and looked at the ruined pyramid. Milo rose and joined him. They both clicked on their flashlights and stood looking at the thing that had caused the girl such distress.

"A pyramid?" murmured Shark. "In the swamp?"

"Yeah," said Milo. "Weird, huh?"

"What do you think it is?" asked Shark.

The shrine.

That's what the girl had called it, but Milo didn't say that to Shark. His friend was already looking at him like he was nuts.

"I don't know."

Without realizing it, they had begun speaking in hushed voices.

With both lights on it, Milo was able to pick out details of the shrine he'd missed earlier. Aside from the carved stones, there were small figures made from woven cane. They looked like corn dollies, but smaller and stranger. Their faces were smeared with colored pigment in dark reds and browns and greens. Despite the unseasonable heat of the day, Milo shivered.

Shark began to reach for one, but Milo touched his hand.

"Don't."

His friend glanced at him, then withdrew his hand without making a joke or asking a question.

Keeping their hands back, they both leaned toward the stones and peered down to see that there was a small empty space revealed by the top stones being knocked off.

"Hunh," grunted Shark. "Kind of looks like there was something in there."

Milo said, "The Heart of Darkness is gone. I think this is what she meant."

Shark gave him an uneasy look, then nodded slowly. "So weird."

They studied the empty space inside the broken pyramid. Whatever had been in there was smaller than a tennis ball. It was impossible to tell if it was round or square. The stones were too badly knocked out of shape to make that call. However, the insides of some of the stones were glazed to a glasslike finish.

"See that?" he said, pointing.

Shark nodded. "The stone's melted. Maybe the crash melted it."

"No," said Milo. "Whatever hit the pyramid crashed over there. This thing was hit by debris, but this area wasn't on fire. I think whatever was inside did this."

"Inside?" echoed Shark; then he cut a look at Milo. "The Heart of Darkness?"

"Maybe. Whatever that is."

"How, though?"

"I don't know."

They looked at each other.

"That's freaky."

"You think?"

After a few seconds, Shark leaned back and said, "Is it me or is it like . . . *cold* . . . all of a sudden?"

Milo shook his head. Not in denial, but because he

was feeling the same thing. He took a couple of steps back and, even though he was still in the shadows under the trees, it was definitely warmer. Twenty degrees warmer, or more. Nearly eighty. Then he stepped forward again, and in the space of two paces, it dropped down to a chilly sixty. Or maybe colder. The humidity stayed the same, but in the heat, it was normal swamp air, and near the pyramid, it was clammy and sticky, like being in a damp root cellar.

"This is *really*, *really* freaky," he said in a frightened whisper.

Shark repeated what Milo had done, stepping back and then forward. He stood chewing his lip for a moment, then started edging around the pyramid. Milo did the same, going in the opposite direction. They met on the far side.

"It's a circle," gasped Shark.

"I know."

"A perfect circle."

Milo nodded.

"That's even freakier," murmured Shark.

Milo nodded again, too creeped out to actually speak.

They stared at each other for a moment and then began backing away from the pyramid and didn't stop until they were in the warmth again. Milo shivered, and Shark rubbed at the skin on his forearms as if trying to wipe away spiderwebs. They stood together outside of the zone of cold and clammy air.

They heard a small sound and turned to see Killer standing ten feet behind them, his ears down, tail curled under his body, hair standing straight up, a low growl of fear and anger issuing from his throat.

"What's wrong, boy?" asked Shark.

The dog looked from him to the pyramid and back again and whined. Then he began backing away until he was out of the burned area. No amount of coaxing would get him to come any closer.

Shark and Milo exchanged a long look.

Then they immediately retreated all the way to the green path outside of the crash site and waited for the rest of the pod to arrive. They did not say a word the whole time.

However, as Milo stood there, he thought about what they were seeing—and feeling. The place felt wrong. Very wrong. The girl had said as much. That he didn't belong here. That it wasn't safe. And Milo had seemed to know that as she said it.

It made him wonder if there were places that could be *wrong*. Places that didn't want people there. Or didn't want certain people there. Places that didn't like people. Places that wanted to be left alone.

That's what it felt like here.

This place wanted to be left alone.

Milo knew it. The *place* knew it. And he was pretty sure that even Shark and Killer knew it.

The pyramid squatted there inside its coldness and dared him to come closer again.

Milo knew that he would not and could not.

He knew that he dared not.

Chapter 13

Barnaby found them a few minutes later, and as soon as he saw the crash site, he clapped Milo on the shoulder. Very hard.

Barnaby Guidry was a fifteen-year-old Cajun teen-ager assigned to train a pod of twelve younger kids in several useful skills. Woodcraft and orienteering were big, of course, because no one could risk living in cities anymore. But Barnaby, whose family were rogues before Mom brought them into the Earth Alliance camp, was a first-rate scavenger. Much better than almost all the adults in camp. A field trip with him might involve infil-trating and raiding a small town or a remote store that was abandoned and overgrown, searching for anything of value while avoiding Dissosterin traps and land mines. Another trip might be like the one they were on today: following up on a report of a downed ship.

Investigate, locate, identify, scavenge. That was the plan.

"Well, lookit that, boy. You done gone an' found it, you," said Barnaby in his Cajun drawl. He was thin, tall, with green eyes and skin the color of coffee with a big splash of milk in it. His wiry black hair was wild and stood out in all directions as if Barnaby had touched a live electrical wire. He shook his head and grinned. "And Mr. Sharkey here was saying that *him* was going to win the prize today. Poor boy gonna cry, cry, cry."

"Bite me," muttered Shark.

The prize for finding a salvage site was first pick out of the salvage barrel. The barrel, which was under lock and key, contained items recovered by salvage teams but which had no value in terms of survival or combat. Books, old comics, toys—some of which still had most of their parts—board games, sports equipment. Like that.

Milo once got a novel that had no burned pages and wasn't water-stained. The book was *The Hobbit*, and it was mostly complete. Only the last four chapters were gone, which was okay. It was rare to find whole books anymore. Weather, mold, and war destroyed paper. Milo liked making up stories to fill in missing pages. However, rumor had it that there was a baseball glove in the barrel. A real one. He wanted that glove very much. Thinking about it had made him excited for this scavenging hunt, and it had spurred him into allowing gut instinct to lead him to the crash site while everyone else followed logic.

Now, though, he couldn't care less about the glove or anything else.

The pyramid, the wolf, the girl, and what had happened to him were all he could think about.

The things she'd said were so strange. He hadn't told Shark everything. Like the stuff about *his* kind wanting to kill *her* kind. He thought his friend would laugh at him. Milo knew for certain Barnaby would.

But it burned in his mind.

Barnaby cupped his hands around his mouth and let out a series of birdcalls that always sounded to Milo like someone strangling a turkey. Within a few moments, the other kids from the pod began emerging from different parts of the swampy forest. Some of them groaned when they saw that Milo had won the prize.

Lizabeth, who, at nine, was the youngest of their pod, came over, scooped up Killer, and stroked the nervous dog's fur.

"What's wrong with you, puppy boy?" she asked. She was tiny for her age, with lots of wavy strawberry-blond hair and those pale blue eyes. Not the same as either the strange girl or the wolf, though. Lizabeth wore baggy jeans and two layers of sweaters despite the heat. She was always cold, even on the hottest day.

Barnaby noticed Killer too. "What *is* wrong wit' him? Dog get himself spooked by a coon?"

The local raccoons were big, smart, and fierce. Even some of the bigger dogs in camp avoided them.

Milo didn't want to explain, but Shark pointed. "He got spooked by that."

"Wha-a-at? Tee-dog been to a dozen crash sites and—"

"No," corrected Shark as he clicked on his flashlight. "*That*."

Barnaby entered the burned area and stopped in front of the pyramid. He straightened, frowned, took a few steps back, then moved forward again. Then he rubbed at the beads of sweat on his forearm and frowned.

"Feel that?" asked Milo. "The temperature?"

The team leader glanced at him but didn't respond. He looked confused and concerned, and his hand rested on the curved handle of a lug wrench he carried when out in the woods. Barnaby called it a "slug ranch."

Lizabeth began to enter the cold zone, but Killer started barking and squirming in her arms. Only when she stopped moving toward the pyramid did the dog settle down. Even then he whined and growled softly.

"What is it?" asked Lizabeth.

Barnaby said nothing for almost a minute. It was a long time, and Milo felt more and more uncomfortable as the seconds passed. Then Barnaby began backing away.

"Turn off da light, you," he said, and Shark complied.

"What *is* that thing?" Lizabeth asked again. "It feels . . . It feels . . . ."

They waited for her to finish.

"Feels what, Lizzie?" asked Milo.

Her eyes met his and fell away. "You'll just laugh."

"No," he replied, "pretty sure I won't be doing that."

Lizabeth hugged Killer. "It feels sad. And . . . really *mad*."

Nobody laughed.

Barnaby turned and studied the burned clearing and the surrounding woods. His green eyes were narrowed, and his face was without expression. He stopped when he was facing the pyramid again.

"You think the Dissosterin built that?" asked Shark.

"No. Dem cockroach din' make dis," murmured Barnaby, his voice gone suddenly quiet. As Shark's and Milo's had before.

"It looks old," said Milo.

Barnaby nodded. He licked his lips as he continued to study the woods. He didn't say what he was looking for. As he looked, though, Barnaby dug into his pocket and clutched something. Milo knew what it was. Like a few other Cajuns in the camp, Barnaby had a small deerskin pouch in his pocket filled with special herbs, stones, chicken bones, and other items that his grandmother had gathered for him as protections against the *gris-gris*. Against evil.

Milo didn't mock. He had his lucky black stone. As everyone always said, the world was pretty short on luck. You held on to any of it you could find.

"C'mon, man," insisted Shark. "What is it? Is something else going on in these woods?"

"Dey's always something goin' on in dem woods, you," Barnaby said without looking at him. "Always been dat way, goin' alla way back."

"What kind of stuff?" asked Lizabeth, her blue eyes huge. The other kids had gathered around now, and they took turns looking at the crash site and then at the pyramid. One by one they clustered around Barnaby.

"When you is out here, you got to be real careful," warned Barnaby. "Most of you ain't never been this far out."

"Why?" asked one of the other kids. "Alligators?"

Barnaby snorted. "Dey's more than gators in dem woods, you."

"Like what?" asked Lizabeth in a frightened whisper. "Stingers?"

"Dey's probably Stingers out dere too," said Barnaby. "But dat ain't what I'm talkin' 'bout. Dey's stuff out here ain't never come down from the sky, no. Tings dat was already here. Stuff dat's been here a long time. Stuff dat live bag dare in the swamp."

Lizabeth looked off toward the east, toward the part of the swamp forest beyond their scavenging patrols. Milo followed her gaze, and his imagination began playing tricks with him. Those vine-draped, mosquito-infested swamplands were no different from where they stood, but at the moment they *looked* different. They felt different. They felt wrong.

Barnaby sucked his teeth as if deciding whether to say more; then he glanced at the pyramid again and nodded to himself. "Dis here's *rougarou* country. Don' you know dat?"

Lizabeth's blue eyes snapped back to stare at him, and now they were wider than ever. "What's a—a *rougarou*?"

"A *rougarou*?" said Barnaby quietly. "Why, dat's a big bad wolf, *cher*. Got long, pointy teet. He bite you whole."

"Wolf?" gasped Shark. Before Milo could stop him, his friend blurted, "Milo just saw a wolf."

Barnaby's head whipped around toward Milo. "What dat you say?"

"It's true," insisted Shark. "Right here."

The older teen grabbed a handful of Milo's shirt and pulled him close. "You tell me exactly what happen, you. Don't be lyin', no."

Milo didn't want to. This was starting to really scare the daylights out of him as bad as what had happened earlier, but there was no way out of it. So he told them all what he'd told Shark.

When he was done, Barnaby looked deep into his eyes as if searching for a lie. Then he let go of Milo's shirt and stepped back. The Cajun teen's brown face had gone slack, and he gave his lips a nervous lick.

"Okay, okay . . . Whatever's goin' on, dis ain't our bidness, no," he said slowly. Then he deliberately turned his back on the pyramid and faced the debris field. "We'll tag da spot and den we're out of here. And I don' want to hear no complainin', me."

The others groaned in protest, but they all knew this was Barnaby's call. The pod-leader was responsible for more than the scavenge trip; it was his job to bring them all home safe.

The grumbling continued, though, because even though Milo had won the big prize for this hunt, there were other things they could win by finding good bits of salvage–extra food, fewer chores, bonus points in their sit-down school. But Barnaby wouldn't budge. He ordered four kids to tie orange markers to trees on the outside of the burn zone.

He didn't let anyone go into the crash site, and he did not step even an inch closer to the damaged pyramid.

While the team was buddy-checking their gear for the hike back, Milo, Shark, and Lizabeth cornered Barnaby. In a hushed tone, Milo said, "What's with you? What's going on? Why are we bugging out like this?"

"What you tink?" said Barnaby sourly.

"Is it because of the wolf?" asked Lizabeth.

"Maybe dat's right, *cher*."

"Why?" asked Shark. "Is it rabid or something?"

"Or sometin'," was Barnaby's reply.

"C'mon, Barn," Shark pressed. "What's wrong? You looked like you swallowed a hairy caterpillar as soon as Milo said he saw a wolf. How come? It's just a wolf. What's the big?"

Barnaby shook his head. "Dat's where you wrong, Mr. Sharkey, you. If Milo saw a wolf here." He pointed to the pyramid. "*Here*. Den maybe it a *rougarou*. And a *rougarou* ain't no everyday kind of wolf, no." When he was scared, the Cajun's accent got even thicker. "The *rougarou*—him's a big, bad wolf."

"Bad?" asked Lizabeth. "What do you mean?"

"I 'member my grandmama tole me when I was little, before dem Bugs come down here. She said I don' do all my chores and don' say my prayers before bed, den da *rougarou* gon' come an' eat me all up. I believe her, too, 'cause everybody down here heard da *rougarou* howlin' on a dark night."

"You're talking about the boogeyman," said Shark.

"Da boogeyman? Him's a puppy compare to da *rougarou*. Da *rougarou*—him knows who you are. Da *rougarou* is all da time watchin'." Barnaby laid a straight finger alongside his nose. "He smell if you been good or bad. You good, he maybe leave you alone, you. Maybe. You never can tell. You bad—well, he knows. You *very* bad, da *rougarou* come and bite you."

"Bite?" echoed Lizabeth.

"He bite you, *cher*, and make you a *rougarou* just like him."

"How . . . ?" she began, but Barnaby leaned close.

Barnaby's green eyes burned as bright as an alien life-light. They shone with a sinister emerald fire. "'Cause the *rougarou*—him's a *werewolf*."

Lizabeth's eyes were so big now that they seemed to bug out of her head. "A were—were—were—"

It was as far as she could get.

Milo was about to say something, to tell Barnaby to knock it off, when the team leader suddenly let out a big bray of laughter. "Look at you faces. You *believe* me, you. Don't tell me you don'."

For a few seconds he was the only one laughing. Then the others joined in. Slowly, reluctantly. Lizabeth too, though hers sounded entirely false and forced. Milo and Shark exchanged a look. They were the only ones who didn't laugh.

"You're a total dipwad," Milo said to Barnaby.

That only made the pod-leader laugh harder. He sauntered away from them, slapping his thighs as he laughed.

Shark leaned close to Milo but nodded toward Lizabeth and in a quiet voice said, "Guess who's going to be wetting the bed for, like, the next month."

Still chucking, the Cajun walked back, waving to the pod to fall in behind him.

Shark and Milo lingered at the edge of the clearing, fuming and angry.

Under his breath Shark muttered, "Maybe when we take a bathroom break, he'll wipe his butt with poison ivy."

Milo said nothing.

He hadn't liked Barnaby's story.

He'd been angry about the joke.

But he did not believe for one second that Barnaby's

laughter was real. It sounded fake and forced to him. It sounded like a lie.

He saw little Lizabeth mouth the word "*rougarou*." There were tears in the corners of her eyes.

Milo held out his hand until she took it. "Come on, Lizzie. Don't you believe any of that stuff. You know Barnaby. He's just messing with you."

She gave him a smile, but from the look in her eye, Milo knew that she didn't believe it was a joke any more than he did.

Chapter 14

Barnaby did not make them leave after all.

After warning everyone to stay well clear of the shrine, he gave orders for the pod to do what they came to do. Examine the debris and search for anything useful.

"Wonder why he changed his mind," Shark said quietly.

Milo shook his head. "I don't know."

"Maybe he's just being annoying."

While the pod unpacked their gear in preparation for examining the debris field, Barnaby stood to one side, his right hand resting on the butt of his stun gun, the other on the leather-wrapped handle of his knife. He was sweating, but he kept a smile on his face. It was the most false smile Milo had ever seen. He said as much to Shark.

"He's spooked," agreed Shark. "Lot of that going around."

Milo nodded. "Yeah."

They began unpacking their gear. Milo dug his pack of microtools of out his jeans pocket, selected a little meter, and attached the leads to a piece of junk. The readout told him that the machine was Dissosterin. Milo used a couple of small tools to remove the cover and isolate undamaged circuits. Then he removed them one by one and put them in his pocket. Shark was doing a similar job, removing booster cells from a communicator. They worked quickly and with great efficiency, using techniques they worked every day to refine. Even at their age, this was something they—and nearly everyone in their pod—could do well. With the tools in their kits, they could dismantle everything from a drop-ship antigrav engine to a complex mechanical door lock.

While they worked, Milo noticed that no one even glanced in the direction of the broken pyramid.

They all feel it, he thought.

He found a clear patch of ground and ran through the standard equipment check they were all required to do. He had his tape measure, portable Geiger counter, digital land surveyor, metallurgic analysis scanner, and a dozen other gizmos. Most of them were secondhand—damaged and refurbished, handed down from soldier-scouts to pod members.

A shadow fell across him, and he looked up to see Barnaby. The pod-leader was no longer smiling. He glanced around to make sure everyone was busy with their own gear checks, and then he squatted down next to Milo.

Before he could speak, Milo said, "That was a rotten thing to do to Lizabeth."

Barnaby glanced at Lizabeth, shrugged. "Didn't mean no harm, me. You know dat."

"Still."

"*Mo chagren*," said Barnaby. Then the pod-leader sighed and repeated it in English. "Sorry. I'll make it up to Tee-Lizzie, me. We're having ice cream wit' dinner. She can have my share, her. Tink dat'll do?"

"Better if you didn't do something like that again, man. Lizzie's got issues. Ever since . . . you know . . ."

Barnaby nodded and sighed again. A little more than a year ago, Lizabeth's parents went missing when one of their previous camps was attacked. Later, when they'd found a new, safer spot, a patrol had gone back to look for survivors. All that was ever found of Lizzie's parents was her mom's left shoe. It was torn and stained with blood. Lizabeth didn't get hysterical or anything. Instead she went into her own head and seemed to get a little lost there. It was shortly after that when she started seeing monsters. Most kids would have been treated harshly for telling lies—after all, the whole Earth Alliance survived on the strength of reliable intelligence. Bad or false intel got people killed. Nobody came down too harshly on Lizabeth except once or twice. Mostly people just smiled and nodded and pretended they believed her. Milo was pretty sure that Lizabeth wasn't lying. He thought she believed that she was seeing these things.

Shark thought so too. It scared him.

It made Milo sad and a little frightened. Not of her, but of the world. He had vivid dreams—nightmares, really—and sometimes things he dreamed about came true. He'd dreamed of his father disappearing the night before he went missing when his patrol tried to raid a hive ship. So, if Lizabeth said she was seeing monsters, maybe she was. Real ones or ones that were coming their way.

It was tough living like they did.

Fingers snapped in front of him, and he jerked his head back—and dragged his thoughts back to the moment.

"Talkin' to you's like talking to a fencepost sometimes, you know dat?" said Barnaby.

"Yeah, yeah," muttered Milo.

"Look," said the pod-leader, "about what you saw. You tellin' the trut', or is you messin'? I mean, maybe you playin' a joke on us?"

"No. You're the comedian around here," said Milo.

"I'm being serious, me. You really see dat wolf?"

"I really did."

"And dat girl?"

"Yeah."

"Who had eyes just like da wolf?"

"Well . . . same color, but yeah."

Barnaby chewed a crumb of skin off the corner of his thumb. "You told me everyting she said, you?"

"All I could remember," lied Milo. In truth, he'd told Barnaby only parts of it. Much less than he'd told Shark.

"What she said," persisted Barnaby, "about conjurin'? She said dat?"

"Yeah. You know what it means?"

Barnaby took a bright red cloth from his pocket and

mopped the sweat on his face. "Dat's old stuff. Hoodoo and black magic."

"Huh?"

"People used to believe dat names—people's true names—have power. If you knew someone's true name, you could stir it up like ingredients in a gumbo pot. Dat's how dey make a spell. Dat's how dem bad people control you. Dat's how wizards used to control demons."

Milo narrowed his eyes suspiciously. "Are you making this up?"

"Hand to God," said Barnaby, no trace of a smile on his face. "All dat hoodoo magic was like dat. Dat's why I wear my dime."

He pulled up his pant leg. There was a sturdy piece of string tied around Barnaby's ankle. It passed through a hole cut into an old dime. Milo had seen it a thousand times but always took it for a simple good luck charm. His scavenger eye noted that this was an old mercury dime, not one of the dimes made after 1965, which meant it was mostly silver. That precious metal was highly prized by the tech teams because it had a lot of uses in their weapons labs. Dimes made after 1965 were composites that had no silver at all. He didn't comment on it even though no one was allowed to have silver or gold. Maybe there was an extra rule for good luck charms.

"This protect me from da *gris-gris*," said Barnaby. "Him keep the *rougarou* away."

Milo could never quite get straight if *gris-gris* referred

to the actual evil or the things used to protect against it. Barnaby seemed to use it both ways, but this didn't seem like the time to ask for clarification.

"I thought you were only joking about that," said Milo.

Barnaby shrugged. "I'm not talkin' about dat right now, me. I'm talkin' about da wolf and da girl who ran with da wolf."

"I don't know that she was even connected with the wolf. I just saw her around the same time. They weren't together."

"But you saw dem at the same time, din' you?"

"No. I saw the wolf first, kind of. Just the eyes, I mean. Then I saw the girl. Then I saw the wolf."

"Not together?"

Milo thought about it, shook his head. "No."

Barnaby started to say something, but then looked away. Milo watched the muscles at the corners of his jaw clench and unclench over and over again.

"Barnaby?" Milo said tentatively.

"What?"

"What's going on? Do you know something about that girl?"

But the young Cajun shook his head and refused to say anything more. He got up and walked back to the pod, leaving Milo to wonder exactly what the heck was going on.

Chapter 15

They set about their work. The crash site was divided into quadrants, and the debris field was far enough from the banks of the bayou for the ground to be firm. No risk of deep mud. However, the squadrons of mosquitoes and biting flies had come up from the flat water and had descended on the pod. Shark, as always, seemed to be the centerpiece of the menu. Every time he swatted a mosquito, he smiled fiercely and said: "Take *that* back to the Swarm."

The Earth insects were not connected in any way to the Dissosterin, but if it made Shark feel better, Milo didn't see any reason to constantly correct him. Over the last few months, some of the other people in camp had started saying the same thing. Shark was always a trend-setter when it came to stuff like that.

So, despite the aerial assault, they focused on the task at hand.

Scavenging sites like this was what the pod was trained for and what they were good at. Locating debris, identifying it, examining it, and salvaging anything that could help his mother's resistance team. The most important items were things like working servos, undamaged computer parts, and any kind of weapons system. Milo looked at the wreckage and thought that it would be a real stroke of luck if they found anything of even minor use.

Milo usually loved the work of scavenging, but as he worked, he kept going over everything that happened. As time went on, he began to doubt some of his memories. Like . . . the hands that grabbed him. How many people could there really have been standing behind him? How had so many grabbed him at once? And how had they all vanished so quickly and completely?

And . . .

What was with the girl? Had she really been able to see into his thoughts? Was that even possible?

And . . .

What was all that about the Heart of Darkness, and the rest?

His dad had once told him, "If it happened, it's possible. In that case, it must have meaning. Just because you don't understand it doesn't mean it can't eventually be understood." Milo hadn't really gotten that when he was little, but he thought he grasped it now. Whatever was going on, it must mean something.

As he moved through the routine of examining debris, he also laid out the facts as he remembered them from his encounter.

The pyramid was built by someone to be a shrine. In the camp's sit-down school, Milo had read something about shrines, and he poked around among all of the information he had in his brain until he came up with a definition. A shrine was a holy place. Usually built to honor a saint or a specific religious figure. There was a Catholic shrine to a saint over in Grand Coteau that Milo had seen once on a long trip with his mother.

Okay . . . so was this a shrine? If so, to who? Or what?

It didn't look like the saint's shrine. This was rougher. Less . . . He fished for a word. Civilized?

And the shrine apparently contained something called the Heart of Darkness. Whatever that was apparently mattered to the girl and her friends. Milo didn't know what it could be, though he once saw a book called *Heart of Darkness*. He hadn't read the book and didn't think that it could be connected.

The girl originally thought Milo had opened the shrine and taken the Heart. Then she changed her mind. But she was still mad at him. How had she put it?

You're probably happy the Heart is missing. Now your kind can finish what you started. Without the Heart, you can finish killing us all.

Milo didn't know what she could even mean by that, but somehow it hurt his heart to know it's what she thought. It was how it must feel to have someone think you did something really bad—like betrayed a friend—but it not be true.

He wished he could speak to her again. To understand what she meant and to set her straight.

Lizabeth wandered past him. She seemed to be spending her time looking at the ground around the junk. Milo shrugged. In his view, girls as a species were strange. Lizabeth a little more so.

"Hey, Milo," called Shark, "look at this."

Milo, moody and conflicted, went over.

"This is wrong," said Shark, pointing to several pieces of debris. "Look at the breaks."

Milo did. Their teachers had taught them about impact, ratios of mass and momentum, variations in resistance depending on surface density, angle of impact, and the rest of the science. He understood the physics of it, the math. They all did. Every good scavenger had to.

Which was why he saw at once what Shark thought was wrong. Lizabeth joined them.

Shark knelt by one large piece. "I think this is a Bug drop-ship," he said. He brushed at the soot to reveal the signature patchwork metalwork. Then he pointed to the fractures in the metal from where it had crumpled. Most of the fractures were dark with soot, but there were plenty that gleamed as bright as polished silver in the sunlight.

"It's not burned," said Lizabeth.

"No," agreed Shark. "And that doesn't make sense. This whole place was on fire. Look at the grass and trees.

The grass was wet. You can see it. A lot of these saplings would have smoked really bad. So how come only some of the breaks are covered in soot?"

No one had an answer.

"It almost looks," said Shark slowly, "like this stuff was busted up *after* the crash. After the fires went out."

"After?" asked Lizabeth.

"Has to be. Unless someone came and polished these breaks."

"No way," said Milo.

"I know what happened," said Lizabeth.

They looked at her.

"What?" asked Milo.

"I think someone came and stomped all over it. After the fire, I mean."

Shark chortled. "They'd have to have some pretty darn big feet."

"I know. Round feet, too."

Shark blinked. "Um . . . what?"

"Look," she said, and touched the ground. There were indeed several large, roundish dents in the dirt. Several similar marks were punched into the twisted metal. "They're all over the field. Something came in and stomped everything."

"That could be anything," said Shark. "It doesn't even look like a footprint."

"Looks like an elephant footprint," mused Lizabeth.

"Lizzie, there aren't any elephants in Louisiana," said Shark with great patience.

"Aren't any wolves, either," said Milo dryly.

"You know what I mean. We'd have *heard* an elephant."

"No, we wouldn't," said Lizabeth. "No one was out here when it crashed."

Shark didn't know how to respond to that. He looked at Milo for help, but Milo held his hands up in a "you're on your own" gesture. He was enjoying this.

Lizabeth bent and spread her fingers over one of the dents. It was as big as a dinner plate and easily dwarfed her little hand. "Something had to do it, right?"

"Yeah, but—"

"Maybe an elephant escaped from a circus or a zoo during the invasion."

"Sure, but—"

"It could be living out here."

Milo and Shark exchanged a look and then shrugged.

"Must have been one angry elephant," remarked Shark. "He stomped the heck out of this stuff. It's all junk now. Maybe we should ask Barnaby about it."

"Barnaby's a poophead," said Lizabeth softly.

"He is, in fact, a poophead," agreed Milo.

"Poophead or not—and, believe me, I'm with you on that," said Shark, "we should show this stuff to him."

They reluctantly agreed, but when he came trotting

over, before he even looked at what they wanted to show him, he said, "It's dat wreckage, right? Da tracks?"

"Yes, how'd you—" But Milo cut himself off. Everyone was gathering now, jabbering about the same thing. They'd seen it in their quadrants, too.

"What is it?" asked Shark. "Lizzie thinks it's an elephant."

Not one person laughed.

Barnaby's face was pinched. "Okay, dat's it. We're done here. Pack your tings and fall in. We out of here in five minutes. And dat's not five minutes and one second. You all hear me? Move!"

They ran to gather up their equipment.

Everyone was lined up in three minutes.

Barnaby gave them a curt nod of approval. "We're out of here now. Ghost pace, *to konprann*?"

Do you understand?

They did. Ghost pace was scavenger lingo for moving as quickly as silence would allow. They were all good at it, even Shark, who was bigger than any two of the others. Big didn't always mean clumsy.

Within seconds the clearing was empty.

From the woods, Milo took one last look back as the leaves closed across the trail. He thought that he saw a single, brief flash of gray.

Wolf?

Girl?

Or his own frantic imagination?

When he paused to take a better look, there was nothing.

He shivered despite the heat.

Then he turned and hurried to catch up with his friends.

FROM MILO'S DREAM DIARY

I had one dream where I was sitting in a cave talking
to shadows.

The cave was strange, because it looked like someone
lived there. It was rock and dirt, but there were
shelves on the walls and a table, chairs, and a cot.
It felt like a lonely place, though. Not sure I know
why. Could what a person feels kind of stick to
the walls? Or hang in the air? It was like that. Like
maybe whoever lived there spent too much time
alone and not enough time playing with other kids.

Funny, but until I wrote that last sentence, I didn't
really know that the cave was where a kid lived. But
looking at what I wrote makes me believe that.

It was where some kid lived all alone.

No other kids.

But <u>not</u> no one to talk to.

She had people to talk to.

She?

Why did I write that?

How come I sometimes know more about my dreams
    when I write them down than when I have them?

Does writing them down help me remember stuff I
    forget when I wake up?

Not sure.

Anyway, I remember sitting in that cave in my dream
    and talking to someone. It wasn't the Witch of the
    World. Not that time.

I couldn't actually hear the voice, either. It was like
    thinking back and forth.

This is all I remember of the conversation:

Me: Where is this place?

Her: It's not anywhere you can find. It has to let you
    find it.

Me: What does that mean? How can a place do that?

Her: Earth is alive. It has feelings. It has thoughts.

Me: It's just a planet.

Her: No, it isn't. It never was. How come you don't
    know that?

Me: Do the Bugs know that?

Her: They didn't when they came here. They do now.
    That's why everything is going bad.

And that was all I remember.

There was more, and I wish I could remember it,
    - because I think it was really important.

Chapter 16

The day didn't get better.

It wasn't a Tuesday, but it was quickly becoming one of Milo's least favorite Mondays.

When they got back to camp, he saw a lot of activity. At first Milo thought the camp was being moved. Again. Since the invasion, no humans set up any permanent settlements. This camp, though home to Milo, had been moved dozens of times, and soon it would be time to move it again. The Bugs were always looking. Milo was surprised at the activity, though, because this camp was so far out of the normal Bug patrol areas.

But then he realized that it wasn't the whole camp that was in motion. It was only the soldiers, and they weren't preparing for a fast evacuation. They were getting their gear together for a mission.

Which meant Mom was going out, too.

Which meant Mom was going hunting for monsters.

Chapter 17

"Why do you have to go?"

It was maybe the eighth time Milo asked his mom that question. He had no doubt the answer was going to be the same. It was the only answer she ever gave at times like this.

"Because I have to," said Mom as she adjusted the Velcro straps of her shoulder holster. "We talked about this. This is my job."

"I know, but . . ."

Mom turned to him. She was short and so thin. Milo could still remember when she was plump. Not fat exactly, but round and soft and full of smiles. That was before *they* came. That was six years ago, back when Mom was a school librarian. Milo had seen pictures of her from before that, when Mom—who wasn't even married yet—had been a soldier in a war somewhere far away. She'd been thinner then, too, but it was different. In those photos, Mom was always in good shape, always smiling, but to Milo she was a different person entirely. Now Mom was thin and hard, with sharp cheekbones and sharp edges everywhere. And she never smiled anymore.

"But what?" she asked.

"But can't someone *else* do it? Just for once? Why can't you stay here and let someone else go? There's Captain Allen and Sergeant Lu. They're tough and—"

"It's not just about being tough, Milo."

"I know, but why can't they go instead of you?"

"Why them and not me?"

He almost said, *Because I don't want to lose you*, but he bit it back. Stuff like that hadn't worked when he was six or eight or ten, and it wasn't likely to work at eleven.

The real truth was that he was still freaked out by what had happened in the forest. He'd planned to tell his mom everything, but when he came in and found her packing, he hadn't. She would have enough to worry about. So would he.

That was half of it.

The other half was that he'd had a bad dream last night. A nightmare of fire and screams. In the dream, everyone in the camp—all of the soldiers, all the refugees, all the others kids—vanished behind huge walls of flame as the Dissosterin shocktroopers swept down from the sky. Grinders and bangers flew through the air, blowing apart the trucks and the Humvees and the last helicopter. And through the fire and smoke, something huge and terrifying came stalking. Even in the dream, Milo couldn't tell what it was. It had to be one of the Dissosterin, but it was too big, too strange-looking, and it was surrounded by other even more freakish shapes.

The dream went on and on until Milo snapped awake, shivering, soaked, his heart hammering like gunfire in his chest. He snatched up a pillow and jammed his face into it to keep from screaming.

You don't scream in the night. Not unless you wanted to get everyone killed. Sound carries at night.

There had been screams in the nightmare, though. Milo's. The other people in the camp.

And Mom.

He remembered that.

Milo remembered the sound of his mother screaming as that big, strange, awful dark shape dragged her away from him.

Now, sitting in her tent, watching her get ready to lead a mission, Milo felt haunted by the dream, but he didn't know what to do about it.

"I just don't think it's fair that you have to go all the time," he said.

"Milo," she said with strained patience, "how many times do we have to talk about this? This is my team. All of these people look to me. Not just to make decisions, but to lead them. Do you think it's fair for me to send Captain Allen and Sergeant Lu out and I stay here?"

"Not *all* the time, but you go out more than anyone."

She nodded. "I know. And do you understand why?"

"Because it's your team," he said. "I know, but—"

She looked at him. Her eyes had changed, too. In a way they were the hardest part about her. Dark, like polished black stones. And there seemed to be shadows there. Or, maybe ghosts. Ever since Dad went missing, her eyes seemed to be filled with those ghosts. It was worse when someone from another camp said they heard a rumor that someone had maybe spotted Dad. Mom got all excited and went looking, but she never found anything. Each time she came back, she was a little sadder and she looked a little older. Like the hunt for Dad was draining away something vital in her. Spirit or life force. Or something.

"Everyone has something they do really well, Milo," she said. "Captain Allen is a very talented tracker, and he's good at figuring out the alien tech. Sergeant Lu is a dependable squad leader. Her people trust her. But they all look to me for something else."

He could think of a lot of reasons the soldiers and everyone else in camp would follow Mom. She was smart, strong, and scary good in a fight. So what else was there?

"What else?" he asked.

"My track record."

"Huh?"

"When I lead a team," she said, "people usually come back." For a moment her dark eyes were hard as stone, and then they glistened with wetness. Mom turned quickly away and began shoving loaded magazines roughly into her canvas rucksack. She cleared her throat, then echoed one word. "Usually."

Milo felt that word like a punch.

He knew it meant Dad.

Dad.

Gone for three years now.

Milo dreamed about him every night, though it was getting harder and harder to remember exactly what he looked like. It crushed him to think that one day he might not remember his father at all. That would be truly awful.

A single lantern stood on the ammunition box they used as a nightstand, and it was turned down to a pale glow that was barely there. Outside the crickets pulsed like the heartbeat of the night. Milo sat on a cable spool that was turned on its side. They didn't have any real chairs or tables. Everything was boxes and bundles and old crates. Nothing was real. Nothing in the camp was being used the way it was meant to be used.

Except the weapons.

Like the gun Mom snugged into the shoulder holster and the rifle that stood by the tent door.

"Besides," she said, almost as an afterthought, "this isn't a combat mission."

"Then what is it?"

She pursed her lips, clearly debating whether to tell him. Milo put on his most innocent and attentive expression, the one that assured anyone who saw it that he was trustworthy beyond reproach. He even gave it a bit of the big puppy eyes that usually worked well on his mother.

It worked this time, too.

"There's been some unusual activity along the bayou," she said at length. "Reports of shocktroopers down around the Atchafalaya River."

"What? But you said that there wouldn't be any fighting—"

"*Dead* shocktroopers," interrupted his mom. "Scouts found two dead 'troopers and a lot of wrecked equipment."

Milo gasped. "Dead?"

The shocktroopers wore a kind of body armor that was impervious to most kinds of bullets. It was tougher than Kevlar. And the 'troopers carried enough guns so they could walk on two legs and fire four guns at once. In a one-on-one fight, a shocktrooper had no equal on planet Earth. Only combined firepower or high explosives could take them down.

"Who killed them?"

"That's one of the things we want to find out. The scouts said they were pretty badly mangled and crushed. Clawed apart."

"'Clawed'?" echoed Milo.

She shook her head. "We don't know what that means, unless it's a bad description of injuries sustained in a crash, but there's no report of a downed ship. And it's too far away to have been the one your pod scavenged today."

"Do you think, um, a *wolf* could have done that to the 'troopers?"

"A wolf?" she grunted, surprised. "Even if there were wolves in Louisiana, I doubt even a pack of them could take down a pair of shocktroopers. It's more likely a rogue resistance group. We're finding people all the time. If so, we'll see if we can bring them into the Alliance."

Milo understood that. There were lots of rogue groups, mostly made up of families, packs of hunters, and others who had managed to survive on their own since the invasion. The Earth Alliance did a good job of working with them, swapping information for supplies and tactical support. Half the people in this camp were originally rogues. Like Barnaby and his brothers.

"What are they like?" Milo asked on impulse. "The Bugs, I mean?"

Mom was feeding cartridges into a spare magazine for her pistol and she paused. "You know what they're like, Milo."

"Not really. I mean, okay, I've seen a lot of pictures. I know some of them look like grasshoppers or locusts; some look like praying mantises. I know. I get that. But what are they *like*. You've been up close. How insecty are they? They can't be exactly like bugs or they couldn't build spaceships. Do they talk? Do they have families?"

Her face was wooden as she finished thumbing the last rounds into the magazine.

"They're monsters," she said. "That's all they are, and that's all you need to know."

"But—"

"The Bugs have no soul, no heart, no pity. They're *exactly* like locusts. They swarm and consume and destroy and they take everything." Her voice was filled with more hurt and bitterness than Milo had ever heard. Mom wore a small silver locket around her neck that held a picture of Dad. As she spoke, her fingers absently touched the locket. "That's who and what they are. Takers. They give nothing back except pain and suffering and leave nothing behind except waste and destruction."

Her words seemed to hang in the air for a moment, unintentionally harsh, filled with pain and old memories.

"Did you go onto the hive ship to try to find Dad?" he asked.

He didn't think she'd answer. She closed her eyes for a moment as she slipped the loaded magazine into its slot on her belt.

"Yes," she said quietly.

Milo didn't ask the follow-up question because the answer was obvious. Dad had never come back.

"No more questions." Abruptly, his mother bent and kissed him. Once on each cheek and once on the forehead. The way she always did when she was about to leave. "Mind the teachers, you hear me? And don't forget to do your chores while I'm away. I'll check when I get back."

"When *will* you be back?"

"I'm . . . not sure. Two days? Three at the outside."

It was a long time. He tried hard not to let the alarm show on his face.

Mom straightened and reached for the tent flap.

"Mom . . . ?"

She paused, the canvas flap clutched in one small, tanned fist. "Yes?" she asked, looking over her shoulder at him.

He wanted to say, *Come back to me.*

He wanted to say, *Don't get hurt. Don't get killed.*

What he said was, "I love you, Mom."

Her shoulders—always rigid and strong—slumped for just a moment.

Or maybe she was just taking a breath.

Milo couldn't tell.

She looked at him for a long, silent moment.

"I will always love you, Milo," she said and then gave him a small, rare little smile. "You know that, right?"

"I know."

She brushed a few strands of his fine brown hair from his eyes. "Be good. Be smart. Be safe."

It's what she always said.

Then she went out.

FROM MILO'S DREAM DIARY

I wonder where Dad is.

Is he alive?

Some of the soldiers say that the Bugs have been
"collecting" people for years.

Collecting.

For what? What's that even mean?

In some of my dreams, I see Dad in a collection, like
the bug collections you see in museums. Sometimes
he's in a big glass jar and there's not enough air to
breathe.

Sometimes it's worse. Sometimes he's on a big board.
Pinned there.

Those are bad dreams.

I hate those dreams.

Chapter 18

Night fell quickly and completely.

Milo stood looking out through the tent flap at the blossoming darkness. Hating it. Wishing the days would last longer.

Milo could still remember things like streetlights and how they pushed back the darkness with glowing walls of soft yellow and orange. He could remember living in a house that had running water, a flush toilet, electricity, a fridge filled with cold food, a yard littered with toys, a street lined with cars in pretty colors. He could remember watching cartoons and funny cat videos on YouTube with his older cousins—Joelle and Rob. He could remember kindergarten and even day care before that. He could still remember all of it. New books, warm beds with fluffy pillows, going to the movies, playdates, and birthday parties.

Those kinds of memories had stopped when he was six, but he remembered all of it because that was how life should have continued to be. His best memories were part of that time.

Joelle and Rob were gone, of course. Their neighborhood was a hole in the ground gouged by the massive pulse cannons on the hive ships. The edge of that smoking hole was only three blocks from where Milo used to live. Every time he thought about how random it was that they were gone just like that and he survived, he got sick to his stomach.

One minute they were there; the next the world had changed.

The Dissosterin Swarm had begun its conquest of planet Earth.

The five years since seemed like they belonged to someone else.

No, that was wrong. Maybe the truth, as much as he didn't want it to be the case, was that the first six years were the things that belonged to a different person. The five years since the invasion were the real world. They were this world. *His* world.

No streetlights anymore. The poles were still there, but the power grid was off. That was one of the first things the Dissosterins destroyed. Before the big hive ships descended from the starry night, swarms of smaller craft came down and attacked the power plants. Dissosterin shocktroopers took possession of every single nuclear power plant. The whole world went dark. Bang, just like that. His mom said that it was the most sophisticated strategic strike in history. From first shot to last, it took the aliens less than two hours to turn off all the lights.

From then on, everything changed. Without power, there was no Internet. Then the hive ships destroyed all of the communication satellites and major cell phone relay stations.

Bang.

Bang.

Bang.

Only places that had their own generators, or that worked off solar or wind power, stayed operational. For a while.

The Dissosterin targeted those next.

The military fought back. Everyone's military did.

Dad said that there were some mistakes at first. The Americans thought that it was an invasion by the Chinese or North Koreans. The Chinese and North Koreans thought it was the Americans. The British thought it was the Russians. The Israelis and the Arabs thought it was each other. That was bad. Dad said that a lot of countries launched missiles—some regular, some nuclear—and did almost as much damage to the world as the aliens were doing. Maybe more. Dad called it "typical human paranoia."

Milo barely understood that because when he was six he didn't know much about those countries. Since the invasion, the whole idea of a "country" was kind of dumb. It was all "the world" or "Earth" or just "us." The humans and the Bugs.

Us and *them*.

The adults in camp, though, still sometimes talked about things as if the world were the way it was when they were growing up. Borders and all that. Milo understood that it had mattered to them at the time. It had mattered in the first hours of the invasion. Borders mattered a lot in the kinds of war that happened before the hive ships arrived.

Soon, though, everyone knew that this wasn't the kind of war anyone on Earth had ever fought before. All of the things countries and people used to fight about suddenly didn't matter. Everyone was being attacked.

Everyone.

So, everyone tried to fight back.

The next wave of missiles were launched against the *real* enemy.

People said that some of those missiles did their job, though Milo had never seen a wrecked hive ship.

Mom made sure of that.

There were plenty of other wrecks, though. The aliens were winning, but they were having to work really hard at it. Humans—especially now that they were all working together—were hard to beat.

Earth Alliance camps like this one were key to human survival. They were combination homes, training centers, repositories of scavenged tech, research and development field stations, and schools. The camps were always moving, though. Settling down and planting roots was too dangerous. The Dissosterin were always hunting.

Their camp was always moving in order to scavenge new tech, launch strategic strikes, and avoid detection. It was the ultimate game of hide-and-seek.

Milo walked over to the duty officer's tent and told him about the girl. Not the whole story—because he didn't think anyone would believe it—but the basic facts.

"You think she's a rogue?" asked the officer.

"I don't know," admitted Milo. "Maybe."

The officer had Milo sit with a soldier who used to be a police sketch artist back when there were police. The result was a good likeness of the girl. Milo took it and pinned it to the side of the food cart, where pictures of all suspected rogues and refugees were placed. That way everyone would see it and be on the lookout for a lost girl.

Feeling depressed about his mom and thoroughly confused about the events at the crash site, he drifted around the fringes of the camp, making a couple of slow circuits before ending up near the food cart again. Spending time inside his thoughts helped only a little. The day still made no sense.

Something moved, and it snapped Milo momentarily out of his glum thoughts. He peered into the shadows near the old falafel cart that was used as a portable kitchen for the camp.

Was someone there?

For a moment—just one quick moment—he thought he

saw a familiar pair of luminous ice-pale eyes staring at him.

Fear clamped a cold hand around Milo's heart, and his breath caught in his throat.

The wolf!

There was a wolf right here in camp.

Though in that split second, the word in his head wasn't "wolf."

It was a *rougarou.*

What was it Barnaby had said?

If you knew someone's true name, you could stir it up like ingredients in a gumbo pot. Dat's how dey make a spell. Dat's how dem bad people control you.

Milo reached for his slingshot and dug a sharp stone out of his pouch. He opened his mouth to give the owl cry that was the camp's alarm call.

Then the eyes were gone.

That fast.

The darkness was nothing but lightless air again.

He found his flashlight and switched it on as he approached the cart.

Nothing. The falafel cart stood there on its bald tires, the window closed and locked. No wolf. No eyes.

No girl, either.

A hand came down on his shoulder and a voice said, "Boo!"

Milo screamed and jumped.

"Geez," said Shark. "You look like you've seen a ghost."

Chapter 19

Milo wanted to punch his friend. Very hard.

Instead he stood there, quivering and breathless, while Shark grinned at him.

"What's *wrong* with you?" demanded Milo. "You keep doing that."

"It keeps working," explained Shark. "Besides, I called your name first. Twice."

"I—didn't hear you."

"No kidding."

Milo picked up the flashlight that had fallen when he'd jumped. His fingers trembled as he shoved it into his pocket. "I thought I saw the wolf again."

Shark widened his eyes and wiggled his fingers. "Ooooh . . . Was it a real wolf or a *rougarou*?"

"Don't joke."

"You're almost as bad as Lizabeth. She swears she saw a monster today."

"A *rougarou*?" asked Milo, smiling in spite of himself.

"Nope."

"What, then? Bigfoot? A *chupacabra*?"

Shark grinned too, because Lizabeth Rose was always seeing stuff like that. She once claimed to have seen the Loch Ness Monster raising its head out of Bayou Teche. "Not this time. She said she saw a Stinger."

Milo stared at him. "No way."

"That's what she told Aunt Jenny. It was after we got back from the scavenger hunt. She was off by herself for a minute, picking pecans in the woods. She said she climbed a tree and one went by right below her."

"Oh, come on. A *Stinger*?"

Shark spread his hands in a "what can I say" gesture. "She said she could see its lifelight glowing. Aunt Jenny had her give a full report to the patrol sergeant. She sent some guys out to look."

"Your aunt thinks this is real?"

Shark shrugged. "Real enough, I guess, but there was nothing."

"If Lizabeth really saw one, then how come there's no alert?"

"You know how it is. They went looking because they have to look. Doesn't mean anyone really believes her. Lizabeth makes a lot of stuff up. She could get in trouble for this."

Milo nodded. That much was true. Once Lizabeth said she saw a Dissosterin shocktrooper in the swamp. She said it was running on all fours, meaning it was using its secondary set of arms as legs in order to run faster.

Two full squads were scrambled to check it out and they found nothing. Not a trace. Lizabeth had some serious "alone time" after that. A week of it. And some kitchen duty. Oddly, she never budged from her story. And the description she gave about what she'd seen was eerily accurate. It was still something she could have gotten from a picture or a sketch, but even so . . .

"Like I said, nobody's seen anything," Shark concluded. "Probably just Lizzie being Lizzie."

"Maybe," murmured Milo.

"Be scary if she was telling the truth, though."

"I know."

Shark changed the subject. "That wolf you keep seeing? You sure it was the same one you saw at the crash site?"

"All I saw just now was a pair of eyes. Same eyes, though. But, like, how many wolves can there actually be out here?"

"Not counting *rougarous*?"

"Come on, man . . ."

"If it was the wolf," Shark asked as he looked around, "where'd it go?"

Milo sighed. "I don't even know if it was really here. My head's all scrambled today. Come on. Help me look for prints."

They switched on their flashlights and hunted around the food cart, but they found nothing.

"Must have been the light reflecting on something else," concluded Shark.

"Sure," agreed Milo, though he didn't agree at all.

They walked back to the tent but stopped and stood outside, listening to the night.

"I overheard Aunt Jenny and one of the scouts talking about the two dead shocktroopers," said Shark after a while. "I was in my bunk, and they must have thought I was asleep. The scout said that the shocktroopers weren't shot or anything like that."

"Okay, then maybe their flyer was shot down. What's the big?"

"No," Shark said again. "The scout said that it looked like the 'troopers had been attacked by an animal."

"Yeah," agreed Milo, "I heard that from Mom. What do you think? Gator?"

Shark's expression was mysterious. "Something with claws," he said. "Great big claws that can somehow tear through shocktrooper armor. Sure as heck not your wolf. Whatever this was, it had to be huge."

Milo thought about it. "Barnaby said he's seen cougars."

"Sure, okay, but when have you ever heard of a cougar taking on two armed shocktroopers?"

Milo grunted, remembering his mother's similar comment about a wolf taking on 'troopers.

"Besides," continued Shark, "if it was just some big

cat, then why send out a whole patrol? And why would your mom go? She's a colonel. Something like that, they'd send a sergeant like Aunt Jenny."

Neither of them had an answer, so they stood side by side and watched the darkness. There was nothing to see—the squad was gone—but they faced that direction anyway. Shark had no parents. They'd gone missing during the initial invasion. His guardian was a woman who used to be his kindergarten teacher. Jenny Lu, now a sergeant in the Louisiana Chapter of the Earth Alliance. He called her Aunt Jenny.

"I don't know," said Milo.

"Yeah, me neither, but something weird's happening. That pyramid thing. Whatever stomped all over the crash site. That wolf, and now this? This is all really, really, really weird."

Shark's level of distress could always be measured by how many "reallys" he added.

"I wish the patrol didn't have to go out," muttered Milo.

"I know. This bites," said Shark. "I mean really bites. Like with big gator teeth."

"Yeah," agreed Milo. "I wish I could go with them."

That wasn't the truth and he knew it. Milo didn't want to go at all. He didn't want to go within a million miles of the hive ship, the crawler camps, Stingers, or anything even remotely related to those monsters. No way.

What he really meant was that he wished he was big enough and tough enough to do something to protect his mother. To keep her from going missing. Like Dad had gone missing.

In a few years, when he was fifteen or sixteen, he'd be allowed to go on patrols. At eleven? Not a chance.

Even though he was three inches taller than Shark, Milo was as skinny as his friend was big. Everyone always made jokes about him having no meat on his bones, about how his shadow looked like a pencil with shaggy hair.

Shark sighed and said, "I wish I could wake up and this whole thing—the invasion, the Bugs, all of it—is just a bad dream."

"Yeah," agreed Milo sadly. "I think Lizzie'll see a live unicorn first."

Shark unclipped the canteen from his belt, took a sip, winced, took another sip.

"What's that?" asked Milo.

"Some kind of herb tea."

"Taste good?"

"Tastes like boiled snot. Aunt Jenny says it'll help my asthma."

"Oh."

"Want some?"

"No thanks."

Shark nodded philosophically, took one more sip, recapped the canteen, and clipped it to his belt.

"Who do you think she is?" asked Shark, nodding to the picture tacked to the side of the cart.

"I have no idea."

"I told Aunt Jenny about her, and she thinks she's from a rogue family. Maybe staking out that area. Could be why she told you to get lost."

Milo grunted. He didn't want to talk about the girl. It scared him to even think about what happened to him. Every time he tried to apply scavenger logic to the experience, he hit a wall. The hands that had held him made no sense at all.

It frightened him as much as thoughts of the Bugs did.

The whole world seemed filled with shadows and mysteries and monsters.

"We have another hike tomorrow," said Shark, interrupting his thoughts.

"What? Since when?"

"Since this evening. It was on the schedule in the mess tent."

"How long?" asked Milo, dreading another trip into those woods.

"Five miles, I think."

"Oh. That's not too bad."

Five miles was within the normal radius of the foot patrols. Not even wolves could do much against soldiers with rifles.

Even so, those woods surrounded them right now. Huge and so dark that anything—*anything*—could be out there. Hiding. Watching.

"What time do we go out?" Milo asked.

"You won't like it."

"I never like it," said Milo.

"Lineup's at six, which means we have to be dressed, fed, and geared up by six, not getting *up* at six."

The way he said it, Milo knew that Shark was quoting someone. Probably Barnaby, who always tried to sound like an adult drill sergeant.

Milo groaned. Sunrise was around six thirty. That meant getting up and ready in the dark. In an empty tent, with Mom gone. In a camp where most of the soldiers were out on the patrol.

"Maybe we could say we're sick," he suggested hopefully. "You could have an asthma attack, and I'd volunteer to stay here and—"

Shark shook his head. "Tried that too many times. Last time Barnaby dimed me out to Aunt Jenny and I got in trouble. And I do *not* want to shovel out the latrines again. No thanks."

"Oh."

"Unless you want to join me. 'Cause, really, shoveling poop is the most fun in the world. You should try it."

"Forget I said anything. We . . ."

His voice trailed off as he caught something out of

the corner of his eye. He turned quickly and thought he saw those pale eyes watching him.

"What is it?" asked Shark. Killer came to point and stared fixedly into the shadows.

"I . . . ," began Milo. "I thought I saw something."

The darkness was blank now. There was nothing.

"What?"

"That wolf," said Milo in a frightened whisper. "I thought I saw it looking at me."

They both peered into the shadows. Killer crept to the edge of the woods and sniffed. After a long time of total concentration, all three of them relaxed.

"Nothing there," said Shark.

"I guess not."

Shark didn't bust on him for "seeing things." Alertness bordering on paranoia was one way for everyone to stay safe in a world where all humans were constantly being hunted.

They stood there and watched Killer shift from looking for mystery dog eyes to sniffing at all the places he— or the other camp dogs—had peed recently. Exciting stuff. The pale eyes did not reappear.

Very weird, thought Milo. *I definitely saw something.*

Shark said, "I remember reading once that we have dogs now because a long time ago wolves used to hang around the camps of early humans. You know, to get scraps and stuff. People started leaving stuff out for them, and after a while, they kind of brought some in."

Milo thought about that. "I don't think that's what this is. I don't think the wolf is looking for scraps."

"Then why do you keep seeing it?"

"I . . . don't know. . . ."

The moment stretched and thinned and faded into nothing, leaving them standing in the night with a small dog and not much left to talk about.

Shark nodded to the locked cart. "Want some leftovers? I know where Mr. Mustapha keeps the key."

Mr. Mustapha was the cook, and finding ways to break into his food cart had become Shark's mission in life. Mr. Mustapha frequently threatened to add Killer to the stewpot, but no one took him seriously.

"Sure," said Milo sourly, "and if we get caught, we'll both be shoveling latrines until we're fifty."

Shark sighed. "I guess." But he gazed longingly at the cart.

Milo knew that this was one of the differences between his friend and him. Shark ate when he was scared and Milo couldn't. In fact, Shark ate all of the food Milo *couldn't* eat. That's why Shark was heavy and Milo was skinny. People are different even when they're dealing with the same problems.

"Then I'm going to bed," decided Shark.

Milo grunted. "You can sleep?"

"Got to. Been a long day and I'm beat."

"I'm too creeped out," admitted Milo. "I don't think I'm ever going to sleep again."

Shark shrugged. "Got to try, dude, or we'll be zombies on the hike tomorrow."

"Zombies," mused Milo. "I wonder if that would be better than aliens."

"Couldn't be worse. But, let's face it, if there were zombies out there, you'd be safe."

"Why?"

Shark pinched his arm. "Nothing to eat."

"Hilarious," said Milo, not meaning it.

But they laughed anyway.

It was false and it didn't last long.

"See ya in the morning. Hope you don't have any dreams."

Milo nodded. "Hope you don't, either."

Both of them meant it. It was the kindest thing friends could wish each other.

Milo watched Shark walk away with little Killer trotting dutifully at his heels, tail wagging as if everything were right with the world. Far above the camp, visible through a gap in the camouflage netting that hid them all from the air, Orion strode across the sky, his belt and sword glittering. Milo wondered how many times the celestial giant had looked down on boys from a war-torn country talking in the night. Probably more than all the stars in the Louisiana sky.

Milo always found comfort in that constellation. He felt that maybe not everything in the universe wanted to hurt him.

Then he remembered that in the myth, Orion had been killed by a scorpion. Even though Scorpius was in the sky on the far side of the world, it reminded him of the Bugs and all the people they'd killed, all the things they'd destroyed.

Depressed, Milo walked over to where his hammock was hung. He could have slept in the tent tonight, but he didn't want to be alone. Out here there were soldiers sleeping in hammocks or bedrolls. Out here he felt safe. Or, safer, anyway.

He took off his shoes, washed his face and hands with a cupful of water, climbed into the hammock, and lay there for more than an hour, trying to fall asleep.

He didn't think he would. Or could.

But sleep found him anyway.

And, sadly, he dreamed.

FROM MILO'S DREAM DIARY

Really weird dream last night.

It started with the same feast. Just like always. But then it changed again.

There was a girl at the table this time.

It was the girl from the woods. Those same eyes and the same smoke-colored hair. Her clothes were all dirty and covered with ashes and blood. She looked sick, too. Her skin was yellow and her eyes were bloodshot.

"What happened?" I asked her.

"The world is dying," she said, "and so are we."

"'We'? Who do you mean?"

"All of the orphans who wander in the night."

"What does that mean?" I asked, but she wouldn't tell me. So I said, "If you tell me your name, I won't conjure with it."

The girl looked at me for a really long time. She looked so sad and scared that I wanted to do something for her. I felt really bad for her.

She said, "My name is Evangelyne Winter."

I told her that it was a pretty name.

"It's an old name. It was my grandmother's name, and she ran with the night winds."

She wouldn't explain what that meant.

I turned to get some food for her, but when I turned back, she was gone. Her chair was empty and all rusted and broken.

Then I felt something push against my knee and looked down, expecting it to be Killer under the table, begging for scraps like he does. But it wasn't.

It was the wolf from the forest, chewing on a beef bone.

I almost screamed. I mean, it was right there, close enough to bite me.

Then the wolf's mouth moved. Not to bite me. It was trying to speak like people do. It couldn't, though, because it didn't have a human mouth.

It scared me. Not because this was an animal trying to talk to me. No, what scared me was that I couldn't understand it.

And I was very, very sure I needed to.

That's when we started hearing the thunder in the sky. We ignored it, though, the way we always do. At first, anyway.

I bent down and ducked under the table. I had an idea
that if I tried to make my mouth make the same
shapes as the wolf was trying to make that I could
maybe figure out what it was trying to say. It wasn't
as stupid as it sounds. It made sense in my dream.

It helped, too. I could feel the shape of the words.
Real words, but I had to repeat them over and over
before they made any sense. "Thayer . . ." That's
what it sounded like.

It wasn't, though. Not "thayer." It was . . . two words
smooshed into one.

They are.

When I said the words aloud, I could swear the wolf
nodded.

It kept speaking, though, repeating that word and
another. I had to sound it out, too.

It sounded like "common."

It wasn't.

It was "coming."

When I didn't understand right away, the wolf got mad
and growled at me. Not like it was going to bite, but
because it was so frustrated.

The thunder was getting louder, the storm coming
closer.

Then I got it.

I said it aloud.

"They're coming."

They?

"Who . . . ?" I began to say, but I didn't need to finish the question.

Suddenly, everyone at the table seemed to finally hear the thunder, and all the laughing and talking just died. It was totally quiet except for the thunder. We all looked up at the storm clouds.

It was the hive ship.

It broke through the clouds, and then all the smaller ships broke off from the bottom and came at us.

Everyone was screaming and running by then. Mom was yelling orders to her soldiers. Dad was yelling to us kids to run and hide.

Then the first wave of burners and buzzers and drinkers hit us. They look like oversized insects. Moths and locusts and dragonflies and mosquitoes. Some were like mashups of different kinds of insects. Centipedes with butterfly wings; ticks with the wings of blowflies. Hunter-killers, all of them. Relentless robots programmed to destroy.

We were all running. The soldiers had guns even though no one had guns while we were eating. Now they all had rifles and handguns and shoulder-mounted rocket launchers. They started firing at the wave of hunter-killers.

The Bugs fired back. They don't use bullets. They fire blue plasma bolts that can burn through anything.

We all scattered. I saw Shark and Lizabeth running with Barnaby, but I lost them when there was a whole bunch of explosions.

Then I saw the girl, Evangelyne, walking through the smoke.

She said, "They've stolen the Heart of Darkness."

"Who cares?" I yelled back. "Get out of here. Get to cover!"

"A great darkness is coming," she said, and her voice was half hers and half the Witch of the World's. "It will consume this world. This world and all worlds."

Then another ship came down. Not a drop-ship. This is the red one I keep seeing. Big and red.

It fired on us and then everything went black.

Chapter 20

Milo woke in the dead of night, gasping, clutching with desperate fingers at the edges of the hammock. He was soaked to the skin with fear sweat, his thin sheet tangled like a snake around his legs.

His skin seemed to burn with the heat of the explosions in his dreams.

He lay there, panting, terrified, totally unable to move.

Listening to the night.

He wasn't sure what woke him up.

Maybe you always woke before you died in a nightmare. Like when he dreamed of falling. He always woke before he smashed himself to jelly.

So, he woke now.

Or, maybe it was something else that woke him.

A sound.

Was it the creaking voice of the Witch of the World?

The world does not want to die. It wants to fight back. It needs an army, child. It needs champions.

No. That was only an echo of an echo of a dream.

This wasn't an echo. He *heard* something.

Distant. Far away, carried by the night winds. Something so faint that it might have only been part of the nightmare.

However, the nightmare was fading, as nightmares do.

The sound, though, was still there, still riding the black breeze that roved over the forests alongside Bayou Teche.

It wasn't a machine sound. No buzzing or clanking or humming.

This was different.

This was an animal sound.

And, though it was so unlikely as to be almost impossible, Milo Silk believed with every molecule of his being that he knew what it was.

It was the lonely howl of a wolf.

Chapter 21

On Tuesday morning Milo woke to Barnaby yelling at him to get up, get his act together, get his head out of his butt, get fed, get dressed, and get in line.

He tried to hurry, but he was worn out by the dream and the hours spent writing in his dream diary instead of trying to get back to sleep. He'd finally fallen asleep with his face on the page and drool smearing the last few lines he'd written.

Milo was not comforted by the thought that it was all a dream and not the reality of the waking world. Too many things from his dreams had come true. He'd dream about people in camp going missing, and within a few days a small patrol was ambushed by shocktroopers. He'd dreamed of choking on food, and the next day twelve people were hit with food poisoning from canned food scavenged by Milo's pod. No one died, but two of them, including little Lizabeth, were deathly sick.

He'd dreamed of Dad getting into his car and driving away, and the next day he and his whole patrol was lost. Presumed dead.

So, Milo did not lightly dismiss what he dreamed about.

Not that everything came true. He once dreamed of angels coming to rescue everyone. And in another dream the Bugs were bug-sized and everyone from camp gathered around to stomp them under foot.

Even so, the fury of the attack and the precision of detail scared him spitless.

The girl's words stayed with him, too. They haunted him.

A great darkness is coming.

It will consume this world.

This world and all worlds.

And in his mind he could still hear the echo of that wolf's lonely cry.

The world needs a hero.

Did any of it mean anything? *You are a dreamer, child of the sun, but it is time to wake up and take a stand.*

He wished he knew what that meant. If it were a question about how much he would actually risk to stop the Bugs, then he knew he didn't have an answer. Milo knew that he was a long way from being anyone's idea of "hero" material.

But what did being a hero actually mean?

He didn't know.

And he dreaded finding out.

Dressed and more or less washed, he staggered

through the darkened camp from the bayou to where the other eleven kids in his training pod were already in line. Shark stood there, fresh and looking rested, grinning like a ghoul. He punched Milo on the arm as he fell into line.

"Overslept by twenty minutes," said Shark. "Smooth." He pretended to sniff the predawn air. "Wait. Is that the sweet smell of a freshly dug latrine I smell? No . . . Wait. You haven't dug it yet. Hope you like poop, dude. If you're lucky, they'll let you use a shovel."

Lizabeth, who stood on Milo's other side, giggled. So did most of the others.

Shark wore a big, toothy grin.

"Why don't you stick your head in a hornet's nest?" suggested Milo sourly. He yawned hard enough to make his jaw hurt, then sighed, long and deep.

A few moments later, Shark took a closer look at him, frowned and leaned closer. "Hey, you okay? You look like you got dragged by your heels down a mile of rocky road."

"Dreams," said Milo, which said enough. Not all, but enough.

Shark nodded. "Sorry, man. Knowing your dreams, I hope to heck I wasn't in them."

Milo didn't answer. Everyone died in his nightmare about the hive ship attack. So instead, he said, "Did you hear something last night?"

"Like what?"

"I . . . I thought I heard the wolf howling."

Shark shook his head. "I didn't hear anything, but Killer was acting weird last night. Kept whining. I thought he wanted to go out, but he didn't want to leave the tent."

"Yeah, well, I heard the wolf." Milo paused. "I think it means something."

"How could that mean anything? It's only a wolf."

Milo had no answer for that. None that he wanted to share right then.

Barnaby turned toward them, gave everyone a truly vile scowl, and stuck out his pointy jaw. He was fifteen, four years older than Milo, but not much bigger. Small, thin, with a beaky nose and eyes like a hawk. He rarely smiled and certainly wasn't doing it now. "Okay, now dat Mr. Silk has decided to grace us with his presence. . ."

"Sorry," mumbled Milo.

". . . we can do dis before we waste da *whole* day."

The sun wouldn't be up for another twelve minutes, but Milo didn't think it was in his best interest to point this out.

"We going along da bayou," said Barnaby. "A hummingbird drone spotted some wreckage by bolt-hole eight. Our job is go out, find da wreck, and den what we do . . . ?" He arched his eyebrows expectantly.

Everyone spoke in bored unison to give the required answer: "Approach, assess, assimilate."

"And how we do dat?"

"Smart, skillful, and sly," they answered.

"What do we do if dey's trouble?"

"Run, run, run."

Barnaby folded his arms and gave them a firm nod. *"T'as raison."*

That's right.

The bolt-holes were steel or brick-lined tubes dug into key spots throughout the region. Some were big enough to hide a dozen full-grown soldiers and all their gear; a few were two-person pits. All of the bolt-holes were shielded from radar and were designed to be invisible unless you knew how to find them. Knowing the locations of each bolt-hole was required for everyone. Checking, restocking, and cleaning them was the job of the learning pods. However, the bolt-hole—BH-8—that Barnaby mentioned was at least four miles southward along Bayou Teche toward the Atchafalaya River. That meant four miles in and four miles back, not counting the time it would take to actually find the wreck. Not exactly the five-mile hike Shark had said was on the schedule. Beside him he heard Shark groan as he realized the same thing.

Barnaby got up in Shark's face. "Do we have a problem, Mr. Sharkey?"

Killer, standing beside Shark's leg, uttered a low warning growl.

Barnaby glared down at him. "An' who asked you, gator bait?"

There was a lot of big dog in Barnaby's tone; Killer shrank into himself and pretended not to be there. Barnaby gave another of his firm nods and repeated his question to Shark.

Milo tensed. Shark had a habit of saying something smart instead of acting smart, and that usually got him in trouble.

But not today.

"No, *sir*," said Shark, his face totally straight even though he had to call a teenager "sir."

Barnaby gave him the stink-eye for a moment, then turned away. He pointed to a row of backpacks that were arranged in front of the food cart. "Supplies for da bolt-hole. Secondary mission is to restock BH-8. Everyone takes a full pack. Everyone carries dere own weight. Nobody helps nobody. *To konprann?*"

"Yes, sir," they all said. Everyone understood.

"Den get ready to pull out, you."

The predawn sky was showing the first hint of color and the temperature was already climbing. It was going to be another hot one. Everyone shuffled over to fetch a backpack. There was a lot of quiet groaning, but they helped one another to heft the packs—which were heavy—and to adjust the straps.

Little Lizabeth staggered and nearly fell backward when Milo hoisted it on for her. He caught her, steadied her, and making sure Barnaby wasn't looking, bent close and whispered in her ear, "First rest stop, I'll dig out some cans and put them in my pack."

She looked at him for a moment as if expecting some kind of prank or joke, but then smiled and shook her head. "It's okay, Milo. I got it. Thanks, though."

"You sure?"

She nodded bravely.

"Okay, my warriors of da wasteland!" snapped Barnaby, clapping his hands together with a sound like a gunshot. "Fall in."

They lined up again, and before they left, Barnaby asked if anyone had any additional questions about the "mission."

Shark couldn't help himself and raised his hand. "I have a question, Mr. Guidry, sir."

Barnaby's eyes narrowed with wary suspicion. "Yes, Mr. Sharkey?"

Uh-oh, thought Milo, but Shark was already in gear.

"Rumor control says there's a Stinger in these woods," said Shark, his tone reasonable. "What do we do if we run into it? I hear they're pretty fast. Do we run, run, run with these packs on?"

The team leader took a moment before he spoke, and in that moment he once more got up in Shark's face. "If we do, *Mister* Sharkey, den we'll feed *your* fat behind to him, and dat'll give the rest of us all morning to stroll to da bolt-hole. Sound like a sensible plan, you?"

Shark, wisely, said nothing.

"Okay," said Barnaby, stepping back and pointing toward the Teche. "Single file. I'm on point. Milo, you have our backs. Standard spacing. Everybody knows who dere escape partner is, so make sure you know where dey are at all times. Grab a stave on da way out. Okay, let's go."

Shark gave a last meaningful look at Milo, who grinned and shook his head.

One by one, they selected five-foot-long walking staves from a barrel at the edge of camp, and they followed one another into the woods.

Even though the woods around them were empty and dawn was starting to chase back the night, Milo felt an itchy spot between his shoulder blades. The way people do when they are sure they're being watched. He glanced around, but if there were pale eyes watching him, he couldn't see them.

That wasn't as comforting as it should have been.

Chapter 22

Everything was great for the first three and a half miles.

The sun rose like a threat. Harsh and glaring. Tentacles of mist curled up from the dewy grass and explored the spaces between trees, creeping along the trails and stretching over the surface of the bayou. The morning birds whispered secrets to one another.

Milo had been assigned to be last in line—not as a punishment but because Barnaby knew that Milo had sharp eyes and was good in the forests. You need a good observer out front and behind any group moving through uncertain territory. Milo was conscientious about his job, and he slowly and steadily let his gaze drift from side to side, watching the bayou, watching the forest, checking behind them, making sure it was all good. That they were all alone out there.

They skirted a small town, where a cluster of buildings was slowly turning to rot and pulp as nature reclaimed it. Milo's pod had long ago scavenged everything of use, from the last kitchen chair to a cell phone that wasn't totally rusted. Some of the chips from that phone had been enough to earn them all an afternoon off from chores.

A mile on they walked through a graveyard of dead aircraft. Leftovers from one of the first air battles against the Bugs. Milo knew that there were twenty-six fighter jets smashed into the landscape and only two of the Dissosterin attack ships. As they passed, he could just make out the line of crosses—each of them draped in moss—that marked where the pilots were buried.

The pod marched on, and Milo followed.

However, once, when he turned to make sure their back trail was clear, he saw a strangely familiar shape standing at the neck of the curve they'd just walked.

It was the wolf.

No doubt about it.

The animal stood there, silent and still, watching with its pale, pale eyes.

Once again, though, the girl's voice whispered in his mind.

A great darkness is coming.

And the whispered words of the Witch of the World.

Would you walk in the shadows if it meant saving the world?

As those words echoed through the corridors of his memory, Milo could swear—absolutely swear—that the wolf bobbed its head. As if it was . . .

. . . nodding?

"Oh, come on," he told himself. "It was just a dumb dream."

Except that his voice was a weak and frightened croak.

Without knowing exactly why he did it—this was only an animal after all—he smiled and raised his hand to give a small wave. His hand trembled as he did so.

The wolf watched him.

"Friends, right?" Milo said. It wasn't loud enough for the animal to hear, but it seemed important for Milo to say it, to put it out there.

The wolf did not nod its head again.

Milo whispered a name.

"Evangelyne."

The wolf watched him with unblinking eyes.

The words of the witch replayed in his head as clearly as if she were real and whispering in his ear.

The world is always half in shadows and half in the sunlight. That's what makes a world. If there were only shadows, the world would die in the cold. If there was only sunlight, it would burn up. It needs both sunlight and shadow to survive. Do you understand?"

The wolf watched as if waiting for him to react to a memory from a dream. It made Milo feel strange, as if there were no longer a solid wall between the stuff of his dreams and the things in the real world.

Behind him, Milo could hear the sounds of the others in his pod growing faint. He quickly turned to make sure they were still in sight.

They were, but only just.

He turned back to the wolf. . . .

It was gone.

The path through the forest was empty.

He knew that if he went to look for paw prints, he wouldn't find any. Just like yesterday.

"So weird," he said aloud.

Chapter 23

Freeze!" hissed Barnaby. He stood stock-still, one fist raised.

Behind him, Milo and the others froze.

It was what they had been trained to do. Like rabbits who want to live a long time in a world of quick-footed predators.

Milo had one hand on his walking stick and the other on the handle of his slingshot. His body was like a statue. The whole swamp seemed to be filled with statues. Everyone stood absolutely still, trying to become part of the foliage. Becoming invisible by not making even a tiny movement that could draw the eye.

Around them the Louisiana wetlands were big and green and noisy.

Frogs thrummed on logs in the bayou. Birds chattered in the trees. Mosquitoes hummed through the air like squadrons of tiny fighter planes. Leaves rustled in the soft easterly breeze.

Milo waited. Everyone waited.

And listened.

Milo prayed this was only an exercise. That it was another drill.

At the front of the line, Barnaby stood with his fist still frozen in the air, his head cocked to listen. Barnaby had been born here in the Cajun swamp country. He knew every inch of the lands all around Bayou Teche. It was impossible to beat him in a game of track-and-trap. So, even though Milo didn't see or hear anything out of the ordinary, if Barnaby said to freeze, then everyone, even the youngest of them, did just that.

Forty feet up and to the right, Shark met his eyes and mouthed the words: *What is it?*

Milo didn't risk shaking his head, so he mouthed, *Don't know.*

Barnaby was taking a long time listening. That scared Milo. If this were a drill to teach them to react to commands—which they did a lot—Barnaby would usually turn and watch his team to see if everyone was doing it just right.

So far, though, he hadn't looked back at the team at all.

That was scary.

This had happened three times before on similar training hikes. Each time they'd waited, waited, and then it was over. All a big nothing.

Now they waited, waited, and *kept* waiting.

Milo could feel his stomach clench into a knot. His legs trembled with the urge to bolt and run, and he could do that rabbit-fast. Milo may not have had a lot of muscle or height or bulk, but he could run like nobody's business. Only Killer was faster.

At the moment, Killer was frozen too, his little body crouched down near the ground, eyes alert, ears swiveling like antennae, nose twitching, muscles rigid. A line of hair slowly stood up along his spine.

Then, as Milo watched, Killer's muzzle slowly scrunched into a snarl. He bared all of his teeth and his nails dug into the dirt, preparing him to attack. Or run.

Past him, Milo saw the expression on Shark's face as he saw that snarl too.

That's when Milo knew for sure that this wasn't an exercise.

A moment later, Barnaby screamed out a single word.

"RUN!"

They scattered like leaves.

The pod, their team leader, and one little dog. Fourteen bodies that blew away from the clearing as if pushed by a gust of strong wind.

"Drop packs!" came Barnaby's order, and Milo felt his heart freeze. Dropping supplies during flight was serious business. You did it only in the worst circumstances.

Oh my God, Milo thought as he hit the release and let the pack fall off as he ran. Without its weight, he moved twice as fast. He cut left and ran toward a tangle of wild bougainvillea, smashed through the spray of purple flowers, and found a deer trail running southeast.

He hadn't taken four steps when he heard Barnaby's voice rise to an even higher shriek.

"No! Not dat way!"

The warning was one step too late.

As soon as Milo crashed through the screen of flowers, he slammed straight into something that rose up to blot out the morning sun. It was like hitting a wall. Milo rebounded from the impact and fell flat on his back, all the air knocked out of him. His walking stave went spinning off into the brush. For a moment all he could do was lie there and stare up at the monster who loomed above him, filling the whole world with horror.

This thing that had no place in the natural world. *Un*natural seemed to define it. Or, simply *wrong*. At full height, it was seven feet tall. Dark. Massive. Hard and cold and so, so wrong.

A green jewel, like a burning emerald, glowed on his chest.

Milo's mind felt like it was coming apart.

It was a *Stinger*.

Chapter 24

This wasn't Lizabeth's wild imagination. This was real and it was here. Right now. A thing he'd never expected, hoped, or wanted to see in the flesh.

If you could call the glistening shell that covered it "flesh."

If it were once a dog, it was a dog no longer. Instead of canine hair, it was covered in black-green mottled armor like the segments of an insect. Specifically, like those of a scorpion. The big barrel of its chest was wrapped in bands of the tough chitinous armor, and over the heart was a round socket set with a glowing green stone. The Earth Alliance had tried for years to acquire one undamaged, but never had. It was believed that these gems might contain valuable alien tech. This one was covered by a network of stiff wire, edged with razors. Small wiry hairs wriggled like black worms along the creature's sides. Its forelegs were tipped with razor-sharp claws, but they were not the worst thing about the Stinger. Nor was the grinning mouth filled with teeth as sharp as screwdrivers. Nor even the pair of secondary forelegs that grew from its upper chest and ended with big snapping pincers. No, the worst part of this creature was the massive tail that rose all the way over the creature's shoulder and was tipped by a bright red barb that was as long and sharp as a dagger and filled with paralyzing venom. One touch of that barb could drop a grown man and leave him helpless and vulnerable for hours. The same dose could kill a kid or a dog.

It was the very first monster Milo had ever seen. The first *real* one.

This wasn't in a book. It wasn't in a photograph or a video. This wasn't something he'd made up for one of the stories he liked to write.

This was real and it was right here. Its lifelight pulsed with the beat of its unnatural heart.

Terror was an icy hand that reached into Milo's chest and squeezed his heart with crushing force. For a moment he was frozen there, unable to move, unable to breathe.

The tail quivered in the air above him, and with a flash, it snapped downward, right toward his heart.

Chapter 25

Then Milo moved.

He moved very suddenly and he moved very fast.

He moved faster than he'd ever moved in his life.

Which is why his life didn't end right there and then.

Milo threw himself into a tight sideways roll, spun like an axle, and as he turned, he brought up his knees and elbows, and then he was on his toes and fingers, and then he was running on all fours like a sloppy dog.

The Stinger struck the ground exactly where his chest had been. The barb hit so hard, it took the Stinger a moment to tear it loose. A blow like that would have stabbed him through and through.

It was a terrifying thought to realize that he'd almost died.

Almost.

Died.

Not tapped in a game of combat tag. Not consumed by fire in a nightmare.

He had almost died for real. Right here. One second ago.

It galvanized him. He moved faster than before,

scrambling clear as the Stinger raised its tail again.

He thought about going for his fallen stave, immediately dismissing that as a suicidal move. He didn't go for his knife, either. A small hunting knife against an armored monster was just plain dumb. His slingshot was no good without time to aim and shoot. So, instead of fighting, he did what he had been trained to do.

He ran, ran, *ran*.

That was the plan. That was the training.

The Stinger struck at him with its tail, but Milo was already in motion and the daggerlike barb chopped into the dirt at his heels, missing him by mere inches. It jerked the barb free and jabbed again, tearing bark off a tree. And again and again, each time coming closer.

Milo dodged sideways and tried to slip around the creature by cutting around a stunted cypress. The mutant turned with him, snapping with one of its heavy pincers. Milo jumped backward, but the jagged tip of the insect claw snagged a fold of his shirt and tore it away with a huge *ri-i-i-i-p*.

Wearing only a collar, sleeves, and the flapping back of the shirt, Milo dodged two more swipes of the pincers and then had to leap over a thick bush as the scorpion tail whipped at his head. Small spots of fire seemed to ignite all over his scalp as droplets of venom from the quivering barb splattered him.

Milo hit the ground on the far side of the bush in a

very bad roll that sent him tumbling and bumping ten feet down the side of shallow ravine. Roots and half-buried stones punched him in the back and chest and ribs as he rolled down to the bottom.

He lay there, gasping and dazed.

Get up and run!

Those words—the voices of everyone who'd ever trained him—yelled in a chorus inside his head.

The scorpion dog began moving along the edge of the ravine, testing it to see if it would bear its weight. Hot drool swung in lines from the corners of its mouth.

Milo struggled to his feet and began running along the bottom of the ravine. A heavy thud behind him told him the Stinger had jumped down, landing hard on the spot where Milo had been lying.

A whimper of shear dread broke from Milo's chest.

As he ran, Milo tore the slingshot from his belt and dug into his pouch for a good stone. Found one. Pulled it free. Fitted it into the leather pad. He twisted around midstride, pulled back on the rubber band as hard as he could, and fired. Milo had won prizes—canned food, baked pies—in games like this. Running and shooting. It was the only thing he could do better than any of his friends. Better than Barnaby. And his skills did not fail him now. The stone whipped through the air and struck the Stinger in the face.

And bounced off.

The Stinger howled. Its green lifelight throbbed with the beat of its heart, urgent and furious. If it felt pain, there was no trace of it in that howl. All Milo could hear was hunger and fury.

Oh no, thought Milo.

The monster dropped down to all fours to chase him, and immediately began gaining ground.

Oh God. Oh God. Oh God.

Milo fired one more shot, hoping to hit the lifelight, but it struck an inch too high. He turned and ran. A fallen tree blocked the ravine ahead, but there was a narrow gap beneath it. Milo dove for it and slid through like a runner trying to beat the throw to first base. As he climbed to his feet on the far side, he felt the ground shudder and pitched sideways as the scorpion tail slapped down over the trunk and buried itself ten inches into the ground.

Milo twisted and fired a stone, then another and another as he backed quickly away. Each rock hit the Stinger in the face, and for a moment, the creature seemed to hesitate. Milo saw a single bloody tear leak from the corner of one eye.

I hurt it, he thought. *I actually hurt it!*

Then the Stinger leaped atop the tree trunk. It bared its teeth and bit at the air with its mouth pincers as its tailed snapped back and forth overhead.

It didn't look hurt at all.

Only furious.

Milo wasted no time looking back. He shot to his feet, grabbed the stub of a broken limb, and pulled himself onto the tree trunk.

There was a massive shuddering impact as the Stinger slammed its full weight into the tree. The shock knocked Milo off and back down into the mud.

"Owww!"

Milo got up, spun, and raced for the deepest part of the ravine. He knew this gulley. It angled down, and there were marshy spots that would still be wet from the morning dew. Down that far, the sun hadn't yet burned off the last of the fog. Milo hoped he could lose himself in the mist and maybe trick the Stinger into the mud pools. With its weight, it might get stuck. Milo knew where the rocks were that would bring him through.

He ran.

The Stinger howled loud enough to shake the world, then leaped from the tree and raced after him.

For the moment, its sheer bulk worked against it. The ravine was narrow and filled with storm-shattered trees and thick vines. Milo was skinny and agile, and this was no more difficult than the obstacle courses he ran in Survival 101 class.

He plunged into a waist-high fog bank and immediately ducked down beneath its surface. He felt for the ground and picked his way, letting his feet follow the trail his fingers discovered. The ground was even marshier than he'd thought. That was good.

Milo reached the point where the ravine split into two directions. The left arm went southeast toward the bayou, the right rose to dryer ground and an easy way out. It was a tough call. Try to trap the Stinger in the swamp or make for flat ground where he could make a run for the bolt-hole.

The Stinger made the choice for him.

It appeared as if out of nowhere, and the poisonous barb slashed past his right ear.

Milo screamed and ran to the left.

Forty feet along that arm, he saw a tumble of rocks on the near side of the ravine. They were bigger than the small stones he carried in his pouch. He jammed the slingshot into his belt, snatched up several of them, and began pelting the Stinger, still hoping to smash the life-light. The Stinger used its pincer arms to swat the rocks aside.

Milo adjusted his grip on the next one and pitched it like a split-fingered fastball. The rock burned past the flailing pincer and hit the Stinger in the mouth. Milo saw something dark pop into the air and realized he'd snapped off the tip of the creature's mouth pincer.

This time the Stinger bellowed in pain.

Green blood flowed from the break. The mutant reared up and tore at the air with its legs and pincers as if demonstrating how it was going to tear him apart.

Milo stumbled backward, dropping the rest of the rocks, and when he tried to turn to run, his sneaker sank to the ankle in mud. It stopped him right there, and Milo pitched sideways. It was only luck—if he could call what he had "luck"—that he didn't snap either ankle or knee.

But he flopped into the mud with his leg stuck as surely as if it were chained to the ground.

The Stinger uttered a cry of triumph that came close to cracking Milo's head open. The leaves on the trees lining the ravine shook as if in fear. With blood dripping into the mist, the Stinger began stalking forward, certain of the kill and delighting in the fear he could probably taste on the damp air.

This was it, and Milo knew it.

He struggled to pull his foot free, but he knew he had no time left.

Then a howl of animal fury split the air behind him, and Milo turned, certain that a second Stinger had come to share in the feast.

As he twisted to look, something leaped over him, coming out of the mists in the deepest part of the ravine, sailing over him, passing between Milo and the distant sun. It was big and gray and it seemed to be made of teeth and claws and hate.

The wolf!

It slammed into the Stinger.

Chapter 26

The wolf hit the Stinger like a gray thunderbolt, and the two of them went rolling and tumbling, snarling and snapping down the slope.

The mist swirled and boiled. Milo could see only part of the fight. The whip of the segmented tail. A clawed and furry foot. The flash of white teeth and the bulk of a dark pincer arm.

The howls and screams rose out of the melee to fill the morning air with horror and pain.

There was a crashing sound to his right, and for a wild moment Milo thought that there was a second Stinger, but then a bulky form crashed through. It was Shark. He held his walking stave in his hands like a baseball bat. He stared past Milo at the battling creatures. For a moment the Stinger's back rose above the level of the churning mist.

"I got him!" growled Shark, raising the stave for a hearty swing.

The Stinger's tail slashed out of the fog and struck the ground directly between the toes of Shark's sneakers.

"Oh, wait. No, I don't," he amended, backing up as fast as he could. He turned and ran to help Milo out of the mud.

Milo's foot came free from the muck with a wet *pop!* His sneaker was a high-top and laced up well, so it stayed on, but it was filled with muddy water.

"Run!" yelled Milo, shoving Shark back the way they'd come.

Killer came yipping and barking out from under a shrub. The little Jack Russell was fierce and brave. He darted toward the dueling creatures as if he were going to join in.

"Killer—*no!*" Shark and Milo both yelled. The terrier ignored them and began edging toward the oncoming monster.

Once more the Stinger rose up from the fight, and this time it bent low and roared at the dog. The green glowing gem on its chest pulsed like a heartbeat.

Killer instantly stopped barking and seemed to take a moment to consider the realities of the situation. Then, as his master had done, he turned tail and bolted, zooming past Shark and Milo and vanishing into the brush.

The boys, no less terrified, followed.

The Stinger's tail quivered in the air, ready to strike, but then the wolf leaped up again and dragged the mutant down. There was a fresh wave of screams and howls.

Then something came flying out of the mist, twisting

and yelping, and went hurtling into the foliage on the side of the ravine.

The wolf.

Bloody and defeated.

With a scream louder than anything that had come before, the Stinger rose up on its hind legs and bellowed its triumph.

Milo pulled his slingshot, twisted as he ran, and fired two more stones, hoping to hit an eye.

He hit the thing's chest and its nose. Blood erupted from the Stinger's nostrils, but the only effect was to make it scream louder, with greater hatred.

"Stop . . . ," gasped Shark, ". . . doing . . . that. . . ."

Milo didn't shoot any more stones because in the next instant, the Stinger was running on all fours, using its dog muscles to devour the distance between them.

Stingers could run very fast.

Way too fast.

Milo and Shark cut left and right, ducking under low cypress limbs, dodging around towering live oaks, trying to confuse the line of pursuit.

"Head for da bolt-hole, you!" came the yell from far off to their right.

Barnaby.

Shark and Milo turned on a dime and slanted down-land, using the slope to build momentum. BH-8 was on the banks of Bayou Teche nearly three hundred yards away. It was a steel-lined rabbit hole waiting for the rabbits. If they reached it and got inside, not even a Stinger could get them.

Three hundred yards, though. Three football fields.

That seemed like an impossible distance.

Milo was already breathing hard, and between sheer terror and exertion, his heart was hammering faster than a woodpecker.

"Come *on*," he growled to Shark, pulling at him.

"I . . . I . . . can't . . . go . . . any . . . faster . . . ," gasped Shark, whose face had turned bright red. With each step, he was doing more staggering than running.

Milo pulled even harder, tried to help Shark run.

Killer raced ahead, stopping to turn and scold them with sharp barks, urging them to move faster. Out of the corners of his eyes, Milo could see other kids racing down to the bolt-hole. Lizabeth was out in front, running like a deer, her blond hair floating on the breeze. Others chased her down to the rally point.

Behind them the Stinger let loose with another of its dreadful hunting cries.

It chilled the blood in Milo's veins.

It was so close.

Then the leaves parted and the wolf jumped out of the brush once more. Its pelt was crisscrossed with slashes, and the gray fur was soaked with the red of her blood and the green of the Stinger's. It landed between the boys and the Stinger and stood four-footed on the trail. The wolf's body trembled—either from exertion or fury or pain. Milo couldn't tell. Probably all three.

The boys slowed to a breathless walk and then stopped to stare.

The Stinger slowed to a stalking pace, and Milo could see that it was also injured. Some of the armor was gouged and slashed. There were deep claw marks and fang punctures as deep and dark as bullet holes. The flesh around its lifelight was torn to ribbons, as if the wolf somehow knew that to destroy that gem would end the creature. However, the gem still glowed its ghostly green.

In Milo's mind, he heard his mother saying that the two Dissosterin shocktroopers had been clawed apart.

She had thought it couldn't have been a wolf, but Milo wasn't so sure.

After all, this wolf, this hundred pounds of fang and claw, had done terrible damage to a mutant more than twice its size.

Somehow.

But . . . how?

The Stinger was wary of the wolf. Perhaps confused by the fact that a defeated enemy had come back.

Even so, it kept moving forward.

Killer cringed down and peed all over the ground.

"Milo," gasped Shark, tugging at his sleeve, "we have to go."

The wolf tensed and sprang, moving with incredible speed as it drove toward the Stinger's throat.

"Kill it!" snarled Milo.

But the Stinger was ready. As the wolf leaped, the Stinger wheeled sideways and snapped out and down with the barb. Even from fifty feet away, Milo heard the sound of the dagger tip bury itself in muscle and bone. The wolf shrieked in pain, and for a moment, its voice sounded more human than animal.

The Stinger jerked its barb free as the wolf landed badly, tried to stand, wobbled, and pitched off the path into the fog.

"NO!" screamed Milo, and if Shark hadn't been there, he would have charged the mutant.

Shark dragged him back, and together they stumbled and fell and got up and staggered along the path.

The Stinger, not content with its victory, suddenly rushed at them at full speed, hungering for more kills, its tail ready for another death blow.

Milo shoved Shark over a blueberry bush, juked left, grabbed a fallen branch, and smashed the Stinger across the face. The monster got its pincer up in time to take most of the blow, but it staggered sideways against a tree trunk. Milo seized the moment and swung again and again, hammering at the Stinger's legs, hoping to cripple it. But on the second swing, the stick cracked and the top two-thirds of it went spinning off.

"Milo—*come on!*" Shark pleaded.

Milo kept hammering at the creature, still hoping to at least smash one leg. That would give them a chance. The Stinger seemed to smile at him, annoyed but amused at the futility of the attack. With a backhand sweep of a pincer arm, it smashed Milo against a tree so hard he struck his head. The stick fell from his hands, and he dropped to his knees, coughing, his chest and back on fire. He looked up with helpless eyes as the Stinger's tail rose above him.

Suddenly, Shark was there too, swinging his stave.

It was a very heroic thing to do.

Very heroic and very dumb.

Even from where he lay, Milo could hear the crunch as Shark's stave cracked against the Stinger's armored ribs. The stave exploded into flying fragments, leaving Shark holding ten inches of jagged stump. There was a flash as the tail snapped out and down, and then Shark was falling, falling, falling.

Something in Milo's mind snapped.

He drew his small hunting knife and jumped onto the Stinger's back. With a cry of desperate, hopeless fury he buried the blade between two segments of armor. Green blood erupted from the wound, and the Stinger screeched in pain. With a furious twist, it flung him off. Milo crashed to the ground beside Shark.

His friend lay in a tangle, his face gray, eyes glazed

with pain. On his arm was a red welt that was already swelling and turning dark.

Shark had been stung.

Shark was dying.

The shadow of the Stinger fell across them both.

Milo struggled to his knees.

Shark's mouth worked as he tried to say something. There wasn't any sound, but the word he kept trying to say was: *"Run!"*

"Shark!" cried Milo. "No!"

The Stinger loomed above them, tail thrashing, pincer arms snapping, dog muzzle wrinkling in triumph, closing in for the kill. All the little hairs along its side twitched and writhed. It bent toward Milo, and pale yellow drool dripped from its jaws to splash on the boy's face and chest. Milo had no weapons left, no chance left.

All he had left was his hatred for this thing and all that it represented.

"I hope I give you stomach cramps, you cockroach," he said weakly as the creature closed slowly on him. Then Milo hocked up a loogie and spat it right into the creature's face. The Stinger recoiled in surprise.

And one millionth of a second later, its head exploded.

Chapter 27

It was an impossible thing to happen.

It *couldn't* happen.

All he did was spit at it.

The Stinger's body remained upright for a moment; then a great shudder swept through it and it toppled sideways to flop onto the ground.

Dead.

Headless.

Ruined.

And it was all impossible.

Then Milo saw that someone stood behind the Stinger.

Only it wasn't someone.

It wasn't a person.

It only looked like a person.

Kind of.

The shape was person-shape. Two arms. Two legs. A torso and a head.

But it was not a person.

It was not . . . *human*.

The thing that stood there was made entirely of stone.

A statue built of chunks of rock pressed together and held by mud and moss. Wrapped in creeper vines and lichen.

The statue still had its fist raised. A fist of stone with which it had struck the Stinger so hard that the blow exploded the mutant's head.

Except all of that was impossible.

Absolutely impossible.

And since impossible things happened only in dreams, they happened only when he was sleeping, Milo obliged by rolling his eyes up in his head and passing out.

Chapter 28

A voice said, "Come on, now. Don't be dead. Don't be dead."

Milo wanted to say, "I'm not dead. I'm just having a nightmare."

He opened his eyes and saw that the speaker was Barnaby, and the Cajun wasn't talking to him.

Barnaby was crouched over Shark.

"Don't be dead," pleaded Barnaby. "Don't you dare be dead here, you."

Shark, however, looked dead. His face was slack, his eyes open and staring at nothing.

If this was another dream, Milo didn't like it.

So he passed out again.

FROM MILO'S DREAM DIARY

The other night I dreamed I was dead.
Didn't really want to put that in my dream diary.
    Other stuff I wrote down came true. But it's been
    bugging me, so I put it down.
I don't remember a lot of details. Every day it's harder
    to remember a dream. I just remember that there
    was a lot of fire, and some explosions, and I was
    running. Shark and Killer were there too. We were
    running from a Bug ship. Not an ordinary drop-ship,
    though.
I kept seeing bits of it above us, through the trees. A
    round ship, like the Bug drop-ships, but this one
    was painted red. The one I keep dreaming about. It
    had rows of pulse cannons sticking out and it kept
    firing.
We ran like crazy. Even Shark. We ran and ran. What's
    nuts is that even though we never got tired of
    running, we never got very far. And even though

the thing that was chasing us was only walking, it kept getting closer.

Then there was a fight of some kind. I don't remember all of it except that it hurt and I lost.

That's when I dreamed about dying. Usually I wake up when I die in a dream. Like when I'm dreaming of the hive ship blowing up our camp. Or falling from a hive ship down to the bayou. I always wake up before I hit.

Except this time I didn't.

I was kind of floating there, looking down at my body. I could see me dead on the ground. So freaky. So wrong, wrong, wrong.

I think that maybe I was inside the thing that killed me. Like somehow I _was_ the thing that killed me.

How messed up am I?

Chapter 29

When Milo woke up again, the world made a little more sense.

There were soldiers everywhere. The perimeter patrol. They tore past him, faces grim and angry as they fanned out and raced up the slope. Looking for more of the deadly Stingers. Barnaby stood a few yards away, his arm around Lizabeth's shoulder. Killer was snugged into the little girl's arms, and her face was streaked with tears.

A medic—a twenty-year-old named Ginnifer—squatted down beside Shark. Her face was tight with concern as she bent to examine the bleeding wound where the barb had struck. Shark's entire arm had turned a livid red and had swollen so badly it looked like it would burst. His fingers looked like tiny sausages attached to a meat loaf. Shark's face was slack and pale and beaded with sweat.

"Is he dead?" croaked Milo, terrified of the answer.

She glanced at him, surprised that he was awake. "No," she said through gritted teeth.

"Is he going to die?"

"Not if I can help it."

She uncapped a syringe, and without even waiting to swab the skin with alcohol, jabbed it into Shark's thigh through the stained fabric of his jeans.

For a terrible moment nothing happened.

Ginnifer muttered, "Come on . . . Come *on* . . ."

Shark lay as still as death.

Milo felt his heart sink.

Then abruptly, Shark arched his back and let out a loud groan of pain and protest.

Ginnifer pushed him back down, pressed her fingers against his throat, waited, counted, then sagged back, nodding.

"He's good," she said, looking greatly relieved. "He'll make it."

Milo struggled to sit up, but the world seemed to tilt on its axis and wobble. He sat there for a moment with his head in his hands.

Ginnifer worked on Shark for several minutes. Then she nodded to herself, satisfied, and turned to Milo.

"Let's have a look at you."

He tried to argue about it, lost, and endured her touches and pokes. There was fresh pain everywhere she touched. She sprayed the back of his head with something cold, used antibacterial swabs to clean the Stinger blood from his face, and checked his pulse, pupil dilation, and blood pressure.

"You're pretty banged up, but you'll live, too."

"I'm okay," said Milo, trying to fend her off. "I'm okay."

For a moment Shark opened his eyes and looked around as if trying to understand the things he saw. His eyes were bloodshot and his face all puffed out.

"M-Milo—?"

"Yeah, man. How are you?"

Shark licked his lips. "This really, really, really, really, *really* sucks."

Milo took his hand and squeezed it. Shark didn't squeeze back. Instead his eyes drifted closed and his hand flopped back onto the ground.

"No!" cried Milo as he grabbed for Shark to try to shake him, but the medic pushed him gently back.

"It's okay," said Ginnifer quickly. "If Shark were skinny like you, he'd be a goner. He has greater blood volume. Probably more than I do. After this, no one's going to bust on him for going for second helpings. He's one tough kid."

Shark groaned like an old man.

"Relatively speaking," amended the medic. "Mind you, he'll be sore, dizzy, and sick to his stomach for a few days. The Stinger's venom causes an allergic reaction, but the epinephrine I gave him is already working. See? The swelling is already down a little. Give it time and he'll be right as rain." Ginnifer studied Shark for a moment and then glanced at Milo. "Tell me again how all this happened."

When Barnaby and Lizabeth realized that Milo was

awake, they hurried over and squatted down. Killer jumped from her arms and tried to lick Shark awake. When that didn't work, he snuggled against Shark's side and whimpered quietly.

"What happened?" asked Barnaby. "How you do dat to da Stinger?"

"Yes," agreed Ginnifer. "How on earth did you do that?"

"Do . . . what?"

"How'd you kill dat *scisseaux*?" demanded Barnaby, using the Cajun word for an insect with pincers. "You have a grenade, you? What you use? I didn't hear nothin' go off, but . . ."

Milo looked at the dead mutant.

All of the details came back to him in a rush. He almost told them what he *thought* happened. What he'd seen.

Almost.

But didn't.

First a wolf.

Then a . . .

A what?

A man made of stone?

How was that ever going to make sense?

So he told them a version of the truth.

"I don't know," he said when they asked him to explain it all. "I really don't."

Barnaby gave him a narrow, suspicious look, and Milo

wondered if the pod-leader had seen some of it. Barnaby said nothing, though. Not about that.

"I have to check on da rest of the pod, me," he said vaguely, and wandered off.

Ginnifer called for stretcher bearers and oversaw the transport of Shark back to camp. That left Lizabeth and Milo alone for a moment.

She helped him get to his feet, and though he was dizzy, the world seemed to be less wobbly.

"You okay?" she asked.

"I guess."

They stood there, looking at the decapitated Stinger. Milo wanted to scream. Not only had he seen his first Stinger, but he'd fought one and seen it killed.

Already the details of the last few minutes seemed to be fading into a confused version of a dream rather than actual memory.

"I saw it," said Lizabeth, jarring him from his thoughts. He turned to her.

"What?"

"I saw it," she repeated.

"Saw . . . what?"

Her pale eyes were huge and haunted. "The stone man."

Milo could feel that familiar cold hand reach into his chest and take hold of his heart. "W-what?"

"I saw him," she said, nodding. "He came out of the mist and hit the Stinger and killed him. I saw it."

"Oh."

"He left footprints," she said, and pointed to a bunch of round indentations. They were identical to the marks they'd found at the debris field yesterday. "See? It must have been the rock man who stomped all over the crash site. Maybe he was mad because someone broke open that pyramid. I think the Bugs did that, and the rock man wanted to get them back for it."

When Milo didn't respond, she nodded as if he had.

"I saw the wolf, too," she said.

Milo ran his trembling fingers through his hair.

"They went off together," said the little girl. She pointed to the south, down toward the bayou. "That way. The wolf and the stone man. They went down there together."

There were no paw prints, but there was a line of the same round indentations.

After a few seconds, Lizabeth said, "Do you believe in monsters, Milo?"

He didn't look at her. He couldn't. He cleared his throat. "You're not asking about the Bugs or Stingers, are you?"

"No. I mean *real* monsters. Like in stories."

"I—" Milo began, but he honestly did not know where to go with the conversation.

Lizabeth smiled and nodded again. Then she took his hand and led him back toward camp.

Chapter 30

Tuesday morning turned into Tuesday afternoon and began creeping its way toward Tuesday evening. So far Milo hadn't liked any of it.

His body hurt everywhere. He was sure his molecules were bruised. And as for his brain, Milo was convinced that either he was totally nuts or the world was.

Maybe both.

He sat with Shark on the tailgate of an old army truck. Shark looked like Milo felt. They both wore clean clothes, but they were still grubby and shell-shocked. The aftereffects of adrenaline made Milo jumpy, and the epinephrine kept Shark on the edge of snoozing.

The only comfort was that someone had sent a runner to notify his mom's patrol. With any luck, she'd be back by morning. Milo would have rather had his fingernails pulled out than admit it aloud, but he really needed a hug. Not just any hug. A Mom hug. Shark would probably get one too. From Mom and his aunt Jenny.

They each had plates of food on their laps, though neither of them had much of an appetite. Every time Milo

177

tried to take a bite, the tines of the fork rattled against his teeth. His hands were shaking that bad.

Despite his reluctance to talk about it, Barnaby convinced Milo to give a full account of what happened. He did, but at first didn't mention the stone figure, but then Lizzie jumped in and ranted—quite loudly—about a boy made of rock. Milo flinched, expecting everyone to laugh at him, but they didn't. In fact, one of the officers, Lieutenant Jeter, floated a suggestion that everyone seemed to accept.

"Must have been some new tech," he said. "Some kind of exoskeleton with hydraulics to give the wearer extra strength."

"Do we even *have* that?" asked Shark.

"They were working on combat exoskels before the war. Maybe somebody built one."

"What about the rocks and all?" asked Milo.

Jeter shrugged. "Camouflage. I mean, what else could it be, right?"

That had been the end of the conversation. Jeter sent scouts out to find whoever had the new tech. Milo, for all that this was a reasonable explanation, was pretty sure they weren't going to find any rogue soldiers in high-tech battle armor.

Lizabeth, who'd been there during that conversation, laughed at the idea and went back to her tent.

Now it was just Milo, Shark, and Killer on the tailgate. Above the camo netting, the sun was tumbling toward the western tree line, and twilight was beginning to paint interesting colors on the sky. Pale purples and vermillion with streaks of yellow. It was pretty, and Milo usually liked the lurid sunsets even though he knew that intensity of colors came from dust and ash hurled into the atmosphere by the Dissosterin mining rigs. The ones that tore great gaping holes in the earth to get at the rich veins of minerals.

The people of the sun . . . your people, the Witch of the World had said in his dream, *hammered in the first cracks. Now the Swarm has come from behind the stars to kill what is already dying.*

Remembering those words made him shudder. They felt a lot less like something from a dream and too much like a statement of fact.

"Well," said Shark, whose face was a ghastly shade of gray-green, "that really sucked."

He was so weak, he gave it only one "really."

"Yeah," said Milo softly. "Yeah, it did."

Shark looked like a sick old man instead of an eleven-year-old boy. He sipped the snot-tasting tea from his canteen, wincing as it went down.

"Really tastes that bad?" asked Milo.

"It's not that," said Shark is a husky voice. "My throat's still closed. Hard to swallow, you know. And I feel like a balloon, which is just what I need—to look fatter."

"You don't look fatter," said Milo. "You look kind of . . . inflated."

"Gee, thanks," said Shark sourly.

"Could be worse."

"How?"

Milo tried to make a joke, frowned at the middle distance, then shook his head. "I got nothing."

They sat there, both of them totally wrung out from what happened.

"A Stinger, dude," said Shark after a while.

"A Stinger," agreed Milo. "Geez."

They both shivered.

After a while, Milo said, "Look . . . about the other stuff. The wolf and all . . ."

"Yeah."

Shark shook his head. "Am I crazy, or did she try to save us from the Stinger?"

"Seemed like it to me. Kept going after the Stinger."

"I didn't get a great look at it, Milo, but I don't think it was a real wolf."

"What do you mean?"

"I mean it's probably someone's dog. Maybe it looks like a wolf or it's part wolf. I don't know," said Shark. "But, c'mon, dude. Wild animals don't just up and rescue kids from alien mutants."

Milo said nothing.

A few minutes passed. The colors of the sunset became more intense, more bloody.

Shark said, "The exoskel tech?"

"What about it?"

"Do you believe that's what it was? That rock guy, I mean?"

Milo chewed his lip.

Shark nudged him. "Say something."

"Okay," said Milo. "I got to tell you some stuff, but you got to promise not to say I'm crazy."

Shark ticked some items off on his fingers. "Wolf. Pyramid. Cold zone. Stomp marks all over a crash site. Stinger. Wolf again. And maybe new tech or maybe a man made out of rocks. Crazy? I don't know, man. How much crazier can today get?"

Milo almost laughed at that.

Then he told Shark everything.

This time he held nothing back. He told Shark every word of the strange conversations with Evangelyne Winter. Her obscure references to the orphans and the spirits of darkness. His dreams about the Witch of the World. Everything Lizabeth said about the round footprints where they'd had the fight with the Stinger. And what he really saw when the Stinger was killed.

It was the very first time Milo had ever totally opened up to anyone. The first time he'd ever mentioned the things he wrote in his dream diary. The whole story took a while. The sunset burned brighter and stranger. Shadows began to grow under the parked vehicles and beneath the reaching branches of the trees. The air around them seemed unnaturally still.

When Milo was done, the two boys sat there and didn't look at each other for a very long time.

Eventually, Shark said, "Wow."

"I know."

"Those round footprints were from the rock boy?"

"I . . . think so."

Shark grunted. "Makes me wonder if that's what the scouts found."

"What do you mean?"

"The patrol your mom and Aunt Jenny went out on. They found two shocktroopers who'd been clawed up and smashed flat, right? Who does that sound like? A wolf and a kid made out of rocks. If that's even possible."

"You think I'm nuts, right?"

Shark shook his head slowly, though Milo didn't know if that meant his friend didn't think he was crazy, didn't believe him, or didn't know how to answer.

Milo never found out.

Killer suddenly jumped to his feet and stared at the sky. His fur stood up, stiff as a bristle brush along his spine. The unused forks on their plates began to rattle again. Then the plates themselves started to shake.

To tremble.

"What the heck is . . . ?" asked Shark, but his words trailed off.

They both heard it then.

A low, heavy rumble.

Milo felt his mouth instantly go dry.

He looked up through the gaps in the camouflage netting stretched from tree to tree over the camp. He could see the wispy clouds far above.

But as they watched, those clouds thickened and darkened. The white edges seemed to boil. The sun grew abruptly dimmer and then vanished behind a pall of darkness.

They were not storm clouds.

This was not thunder.

"Oh no . . . ," he breathed.

He had never seen this in real life. Neither had Shark. But in dreams . . .

In last night's dream.

They stared in slack-jawed horror as the clouds suddenly boiled away to reveal a dark patchwork of fused metal. It filled the whole sky. So huge. So ugly.

So close.

"God . . . ," he heard Shark say in a tiny, faraway voice.

This was no dream.

It was a hive ship.

Chapter 31

Someone yelled, *"They found us!"*

That's when the screaming started.

And the gunfire.

Milo was trapped inside the moment, unable to determine if this was really happening or if he was dreaming. Was he still back where he'd found the Stinger? Was this another nightmare?

It had to be.

This was exactly what happened in his dreams. He'd written this down a hundred times. Even though the camp had been moved so often and was so well hidden under the camouflage canopy, the Dissosterins had found them.

That was always the fear. The Bugs never stopped looking. Never. They were as relentless as they were merciless. They hunted for EA camps to steal supplies, to end resistance, to take captives. To destroy.

Milo's heart sank.

The hive ship burst through the clouds. The swarms of hunter-killer machines. Soon the shocktroopers themselves would come flying over the trees, squads of them clinging to the sides of their drop-ships like wasps on a nest.

This was only a dream.

Except that it wasn't.

The sounds were different. Everything was more confused. Muddier, overlapping, deafening. There was the stink of smoke in the air, and he never remembered smells from his dreams. Goose bumps rose on his skin. His heart began racing.

Real.

This was real.

Oh my God. This is real!

Suddenly, Milo was in motion.

He flung his plate away and jumped off the tailgate. The ground seemed to ripple under him as the shock waves shook the camp. A hunter-killer drinker—a flying foot-long tick that could suck all the life out of a person— flew directly at him, and Milo swatted it out of the air. The impact numbed his hand. The drinker struck the fender of the truck and dropped to the dirt, the wings beating furiously to regain altitude. Milo stomped down on it. Once, twice, again and again until the metal shell split apart and the green lifelight burst into a cloud of glittering crystal dust. Fire and sparks shot upward from the machine.

The sky seemed to be filled with glowing green lights. There were more of the hunter-killers in the air. So many kinds. More of the drinkers as well as iron-toothed biters that were as big as bobcats and clouds of mechanized gnats whose tiny mouths carried drops of a neurotoxin that could paralyze a grown man. Poppers exploded in the air, blowing apart the camouflage netting, exposing the camp to the Swarm.

"Shark!" yelled Milo as he grabbed his friend's arm. "We got to go!"

He pulled Shark off the tailgate, but Shark was still so sick and weak that he stumbled two steps and dropped to his knees.

"Go!" gasped Shark. "Milo, run. Don't worry about me."

"Oh, *shut up!*" Milo grunted as he jerked Shark to his feet again, wrapped his arm over his shoulders, and began to half carry him.

A grinder—nine feet long and driven by a frenzied high-speed engine—ripped across the camp, the chain-saw blades scything through poles that supported clothes-lines and tents. It whipsawed in the air like a snake, and when it caught their movement, it changed direction and flew straight for them.

"We'll never make it. Get out of here," insisted Shark, trying to shove Milo away.

Milo grabbed him and spun Shark's bulk around and down just as the grinder tore through the air where they'd been standing. Milo felt the grinder's whirling blades snip off a good inch of his hair as they fell. The hunter-killer slammed into the truck and immediately began chewing its way through the metal and glass.

A jumper—a hunter-killer shaped like a rabbit-sized grasshopper with rotating rows of steel teeth—came hopping toward them. Just as Shark began to fight his way to his feet, Milo shoved him down again and half pushed, half kicked him under the truck.

"Sorry!" cried Milo, but he wasn't. Not really. All he cared about was getting them both to safety. Killer was barking furiously at the approaching craft.

Milo tore the slingshot from his belt, snatched up a chunk of torn metal that the grinder had spat out as it devoured the top of the truck, slapped it into the pad, pulled, and fired. The metal was lumpy and awkward, but it also heavy and sharp. It hit the jumper in the mouth from seven feet away. Hard. The steel teeth chomped down on it but couldn't bite through it. Milo could hear the engines racing as they tried to bite through something as tough as its own teeth.

Milo stepped forward and kicked the jumper in the side of the head, and when it fell, he jumped up and down on it until it burst apart.

A boomer—a machine like a yard-long metal centipede—raced toward them on a hundred tiny red legs. Milo didn't dare kick that one because each segment of the boomer was actually a small explosive. Killer made a dash for it, barking his head off, but Milo shot a hand out, grabbed the edge of the little canvas harness the dog wore, and jerked the terrier off its feet. With his other hand, he scooped up the boomer, twisted, and flung it at the grinder atop the truck.

He was hoping for them to destroy each other, but as the two machines collided, they switched off and fell inert on the ruined truck hood. Aunt Jenny had told them about this. The Bugs had programmed their machines to go into a temporary safe mode at times to prevent damaging one another. As soon as the two hunter-killers rolled apart, though, their green lifelights flared back on. The boomer scuttled over the far side of the truck and disappeared. A second after it was gone, the grinder fired up again.

Above them, something exploded with such sudden force that the truck rocked side to side on its tires, one set of wheels lifting completely off the ground. Then it thumped down and jounced on its tired old springs. A moment later, a string of smaller explosions popped all around them.

"We got to get out of here!" cried Shark weakly, his eyes wild with fear.

Milo wormed to the edge of the chassis and peered out at a scene of absolute horror. The camp was under full assault. He couldn't see any place to run to.

Then he saw the worst thing of all.

An attack by hunter-killers could be dealt with. Most of these soldiers had faced that before in different camps across the American south. But now there were shapes moving at the edge of the burning camp. Hunched, nightmare shapes that scuttled on four spidery legs, but instead of the bulbous bodies of arachnids, they had torsos like men. Big and muscular and coated with a blend of their natural insect armor and alloy plating. Each of them had a green lifelight glowing on their chests and blue pulse rifles in their deformed hands.

Milo mouthed the word.

Shocktroopers.

There had to be a hundred of them, with more descending on steel lines from the drop-ships.

Their armor was as ugly and patchwork as their ships.

People were running everywhere. Some of them had guns; others were trying to find guns. The old people were herding the little kids toward the armored vehicles. All around them, and filling the whole sky, were machines of every kind. Dragonfly buzzers that dropped grenades. Short-range jabbers that looked like hornets and attacked with stingers as long as bayonets. Jumpers that bounded like wolf spiders and exploded as they landed. Spitters that shot tiny marble-sized stunner devices from their tubelike mouths.

These and so many others. Too many for his reeling mind to catalog.

It was a full-scale invasion of the camp.

This was the *end* of his camp.

This was the end of everything.

FROM MILO'S DREAM DIARY

I had another one of those dreams about the Witch of
    the World. She kept trying to whisper stuff to me.
    Things that didn't make sense.
Stuff about evil. Stuff about saving all the worlds.
    That's how she put it: "all the worlds."
I asked her why she thinks I could do anything about
    that. I mean, who am I? I'm nobody special.
She laughed at me. Or maybe she thought the question
    was funny.
Then she said something I didn't really understand.
She said, "Not everyone is the hero of his own tale.
    But everyone should try to be."
Before I could ask her what she meant, I woke up.

Chapter 32

A figure broke from cover and ran toward him, zigging and zagging to dodge explosions and frustrate any attempt to hit him. It was Barnaby. One side of his face was bloody, but his eyes were clear and filled with anger and determination. He had a Dissosterin pulse rifle in his hands and fired as he ran, blowing jumpers and grinders to fiery bits.

Now, that's a hero, thought Milo, envying Barnaby for being everything he felt he himself was not.

Barnaby skidded to a halt and ducked low to peer at them.

"*Bonsoir, mes amis*," he said as he half slid under the truck. "You alive or dead, you?"

"Alive," they gasped.

"Well, you're gonna be dead if you stay here. Dem Bugs mean it dis time."

"I don't think I can make it," said Shark. "Can't . . . breathe . . . and my arm . . ."

"Yeah, yeah, your arm. Dat's what you get for standing too close to a Stinger, you. Now, come on, chunky. We got to get your butt out of here before we all Bug food."

A pair of soldiers ran past the truck, both of them firing heavy machine guns. Beyond them, lost in the swirling smoke, a Stinger screamed in pain.

"Are we winning?" asked Milo hopefully.

"Dat's a hive ship up there," said Barnaby. "Dey probably got a million Bugs on dat. Do you tink we gonna beat dat with machine guns and a few rocket launchers, you?"

"What do we *do*?"

Barnaby didn't look at him and didn't answer. Instead he began pulling at Shark. "Come on, Mr. Big. We need to get you out of here."

"I can't . . ."

"Shut up and try, you," said Barnaby; then he flinched as a nearby stack of crates exploded. "We can try for da bolt-hole or head northwest to rendezvous point Delta. Take your pick."

"What about the others?"

"Pretty much every man for himself," said Barnaby. "C'mon. Less talk and more walk, you. Or, run."

When Shark still hesitated, Milo leaned close and said, "You can lean on us. C'mon. We can do it."

Killer barked loudly as if agreeing.

There was so much fear in Shark's eyes that Milo didn't think his friend would—or perhaps even *could*—move; but he did. He clamped his jaw shut, pulled his mouth into a tight line, and began to crawl.

There wasn't a lot of room under the truck, and Shark

filled most of it. The pipes and struts impeded their prog-
ress, but together they crawled through the dirt toward
the front of the truck. The closer they got, the more of
the battle Milo could see.

It wasn't good.

It didn't look like they were winning.

Trucks and equipment carts lay on their sides, or were
wreathed in flame, or exploded as the hunter-killers targeted them. People ran and fired.

And died.

Milo saw soldiers go down. Shot. Speared by Stinger
barbs. Blown to gray dust by the pulse weapons fired by
the shocktroopers. Here and there lay a fallen Stinger or
a crumpled hunter-killer.

There were no dead 'troopers, though. Milo saw bullets ping off their armor and ricochet into the smoke. He
saw an arrow whistle through the air to strike one in the
chest two inches from a lifelight and then be plucked out
and cast aside by the 'trooper as if it were as harmless as
morning dew. A few of the 'troopers stood on two powerful legs, firing strange little guns that fitted around their
four insectoid hands.

He heard a small sound and turned to see Barnaby's
dead-pale face beside him. The Cajun was muttering a
string of prayers.

"How come nobody's trying to hit the shocktroopers'
lifelights?" demanded Milo.

"Dem things are shielded. I hit one dead square with a shotgun, but I might as well have been trowin' kisses at it, me. Din' do nothing." He shook his head. "Dey must know we got some pulse rifles. Dey came ready for dis fight."

Then they all jumped as a grinder smashed through the cab of the truck and began chewing its way through the metal.

Downward.

Toward them.

"Got to go," grunted Barnaby in a voice that was all fake calm.

"Shark, c'mon, move," yelled Milo as he twisted around and pushed, shoved, and kicked Shark out from under. Barnaby scrambled out, nimble as a monkey. He hooked Shark under the armpit, hauled him to his feet, and instantly they set off together, calling for Milo to catch up.

Milo tried to slide out, but his belt caught on something in the undercarriage. He jerked to a stop, unable to pull free.

"Milo—come *on!*" screamed Shark.

"Haul it, you!" yelled Barnaby.

"I'm trying!" cried Milo. He tried to tear loose, but he was caught fast. So he dug his knife out of its sheath and twisted it behind him so he could saw at the belt.

Shark and Barnaby were heading for the far side of

the camp, where a path led off to a game trail at the end of which was a bolt-hole. BH-2. They kept turning to wave at him, urging him to hurry up.

The world needs a hero.

The Witch of the World's voice was right there in his mind.

"I'm not a freaking hero," Milo growled back.

The blade sliced through a belt loop and then through the belt itself, and he dropped flat on his stomach. Free.

"Coming!" he said as he crawled like a frog out from under the truck. "Wait for me!"

But they were gone, and there was too much noise for them to hear.

Screams of rage and pain filled the air as the soldiers and students and camp followers fought for their lives and tried to flee. A soldier ran at him and shoved Milo away from the truck.

"Get back, kid," he yelled as he brought his rifle up and fired at the grinder. It twitched under the assault and turned toward the soldier the way an angry snake would, its body coiling, blades whirling. Then the soldier hit the lifelight on its central column.

The grinder exploded.

Everything has a weak spot, his mom had said. *Find it, and you have a real chance to win.*

For the hunter-killers, the green disk was the key. He turned to watch the soldier fire at several other devices.

Most of the rounds did nothing beyond surface damage. Until a bullet found the right spot, then—*boom!*

"Milo," snapped the soldier, "get to cover. BH-2. Go!"

A second later a pulse of blue plasma struck the soldier and sent him flying backward, his rifle twisting into metal slag as it fell.

Milo flung himself sideways and lay behind the cover of the ruined truck, staring in absolute horror.

He had seen death a thousand times in dreams.

Never before in real life.

Not until today.

Not this close.

He tried to remember the soldier's name.

Farley. Or Fraley.

Something like that. He couldn't remember exactly, and he couldn't remember the man's first name at all.

He wanted—*needed*—to remember that name. This soldier—this person—had saved his life and then died for it.

Tears burned in Milo's eyes. The soldier was maybe thirty. He'd had a life. He'd had a full name and maybe family. He'd been part of the camp, one of his mother's soldiers.

He'd been brave enough to face down a Stinger, to fight it and kill it.

And he'd been snapped out of the world by a single dot of blue light.

Just like that.

Like he didn't matter. Like his life was of no importance at all.

It shocked Milo.

It *hurt* him.

And it made him mad.

So incredibly mad.

Was this what happened to his father? Had the Dissosterin insect minds discarded him without thought or feeling? Had they thrown his life away like it didn't matter?

He snatched up a piece of broken metal and hurled it upward. He threw it with every ounce of strength, aiming for one of the small flying insect machines. The metal chunk clipped one wing, and the teapot-sized flying bug tumbled to the ground. Milo ran to reach it, and as it landed, he stomped it with his heel.

The internal workings exploded, blowing out the lifelight and shooting a spike of fire upward. Milo, luckier than he deserved to be, was knocked backward, but that was all it was. Many of the insect craft were bombs. This one was not. He didn't know its purpose, but as he fell, his heel throbbing from the shock, he realized how incredibly stupid he'd just been.

"Milo!" called Shark, his voice faint through the din. "Come on!"

Milo wheeled and ran. There was ninety feet of war

zone to cross to where Barnaby and Shark crouched at the head of the game trail. They waved him on.

"I'm coming!" he shouted again.

Suddenly, a ship descended through the smoke. It was round, like a drop-ship, but the design was different. The metal was smooth and orderly rather than the ugly patch-work design of the other Bug crafts; and that gleaming metal was painted a bright, bloodred. Unlike every other Dissosterin machine that Milo had ever seen or heard about, this one had a design painted on it: a silhouette of a Stinger rearing onto its back legs so that it could strike with claws, pincers, and barbed tail simultaneously.

As Milo watched the craft descend slowly to the ground, his heart immediately was filled with a super-stitious dread. It was as if this craft—and whoever was aboard—was something more terrible and frightening than anything else. More frightening than the shock-troopers. More frightening even than the Stingers. It was a reaction born of total instinct.

It was a reaction fueled by the fact that Milo had seen this very craft in his dreams. It had landed just this way—slowly, as if it didn't care that there was a battle. As if it feared nothing and no one. As if the world onto which it alit should instead tremble at its coming.

Barnaby and Shark saw it and veered away, and the Cajun turned and fired his weapon at it. It was an act of defiance that did no harm to the machine. As if in response, a wide gun port opened on the rim of the craft, and the blunt snout of a pulse cannon emerged.

Its lens flared with indigo light.

And then that whole side of the camp exploded.

One second there was a wall of green and the hobbling figures of his friends; then there was a whooshing sheet of brilliant flame that engulfed everything.

Everything.

Milo caught one last, despairing glimpse of Shark and Barnaby flying like rag dolls through the burning forest.

Chapter 33

*N*ooooooooooooo!"

His cry was lost in the thunder as explosions tore apart the camp. Walls of flame sprang up, creating a labyrinth of destruction all around him. They were like curtains going up on a scene from the end of the world. One minute the swamp foliage stretched before him, offering safety and cool shadows in which to hide; and in the next second there was fire everywhere.

Just like in his dream.

The walls of fire shot upward a hundred feet, and the heat they generated was like a fist that punched Milo off the ground and flat on his back. As the flames rose, he could see it carrying bits and pieces of the things he knew. The food cart rose as if pulled by strings from above, and its doors and windows flew open, spilling sacks of potatoes that instantly burned to coals and cans of soup and beans that swelled and then exploded like grenades. Weeks' worth of food, some of it scavenged by teams that hiked inland for more than fifty miles—gone in an instant. Tents rose with it, their canvas coverings whipping and turning inside tornadoes of flame. Even vehicles rose up—two Jeeps, an old SUV used for supply runs, and the command Humvee his mother usually drove. They seemed to jump into the air, and as they rose to treetop height, their gas tanks detonated—one, two, three, four.

Milo saw all this with shocked numbness. Then his eyes snapped wide as he saw the burned debris reach the height of its rise, pause, falter, and then succumb to the inexorable pull of gravity. Tons of blackened, twisted metal began plummeting toward where he lay.

The wreck of the SUV whumped down less than two yards behind him, and the shock wave picked him up and hurled him back toward the center of the camp.

He hit, tried to curl and roll like he'd been taught, bungled it, went bumping and thumping sideways, and came to a bruised stop against the burned skeleton of the tent his mother used to manage the resistance. All that remained of it now were charred poles that curled toward one another like the rib cage of some ancient giant. Everything else—the shortwave radio, the chests of arms and ammunition, the personal trunk with family photos and all of the pictures of Dad—was gone. Burned to a pile of ashes atop which small, fading fires danced.

Milo lay there, sprawled, hurting, shocked, and dazed.

And then he heard the roar of heavy engines, and he looked up to see a round drop-ship descending from the smoky sky. It had a glowing green engine core ringed by pads that sprouted like petals from a daisy. On each pad stood an armored shocktrooper. As Milo watched, the pads detached from the hovering landing craft, and the 'troopers began floating downward between the walls of flame, firing blue pulse weapons as they descended.

Milo forced himself to his knees and stared across the camp.

Across what was left of it.

The soldiers and everyone else were gone.

Blackened shapes lay sprawled on the burned grass. There was no sign of Shark or Barnaby. Nothing.

Even so, the Dissosterin hunter-killer devices kept popping explosives, which kept everything burning. There were several barriers of fire, each of varying heights. It wasn't a complete box, but there were enough of them so that the air inside the camp had become too hot to breathe.

He heard the bays of the Stingers. Very loud and very close.

Milo turned toward the nearest wall of flame—thirty feet away but feeling like it was an inch from his face—and within it, or behind it, something moved.

Once more Milo was trapped in a brain-twisting dilemma. Was this real or was it a dream?

He'd *seen* this last night.

He'd seen it on other nights.

This is nuts, he told himself. Then he shouted it aloud. "This is nuts! This is only a dream!"

Except that he was positive it wasn't.

A massive shape, bigger even than the scorpion dogs, moved inside the flame. Around it, the Stingers clustered like a pack of hunting dogs.

Run, child of the sun, warned the voice of the witch. As before, it was as if she stood just behind him, but this time there was a note of panic in her voice. *You cannot face this thing.*

"What is it?" Milo asked, aware that he was asking a question of a fantasy from his dreams. The hinges of reality seemed to have fallen off the day, so he figured why not? Nothing else seemed to make sense anymore.

He is what we all fear most. He is the monster that monsters fear.

Those words stabbed Milo through and through.

He stumbled backward, almost falling.

"Wh-why—?" stammered Milo, speaking aloud to a voice in his head.

He is looking for answers, whispered the voice. *He can sense that the Nightsiders are near.*

"W-who?"

The children of the shadows have accidentally led him here, and now you are all in mortal danger. Run!

The thing came directly toward him, and with each step, it became clearer that it was man-shaped.

Tall, broad-shouldered, with muscles crammed atop muscles so that his torso looked like a deformed ape. Gigantic.

But definitely human. Not a Bug.

Or, that's what Milo thought as he watched it draw closer.

He didn't stay to find out.

Run, run, run! shouted all of the voices in his head. The witch, Barnaby, his mom. Everyone.

Run, run, run!

Milo shot to his feet, cast around to find a way out, saw a narrow gap between two of the smaller flame walls, and ran for it as fast as he could run. He'd never run faster in his entire life.

As he reached the gap, he caught movement off to his left and behind him. The shape was about to pass through the wall of flames.

Milo turned away and ran.

"What is he?" Milo begged of his inner voices.

This is the destroyer, cried the Witch of the World. *This is the Huntsman who will hang us all like trophies on his wall. Run, child. RUN!*

Behind him, the howls of the Stingers tore the air.

Chapter 34

Racing down the narrow lane between the fiery walls was like running through a furnace. Steam rose from his clothes. His skin grew red. His eyes dried out and began to ache.

Run, run, run . . .

He had no idea who was yelling at him, urging him on. The witch, his mom, or maybe his own need to survive. It didn't matter. He ran.

The path between the flames could not have been longer than fifty feet, but it felt like fifty miles.

When he burst out into the clear ground beyond the camp, he staggered and went down onto his knees, gasping and gagging. The grass was damp, and he wished he could lie down in it, roll in it. He gulped lungfuls of cool air into his parched chest, blinking fresh tears into his eyes to moisten them. The tears, though, kept flowing. Two fat ones rolled down his cheeks, and all he wanted to do was curl up and cry.

Behind him, the Stingers bayed. Closer than ever. That terrible sound did not stop his tears, but it got his butt off the ground.

He ran.

Somewhere off to the north, on the far side of the camp, he could hear gunfire and shouts. This wasn't a slaughter. It was still a fight. He pawed the tears from his face and felt his mouth curve into a rough smile. The thought that his friends were still fighting put iron in his legs.

He ran even faster.

He shot a quick look back to see how close the Stingers were.

They weren't there.

Had he lost them when he ran between the flames?

He hoped and prayed so.

Be smart. Be safe. This time it was definitely his mom's voice, echoing in his head. Almost the last thing she'd said to him.

It steadied him. And it made him think. Really think.

The forest was dense, but there were several clear paths used by patrols, hunters, and just about everyone else in the camp. Some of the paths had been so heavily used that the brush was pushed back at and beaten down; others were so infrequently used that they looked like natural game trails.

Milo immediately cut left and ran down one of the well-trodden paths. This was something his mom had taught him: "When you're in a hurry and you don't have the time to erase your tracks as you go, then use a trail with so many prints and signs that yours will blend in."

He didn't run straight down the center of the path because that would leave too clear a sign. Instead he ran on one side, then the other, then jumped forward and to one side, constantly breaking up his rhythm so that his footprints weren't obviously the most recent. No one knew if the Dissosterin even understood trail sign, but it was the only skill Milo could think of that might give him a little edge.

The Huntsman can follow any trail, whispered the Witch. *He will follow you to the gates of—*

"You're *not* helping," Milo snapped irritably, and for a moment the voice in his head fell silent.

He hoped that the smoke and the stink of burning oil from the attack would clog the Stingers' noses and make it harder for them to track him. If he could shake them for a bit, he knew some ways to hide his scent. Barnaby had taught them all a lot of tricks, but those things would take time.

Time.

It seemed to burn away, too.

He ran on, leaving that trail, taking another, sometimes going through unmarked foliage. He found a stream that trickled down to the bayou, and he splashed through that until he saw a huge, lumpy green shape pretending to be a fallen log. It wasn't the biggest alligator he'd ever seen, but it was big enough. Ten feet from teeth to tail.

No thanks.

He went up the bank and slipped back into the forest, hoping the Stingers would run into ol' Mr. Gator.

Then, after he'd run at least a mile and maybe two, Milo stopped to listen. He needed to know how much trouble he was still in.

Listening was something Barnaby taught. The bayou is always noisy, so you have to filter out the sounds that are always there and listen for those sounds that aren't. They practiced it on every hike. It was a major survival skill.

Milo stood very still, looked at nothing in particular, and listened.

He heard the birds who were all chattering in alarm at what was happening. He heard the normal Earth insects, who didn't know or care about what their alien counterparts were doing. He heard the rustle of a nutria on the stream banks.

Milo let all of those sounds fade out of his consciousness.

Beyond them, behind them, he heard the other sounds.

The low rumble of the alien craft. It was still up there, but he couldn't see it through the dense canopy of trees.

The engine sounds of the smaller hunter-killer crafts were so faint now that he wasn't sure he could actually hear them.

There was no gunfire now. No new explosions.

He did not strain to hear. Barnaby warned against that. If you tried too hard, you sometimes heard things the wrong way.

He wished his mom were there. Not just to hug him and take him somewhere safe. No, he wanted her there because she was the best fighter. She said it herself.

When I lead a team, people usually come back.

Could she have turned this around? Could she have fought off these monsters—the Stingers, the shocktroopers, the grinders and poppers and all of the other alien tech?

Where was she? Where were Mom and her team?

They said she'd be back by morning.

What would she find? Would it be a burned-out shell of a camp and blackened bones? Would she find survivors? Or would the Bugs be waiting for her?

For a wild moment, Milo very nearly turned to run back to the camp, wanting to intercept his mother, to warn her. To save her.

The world needs a hero.

"I'm not a hero," he growled.

At the same time, he wished with all his might and will that he *was* the hero this world needed. A hero could save his mom.

A hero could stand up to that creature that came out of the fire.

A hero would have fought off the shocktroopers and . . . And . . .

You are a dreamer, child of the sun, but it is time to wake up and make your stand.

Tears burned in Milo's eyes and rolled crooked through the dirty landscape of his cheeks.

He felt very small in a world that was far too big.

The woods were strangely quiet for almost a minute.

"Okay, Miss Witch," he said softly, "if you've got something to say, now's the time.

The only voice in his head was his own.

"Great," he said sourly. "Very helpful."

He pawed away the tears and forced himself to keep going. There was a bolt-hole pretty close. Maybe a mile along the bayou. The question was whether he could he risk heading that way yet. The woods had been on fire over there.

There was something on the trail ahead. Milo paused, afraid that it was a body. But as he crept close to it, he saw that it was a soldier's gear bag, lying partly hidden by bushes that were withering and steaming from the heat. The canvas was scorched in places, and some of the contents had spilled across the path. There was a rifle with a bent barrel. A shotgun with a splintered stock. A handgun but no bullets. A military combat knife in a durable plastic sheath. A net bag of round metal globes that Milo recognized as S&F grenades. The letters stood for "sound and fury." They were designed especially for combat with the shocktroopers. Milo had heard about them but had never seen them used. All he knew was that they were very dangerous, and Mom had given him a long lecture about never—*ever*—touching one.

The rest of the stuff in the bag was either melted or broken. He took the combat knife and began to move off, paused, thought better of it, and snatched up the bag of grenades.

He figured his mom would understand.

Milo headed into the gloom, keeping low, running lightly along the secret paths, using the skills he'd been taught. With every step, though, he felt pain deep in his chest. Not physical pain, but heartache. Shark and Barnaby and Lizabeth and little Killer. The others in the camp. His friends. His extended family made up of a couple hundred survivors. Tough, good-hearted, incredibly brave people. Soldiers and teachers, cooks and scouts, scientists and medics. Everyone doing their part to help the whole community survive. Everyone doing their part to help humanity survive.

Were they all gone now? Were they dead or captured?

If they were, what chance did he have? What *point* was there to fighting for survival if he was all alone now?

A humming sound made him turn, and he saw the red craft lift above the trees, its polished crimson paint glistening like fresh blood. It was the ship belonging to the alien Huntsman. All around its rim, the snouts of pulse cannons peered out, looking to do more harm.

He glared hatred up at the ship as it passed overhead and then dropped down to land beyond a line of cypress trees. Tears burned hot lines on his cheeks. Right then, if he had possessed the power, he'd have leaped up and torn that ship from the sky.

Right then he would have given his life to destroy it.

"Shark," he said, putting his friend's name on the wind. It hurt to say it.

Then he heard two sounds that changed both the shape of his thoughts and the pattern of Milo Silk's destiny.

He heard the roar of a Stinger. Close. So horribly close.

And then he heard the high, shrill, terrified shriek of a young girl.

Chapter 35

Milo tensed and raised his head to listen.

The scream had been close. Somewhere here in the forest. Was it Lizabeth?

No.

He thought it sounded a little older than that.

The Stingers howled. Then something else roared. It was weird, more like a man trying to roar like a Stinger. So strange.

The woods were too lush for him to see much, so he began creeping along the side of a shallow drop-off toward a spot where the plants were sparser. The scream seemed to have come from that way. Beyond the woods, he could see the red hulk of the Huntsman's ship standing on eight hydraulic steel legs like a big metal spider.

There was no movement for a few seconds. No sound. Then . . .

The scream was so loud and close that he jumped and almost tumbled down the drop-off. He crouched down to catch his balance, and as he did so, he saw, between the stalks of wild sugarcane, a pair of feet running past.

Bare feet.

Girl feet.

Running fast.

A slim form whipped past, stirring the leaves, racing at full speed along the curving rim of the drop-off. The path angled around and down to the muddy banks of the bayou.

Milo parted the cane stalks and leaned out to see who it was.

And gasped.

He'd expected it to be one of the girls from camp.

It wasn't.

The slim figure that raced through the woods wore a dress of old linen, and her hair was the color of smoke. Her eyes were wild and filled with fear, but they were as pale and cold as moonlight on snow.

Evangelyne! And even as he thought that and remembered that he knew the name only from a dream, he was absolutely certain it *was* her name.

Evangelyne Winter.

With a pack of Stingers chasing her.

She ran very fast, wasting no time, moving like she meant it. But even with that, Milo thought there was a hint of a limp in her running gait. Like someone who was hurt but was fighting through it, running like the pain didn't matter.

As she raced along, Milo saw with growing alarm that she was hurt. Her dress was streaked with red, and there were long half-healed cuts on her arms and face. Something bad had happened to her.

Milo ducked out of sight as fresh sounds came from the other end of the path.

The grunt and wheeze of big dogs.

Dogs who weren't dogs at all. Not anymore. Dogs that also clicked and clacked as their armor plates rattled with each loping step.

Milo clutched the bag of grenades to his chest and let himself slide down the bank, allowing the rich, fecund, muddy dirt to partially cover him. Camouflage for eye and nose and mud to mask thermal scans if there were any shocktroopers here.

On the ridge, a Stinger raced past.

Then another.

And another.

Four in all. Each of them as massive and hideous as the one that had chased him only hours ago. Just seeing them sent shivers through Milo's body.

Then something *else* moved past.

Huge, tall, manlike.

Milo instantly knew that this was the dark and sinister shape he'd seen through the wall of fire, though now he could see it clearly. In all its terrible majesty.

This is the monster that monsters fear.

That's what the Witch of the World said, and there had been panic in her voice.

Now he could see it clearly, and if he'd been scared

before, he was suddenly nearly frozen with stark terror.

It walked on two legs, like a man. It had a man's torso and human arms, but that's where its connection to humanity ended. The body was wrapped in layer upon layer of chitinous plates, just like the Stingers. And, like those beasts, it had a set of pincer arms sprouting from its sides, just below the more human arms. The pincers snapped at the air as if practicing how to crush the limbs of the fleeing girl. There were plates and ridges along the human arms, too, and sticking out from each separate plate was a spike. Not metal—these were made of the same material as its insect armor. Dark and horrible. A green jewel burned like emerald fire on its chest.

Its face was the most horrible thing of all, though.

There was human flesh there, and maybe this whole thing had started out as a human, but then things were *done* to it. Plates of shell grew around it and over it, cutting into the skin, hiding most of it, replacing humanity with inhumanity, transforming man into monster. Antennae rose from the sides of its head, and the eyes were the multifaceted eyes of a blowfly.

But its mouth . . .

Milo swallowed to keep from throwing up.

The lips were stretched back to accommodate a huge pair of mandibles that snapped at the air as if tasting fresh meat.

Here was a monster a thousand times more terrifying even than the Stingers.

The creature's chest and hips were crisscrossed with equipment belts from which hung guns and other devices whose nature Milo could not even guess. In one armored fist, though, it held a whip made of leather studded with chunks of jagged metal. The thing raised its arm and flicked the whip at the slowest of the Stingers, leaving a two-inch gouge in its flank. The Stinger screamed and ran faster.

This creature—this alien-human hybrid of a Huntsman—passed along the ridge without noticing Milo. He strode behind a howling pack of scorpion dogs, snarling at them in a language that could never have been spoken with a human tongue. The Huntsman and his pack raced on, and far down the slope the running girl was losing ground. She kept having to cut right or left to avoid the Stingers.

Milo realized that the Huntsman and his pack were herding the girl the way dogs do with cattle and sheep. With every forced turn, it brought the girl closer to the clearing where the red ship squatted on its eight legs.

Why?

Were they trying to kill her or . . . ?

Or capture her?

Yes, whispered the Witch of the World. *The Huntsman very much wants to capture one like her.*

Milo tried to project a question to her without speaking. *What do you mean, "one like her"?*

There was no answer.

The girl cut left away from a leaping Stinger, and Milo could almost feel her frustration and fear as she realized what they were doing. She was so fast, though, that the pack had to work hard to keep her contained.

"All she needs is chance," he murmured to himself. One distraction and she could break through their line and get away.

If only there was a way to distract the Stingers.

"God . . . ," murmured Milo in a hoarse whisper.

Milo Silk had no intention of being a hero.

A hero was someone big and tough. Someone older. Someone who knew how to use guns or do karate.

A hero was Mom. The soldiers in the camp were heroes.

He wasn't; he was sure of it.

A hero would have gotten up and done something to help that girl, even though she was a total stranger.

That's what a hero would have done.

And Milo Silk was no hero.

Chapter 36

That's what he told himself. He even said it aloud.

"I'm not a freaking hero. I'll get killed."

It's what he'd tried to tell the Witch of the World.

It's what he believed.

What he didn't understand was why he was no longer hiding. Why he was running as fast as he could along the path behind the alien Huntsman and his pack.

Why on earth was he doing that?

Chapter 37

He raced along, low and fast, making maximum use of cover. The pack was focused on the girl, and she was simply running for her life.

The girl could run. Milo was impressed. Even injured, she could run like the wind.

Evangelyne ran barefoot through the woods, pulling her dress up to her knees when she leaped a creek or jumped onto and over a falling log. She ran like she had been born to run.

The Stingers, though, ran faster.

They spread out and ranged far ahead and to either side, angling around in a classic trap pattern to cut her off. Milo and his friends did that in their games of swamp tag. He heard the girl cry out when she spotted the closing arms of the trap. She paused for a breathless moment, casting wildly around for a way out and finding every exit blocked by a monstrous form, while behind her the Huntsman closed in for the kill.

The kill.

Milo knew that this was what he was seeing.

This is the Huntsman, who will hang us all like trophies on his wall.

A hundred plans formed in his head, and he dismissed each one as being silly or suicidal. A pack of Stingers and the Huntsman against a girl with no weapons and a boy with only a pouch of throwing stones, a combat knife, and a . . .

The bag of grenades was heavy in his hand.

He licked his lips, afraid of the thought that had stuck in his head.

The only possible plan.

He jerked open the drawstring and removed one of the green globes. It was about the size of an apple and weighed only a little more. The skin was a drab olive and *S&F* was stenciled on the shell. There was a plastic cap on the top. Milo knew that all he had to do was twist the cap and throw.

It sounded simple enough, but it wasn't. Did he have to count to four like the soldiers did while practicing with regular fragmentation grenades? Was it better to twist and throw right away, like they did with the nonlethal flash-bangs? And what about the blast radius? Milo remembered a safety lecture about grenades. The standard M67-X fragmentation grenade could hurl crippling or lethal fragments up to fifty feet, though some soldiers said that they'd known shrapnel to fly as much as six hundred feet, depending on elevation and terrain.

Milo's longest pitch was about one hundred and fifty feet, and that was playing outfield. He was better at close, fast pitches. He could never hurl a grenade six hundred feet.

These calculations buzzed through his head in a microsecond.

The Stingers howled.

The girl screamed.

The Huntsman threw back his head and roared in triumph.

"Hey . . . *girl!*" Milo bellowed, trying to get her attention so she could see what he was about to do.

She didn't even glance in his direction.

"Girl!"

Nothing.

So he thought, *What the heck.*

At the top of his voice, he yelled, *"EVANGELYNE!"*

Her head whipped around, and she stared at him with wide-eyed shock.

"Duck!"

With that, Milo twisted the arming cap, cocked his arm, and threw. The grenade rose in a high, high arc toward the gap between two of the Stingers, farthest from the terrified girl. One of the Stingers saw it and whipped around. It even hissed at the small green metal apple.

The Huntsman saw it too. He bellowed out a command to his pack.

The girl did not hesitate. She ducked.

Just in time.

The grenade hit the side of the red ship, bounced high, and exploded.

Sound and fury.

Very well named.

The sound was like all of the thunder that would ever trouble the sky compressed into one gigantic *BOOOOOOOOM*.

The fury was the shock wave.

Even from a hundred and fifty feet away, the force picked Milo up and flung him into a stream of muddy water. The shock wave flattened bushes and tore apart small trees. It bent two of the red craft's landing struts, and with a squeal of protesting metal, the ship canted sideways and bowed to the ground.

As Milo splopped down into the mud, he saw pieces of one of the Stingers go flying in all directions. Another of the creatures reeled back, mortally wounded and screaming out in pain.

The other Stingers screamed too, their bodies trembling with agony, their senses totally overloaded by the effects of the grenade. Even the Huntsman was staggered, and he leaned sideways against a tree, hands pressed to his ears, eyes squeezed shut, mouth open in a prolonged scream.

Milo looked to see what had happened to the girl. He'd tried to throw the grenade as far from her as possible.

He looked.

And looked.

But the girl was gone.

In the midst of the sound and fury, she had escaped.

Milo grinned despite the ringing pain in his own head and the muddy water in his mouth and ears.

He'd done it.

He'd saved her.

The growl behind him, though, told him that being a hero was going to come at a cost.

More than he ever wanted to pay.

A shape blotted out the twilit sky. Milo's head swam with dizziness and shock as the Huntsman glared raw hatred. He tottered on the edge of unconsciousness and lingered only long enough to see inhuman hands reaching down toward him and a green light, like the burning eye of a dragon, flashing at him.

The Huntsman turned for a moment to look at the dead Stingers and then at his damaged ship. His chest seemed to swell with fury. He turned back to Milo as he cocked his fist back. Milo had one microsecond to try to avoid what he knew for sure would be a deathblow.

The fist filled his whole world.

There was a white shock.

There was incredible pain, worse than anything he had ever imagined. White hot. Going all the way through him.

And then darkness closed around Milo like jaws and swallowed him whole.

FROM MILO'S DREAM DIARY

I always wonder if I'm crazy.

I dream of things that sometimes happen.

I talk to a witch in my dreams.

I don't know if I'm normal or not. There's not enough
   kids left to decide what normal looks like.

Part
Two

Six Years from Next Tuesday . . .

"There are very few monsters who warrant
the fear we have of them."
—ANDRÉ GIDE

Chapter 38

Milo dreamed that he was dead.

Or maybe he was dead.

He couldn't tell. He lay on the burned ground, his limbs cold and stiff, his breath stilled, his heart silent.

Only his mind remained.

But it was not connected to his body anymore. He seemed to float in the air above his corpse. He could see all of him and the ground around where he lay.

I dreamed this, he thought. He remembered writing this in his dream diary.

From up there, he could see the burning swamp.

And he could see the manlike thing—the Huntsman, as Milo now thought of him—and his pack of Stingers.

Several of the Stingers were bleeding and injured. Not far away, a pair of them lay dead.

I did that, thought Milo. *I killed two Stingers all by myself.*

Shark would think that was so cool. Maybe really, really, really cool.

If Shark was alive.

He thought, *Mom would be so proud of me.*

If Mom was alive.

If, in fact, *he* was alive.

From where he floated, Milo was pretty sure that, yes, he was dead.

So much for being a hero, he thought.

He hoped the girl was still alive. That, at least, would make his death mean something.

Then he thought, *What am I?*

A ghost?

No!

Milo didn't want to be a ghost. Small and invisible and powerless, wandering the ruined Earth forever. Unable to find his mother. Unable to hug her. To feel her kisses on his head and cheeks. Never again to share her warmth.

That made him so sad he wished he had eyes so he could cry.

It also made him furious, because he wanted to fight back against these monsters who had killed everyone he knew.

Rage was the only heat he could feel, and it burned like a small sun in whatever ghostly body he possessed.

Below, the Huntsman bent low over Milo's body and poked at it with a clawed finger. The body rocked limply, the way a corpse will. The flesh was pale, the lips bloodless.

There was a strange sound. Deep, creaky, and nasty,

and it took Milo a few moments to realize that the sound was coming from the alien Huntsman. He saw the creature's shoulders tremble.

He was laughing.

Laughing?

Laughing at a dead body on the ground.

At *his* dead body.

At him.

The heat in Milo flared hotter and hotter still. It pulsed and throbbed, and for a moment he imagined that his ghostly fists were solid enough to punch this monster. To batter him. To knock the laughter out of its hideous mouth.

With thought came action, and suddenly Milo felt himself moving. His spirit dropped from the empty air toward the Huntsman, driven by rage and grief and frustration. Milo could not see his own hands, but he imagined that he was clenching his fists and then he struck.

Or *thought* he struck.

There was no point of impact. There was no thud of knuckles on insect armor. No shock running up his arm from the force of the blow. No actual sensation of touch.

And yet . . .

And yet.

Something happened.

Milo seemed to pass through the Huntsman.

No. Not through him.

Into him.

It happened all at once, and it was instantly and completely bizarre.

A thousand strange and inexplicable images flashed through Milo's mind. They felt like memories, but they weren't his. He remembered touching things that he had never touched. The handle of a whip. The controls of a flying machine. The edge of a blade. The . . .

Milo's internal vocabulary failed him as the images became more exotic, and they overlapped with things his eyes had never seen but that his mind now "remembered." It was as if he was suddenly thinking the Huntsman's thoughts. Or remembering his memories. It was like peeking into someone's diary. All of those secrets opened to his eyes.

The images came in waves, and Milo was sure that the first wave was not those of the Huntsman. Not really. They were borrowed by him in some way. These images were of the broken and barren wastelands of alien worlds. Devastated mountains of silver and gold. Burning volcanoes rising through the melting streets of crystal cities. Rivers running black with pollution and flowing down to oceans devoid of all life, even to the smallest bacteria. Moons strip-mined and blown apart, hanging like debris above dying worlds. Valleys filled with bones that could never be assembled into shapes Milo would recognize.

There were views from windows. A final assault on

a green planet that loomed close as great ships hurtled toward it. The aching feel of a hunger that could never be satisfied as that world was devoured. Races of ape-like creatures and others that looked like evolved otters were hunted down, enslaved, and then consumed. Milo saw vast deserts of skeletons. He saw the last desperate survivors as viewed through the crosshairs of targeting mechanisms and then the harsh glow of blue pulses of destructive force. And just when Milo thought no more harm could be done to this world, the Dissosterin aimed their biggest guns yet into the deepest valleys and into holes they'd dug. The pulse cannons hammered at the bedrock, cracked the crust, shattered the mantle, and split the planet open to expose the white-hot core of molten metal. As the world exploded, the incalculable energies released were sucked into the hyperdrive engines of the hive ships. Absorbed, stored, ready to power their fleet for the centuries-long flights across the stars. Toward new stars and new worlds.

Between each conquest there was a dreaming time. A dying time as the drones and the shocktroopers and all of the workers grew old and shriveled into dusty husks. Leaving only a few slumbering queens who, even in their sleep, laid millions of new eggs for another swarm that would hatch when the hive ships found another world to plunder.

Then Milo saw Earth.

He saw it from space. A blue speck on a tapestry of diamonds and black velvet. Growing, growing, taking on the shape of a small world with green lands and brown deserts and sparkling oceans.

Earth.

This world.

His *home*.

Milo saw the hive ships cleave through the atmosphere, firing massive antigrav engines, releasing their scout and attack ships. Attacking the planet. Turning off the power. Shattering the cities. Wiping out so many people.

Beginning the process of consuming everything.

Everything.

Milo wanted this to end. He wanted to not see these things. They were too close to the horrible visions in his nightmares.

And for a moment the images did, indeed, stop.

Only for a moment.

Chapter 39

It was as if he stood in a lightless place and then a hand swept across a row of switches and turned the power back on.

Milo was no longer looking down at the destruction the Dissosterin had caused.

Now it was as if he were awakening inside the hive ship.

A familiar voice spoke in his mind.

See this, child of the sun. See and understand.

He wanted to ask, "Am I dead?"

Maybe he did. The witch answered him.

You are between worlds. Neither life nor death has claim on you.

If Milo still had a mouth, he'd have screamed.

Instead, he floated. And he saw so many things.

He was inside a great dark shell of metal. Functional in structure but ugly, without the slightest thought to elegance or beauty. A massive central column to which hundreds of thousands of leathery sacs were attached. Each sac twitched and throbbed as *things* within them moved, jostling with others for space, for food, for air. Long strands of gleaming metal wire that Milo *knew* were webs spun from some fantastic creature that was like a nightmare version of a spider. A dozen hairy legs and bodies swollen with venom and undigested food. And all around, clinging to the walls of the ship, were smaller hives of a hundred different kinds. Creatures like insects crawled around them and over them and over one another. There wasn't just one kind of alien here, but many. Not one dominant species, but a collective governed by a single, cold intelligence. A hive mind.

This is what came from the stars, murmured the Witch of the World. *And it is terrible enough. Witness now something even more terrible.*

He wanted to tell her no, to refuse to watch, or see, or know.

A ghost does not have the luxury of closing its eyes.

As if a page were turned in this strange diary of memories, Milo felt everything change. The mind became less insect and more human. Milo saw glimpses of a childhood that was not his. Growing up on a series of military bases here on Earth. Guam, South Korea, Germany, several places in America. Each new memory was seen from a slightly different height, as if witnessed by a child, then a teen, then a young man, and finally a grown man. Then there were memories of basic training, of specialized combat drills, of real combat in places Milo didn't know—deserts and wind-swept mountains, caves and coastal towns. Milo watched through the eyes of this man as he fought and killed, over and over again. He also felt what this man felt. Milo knew many soldiers, but he prayed he did not know anyone like this. This man loved the combat. The fighting. The killing. He was not an ordinary soldier. This man was born for war, and he embraced his destiny with a red glee.

The Huntsman was not an alien. Not born as one anyway. Milo had suspected it before, but now, knowing for certain, filled him with horror.

He's really human, gasped Milo.

Human, perhaps, said the witch, *but his mind was always a furnace.*

And then those memories were overlaid with those of witnessing the arrival of the hive ships. Of the Swarm. Of battles with shocktroopers. Of killing shocktroopers with guns, bombs, knives. And once even with his bare hands. Milo goggled. He didn't think that was possible. Everyone said that one-on-one, a shocktrooper was unbeatable. And yet these memories told a different tale. They told the truth because these were memories, not stories being told by someone who wanted to brag.

It both excited and appalled him.

To know that the shocktroopers could be defeated by ordinary people was huge.

To know that someone enjoyed it, though, was disgusting.

It was as bad as what the Dissosterin had done. Or maybe worse. The Bugs were not evil. They seemed to have no specific emotions. They were pure drive, pure instinct. But this man was different. He was corrupt. His deep joy in slaughter was warped before this war began.

Then there were other memories. More confused, muddied by shock and pain and horror as this man was ambushed by the Bugs, captured, drugged, studied, probed, operated on, and ultimately changed into something that was even worse than either a war-happy violent man or a dispassionate insect alien.

As if it were happening to his own body, Milo could feel leather straps restraining quivering arms and legs. He could see different kinds of insects bending over him. Not the mindless drones or the brutal shocktroopers. These were more intelligent. Six-foot-tall locusts. These, he suddenly knew, were the scientists, the medical elite. Cold minds, though. All of that knowledge and no feelings to go with it. He could feel the stab of needles, the icy heat of surgical blades cutting into him. He screamed along with the person whose memories these were.

The pain went on and on, but it changed as drugs were pumped into veins and implants drilled into his skull and brain. Milo could feel the process of human mind changing to become closer to an insect mind. It was not a compatible fit. There were no similarities in thought, no shared point of reference to allow for compatibility.

It should have driven the man mad. It should have shredded his sanity.

Except Milo understood that this man was never sane.

He is the monster that monsters fear, said the Witch.

But then something happened, and Milo felt a deep chill sweep through his mind. As the hive consciousness was forced into the soldier's mind, all of the rage and hate and bloodlust he felt, those dark emotions that defined him, were somehow transferred into the hive's shared mind.

It was like a collision of suns. Fiery, mutually destructive, and yet . . .

And yet.

Afterward the man—the Huntsman—was changed. He was more powerful than any human. More powerful than any shocktrooper. Milo knew that this was a surprise to the Dissosterin. This had never happened.

However, the change didn't stop there.

The Swarm was changed. It was polluted by the towering, murderous anger of this man.

This *evil* man.

That's what he was, Milo knew. He understood that. This was true evil.

Where other men join the military to fight for their families or their countries, this man joined because he wanted to fight. To hurt. To kill.

It's what fed him. Like some kind of emotional

vampire, he devoured the pain of others. Milo had read about people called serial killers. That's what this man was. But he was one who hid his hungers inside his job of a soldier. This is what the Dissosterin had captured and surgically enhanced to be their slave.

Only he was not a slave.

He was *part* of them now.

The witch—that unrelenting voice from his dreams—spoke horrors to him.

Witness now why the Swarm came to our world, she said. *Understand why the universe trembles now at this man's footfalls.*

There, inside the mind in which he was an accidental and unwelcome passenger, he saw the memory that explained so much.

Too much.

It was the Huntsman's memory of why he existed. Of why the Dissosterin had trapped him instead of killed him. Him, specifically. This evil man.

They were not evil. They were cold and logical and destructive, but not evil. However, they understood that evil existed.

They understood its power.

There were fragments of memories there. Of evil encountered on other worlds. Of the Swarm's attempts to understand it. Of the hive's desire to embrace it because of its power. They were a stale race. The same, unchanging, for millions of years. Now they wanted to grow. To become more powerful. To become something more than they could ever be if their growth was left to evolution.

They wanted to force their own evolution. To take on emotions. Not love and compassion. But the emotions of the conquerors. Hate and greed and other emotions so dark that they had no name. Not even to humans like the Huntsman.

They wanted to become that.

They sought out the most evil man they could find and they *joined* with him.

But even that was not enough for them.

No, because that man had more than a psychologically damaged mind, more than a sociopath.

He believed in evil.

He believed in darkness.

He believed in darkness as something real and magical.

Milo understood now what *he* wanted. He understood what the Huntsman had shared with the hive.

Even without the witch telling him, Milo understood what the hive wanted to do.

And it was the most terrible thing that had ever or could ever happen.

Ever.

Ever.

Ever.

FROM MILO'S DREAM DIARY

I dreamed I was with Dad. He looked the way he did
before the Bugs came. He was smiling, and he
didn't have scars on his face.

He asked me if I liked who I was.

I didn't know how to answer that. It's a really hard
question.

Then he asked me if I was afraid of the dark.

I said I was, kind of.

He looked really sad. When I asked him why, he said,
"Because the dark is coming, Milo."

"You'll be there if I get scared," I said.

But he just shook his head.

That was the dream I had before Dad went on the
patrol and never came back.

Chapter 40

As the dreadful awareness grew in Milo's mind, it somehow triggered a similar realization of his accidental occupancy to the rightful owner of those memories.

With a jerk and a growl, the Huntsman became instantly aware that he was not alone with his own thoughts. He howled his outrage and turned toward the corpse on the ground. Once more he drew back his fist and struck with savage force.

Milo felt a huge burst of pain as that fist struck him in the chest.

Not in his floating bodiless nothing of a spirit.

He *felt* it in his actual body.

The corpse was not a corpse at all.

A split second later, Milo's body arched upward and Milo let out a scream of pain and confusion. He was immediately torn from the mind of the Huntsman and felt himself dropping an impossible distance down, down, down, as if he were falling a million miles.

He slammed back into his own flesh. Every fiber of muscle, every bone, every atom in his body seemed to scream out in pain as spirit and flesh collided. There were two huge points of pain from where the Huntsman had punched him. Milo coughed and sputtered, choked and gagged.

He opened his eyes.

The Huntsman stood above him, powerful and deadly against this lurid skyscape, and far overhead, the hive ship glowed like a drop of blood in the light of the dying sun.

An armor-plated hand reached down, knotted itself in the fabric of Milo's T-shirt, and plucked him off the ground like so much boneless meat. The Huntsman pulled him close, so close Milo could smell the slaughterhouse stink of the creature's breath and see the burning lights in his eyes. Those eyes were so weird—multifaceted like an insect, but with hundreds of tiny human eyes compressed together to make up each of the mutant's large two eyes.

Milo screamed.

The Huntsman listened to his scream.

And laughed.

Then he shook Milo until the screams stopped, until Milo was jolted to a teeth-clenching silence. The Huntsman studied him, searching Milo's boy eyes with his own monster eyes. The creature's mandibles clicked and clacked, and its human lips moved as if trying to speak.

It did.

But the words it spoke were badly misshapen by that hideous mouth. They came out broken and wrong, as if this were the first time he'd tried to speak since his trans-formation.

"How . . . ?" whispered the Huntsman. "How . . . did you . . . do . . . that?"

"I—I d-don't know," stammered Milo. It was the truth. The entire experience was a million miles beyond anything he could begin to understand. "It . . . just hap-pened."

Hot drool swung from the Huntsman's lips and splashed onto Milo's face. He winced and gagged, trying to twist away.

"The . . . black jewel," whispered the Huntsman, and already he was speaking more normally, though his voice was still horrible to hear. "I see it in your mind. The pyra-mid. You were there. The wolf. The girl. You were there."

"I . . . I . . ."

The Huntsman touched a small pouch attached to a strap on his harness. The pouch had a bulge about the size of a robin's egg. "This stone. You know what it does, don't you, boy?"

It took a moment for Milo's terrified brain to make sense of the question, but the answer was there. As the Huntsman touched the pouch, his memories flared brighter for Milo to see. There was a fractured image of a broken tower of stones and an armored hand reach-ing out to tear something small and dark from the cen-ter. The thing was round and faceted like a diamond. It glittered as the Huntsman turned it over to examine it. The Huntsman put it into the pouch he now touched. Milo relived that memory as if it were his own.

A black jewel taken from the shrine.

The Heart of Darkness.

That's what this was about.

That's what all of this was about. The Dissosterin had the Heart and they wanted to know what it was. What it did. And because the Huntsman had seen Milo's memories—or some of them, at least—he'd seen the boy at the pyramid only yesterday.

"What is it?" demanded the Huntsman in a voice like a graveyard wind. Low and cold. "Tell me what it does and I will kill you quickly. Without pain. Lie to me and you will spend years screaming."

Be strong, cried the witch. *Be the hero and not the dreamer.*

He tried to tell her that he was just a boy. No hero. No dreamer. Just a boy who should never have been a part of this. A boy who had no idea at all what the Heart of Darkness actually was. How could she not know that?

It did not even occur to him that she was only the product of his dreams, that she was not real at all.

"Tell me!" The Huntsman shook him like a rag doll.

I beg you, child of the sun, the witch pleaded. *The world begs you. Speak and the Swarm will conquer all of space, all of time, and all the worlds between. Universes will fall.*

Universes. Not universe.

Milo had read about that. About how there might be an infinite number of universes instead of the one he knew. About how there could be worlds where anything was possible. Worlds in which even magic was real.

Worlds that, at the moment, were closed to the unending appetites of the Swarm.

"Tell me, boy," growled the Huntsman. "Tell me, or I will tear the life from you."

If Milo knew, he might have told this creature everything. Anything. He was that terrified. He was eleven. Small, skinny, not any kind of hero. And this thing was the most awful monster Milo could even imagine. How could he not tell him whatever he wanted to know?

"I don't—"

That was as far as he got.

Because at that moment the sun fell below the far horizon.

And a split second later the wolf attacked.

Chapter 41

There was no howl, no snarl of warning as the wolf hit the Huntsman. Milo saw white teeth in a red mouth, and then the impact knocked him flying. He hit hard and rolled into a painful sprawl. Three yards away, the Huntsman staggered sideways, bellowing out a cry of pain.

For a moment Milo could not understand what was happening because he could still feel the monster's fist clutching his shirt, but the monster was now six feet away. Then he looked down and saw the fist and two inches of wrist and then . . . nothing.

With a cry of disgust, Milo slapped the severed hand from his clothes and scuttled backward from it. The hand fell to the ground, and the fingers slowly opened like the legs of a dying tarantula.

The Huntsman stayed on his feet even though blood—mingled streams of red and green—shot from the stump of its wrist. He clamped his other human hand to the wound to stanch the flow of blood.

The wolf landed and turned, crouching low as it wrinkled its muzzle at the monster. Milo was amazed to see that the animal was no longer injured. The terrible wounds it had sustained in the fight with the Stinger were gone as if they'd never existed. If it hadn't been for those luminous eyes, Milo might have thought this was a different wolf.

It wasn't, and he knew it as sure as he knew anything.

The Huntsman bellowed out a call, and immediately the sound of approaching Stingers tore through the air. Milo got to his knees and cast wildly about to see from which direction the scorpion dogs were coming. Their hunting calls seemed to come from everywhere.

The Huntsman stood wide-legged, chest heaving, pain etching deep lines in his hideous face. He released his maimed arm, drew a pulse pistol from his belt, ignited the glowing blue blaster lens, and then jammed it against the stump of his wrist. He threw back his head and howled out his anguish. But his hand was steady as he held the lens there to cauterize the wound. The stink of burning flesh filled the air.

"Stop gawking and get up off the ground," someone said from behind him.

Milo twisted around, startled to hear this voice so close to him.

Standing where the wolf had stood was a slender figure who casually wiped red and green blood from her lips.

Milo mouthed her name. "Evangelyne."

She frowned. "How do you know my name, boy?"

There was no time to answer that question. The Stingers were getting close.

"I will hang your skulls on my belt," hissed the Huntsman through his pain. He shoved the gun into its holster and reached for a coiled whip that hung at his side. He shook it out with a snap of his wrist. Milo saw that its entire length was set with gleaming metal hooks, and the tip was a Stinger's barb sheathed in steel. Another flick and the whip cracked like a gunshot in the air between Milo and Evangelyne.

Evangelyne, despite overwhelming odds, smiled. She had a pretty face, but it was not a pretty smile. Her teeth were very white, and Milo thought they looked very sharp. She dabbed at the blood on her chin, tasted it with the tip of her tongue, and spat it at the Huntsman. Then she straightened, trying very much to look like an adult—tall and imperious and confident.

"You taste like a stinkbug," she sneered.

Despite his agony, the Huntsman smiled back.

Milo didn't think anything good was going to come from all those smiles.

"My pack will tear you to pieces and gnaw on your bones. I will . . ." His voice trailed off because the forest around them suddenly seemed to twist and change as if the trees themselves were coming to life. The Huntsman stiffened and looked around. The Stingers all turned and sniffed the air, clearly disturbed by whatever was in the trees.

Something was coming. Even Milo, having only ordinary human senses, could feel it.

One of the Stingers whined nervously.

Evangelyne edged toward Milo.

"Get ready to run," she murmured to him.

He wanted to say something. To make a joke about how he was born ready to run. Or something snappy. But his brain and his tongue were in separate gears, and neither was the right gear. He said something like, "Um . . . oh . . . yeah."

It was the best he could manage.

The Huntsman laughed. It was a small thing. A faint chuckle, but it was enough to show his utter contempt for whatever was about to happen.

"You've actually set a trap, haven't you?" He shook his head. "That's almost charming."

"See how charming it is when your bones lay bleaching in the s-sun."

She stuttered on the last word.

The Huntsman yawned. "You can't even make a threat without your voice shaking. So sad."

Evangelyne hunched forward, eyes filled with hatred. "This is our world."

The things in the shadows growled.

They all looked toward the woods for a moment; then the Huntsman smiled in a mockery of humanity. His steel teeth dripped with saliva, which ran down over his chin.

He held out the severed stump of his arm and showed her the burned flesh. The way he did it was like a threat. Or a promise. His mouth pincers snapped and clacked in what Milo could only interpret as some kind of laugh.

"I've already taken your heart, girl," he told her. "Now I'll take your life. No—maybe I'll kill everyone you love and keep you on a leash so you can watch."

The Huntsman cracked the whip again, and this time the pack of Stingers burst from the woods and rushed in for the kill.

Chapter 42

Evangelyne stood her ground.

As the pack rushed toward her, she raised one small fist in the air.

"Orphans—NOW!"

She slashed downward with her fist as she let out a fierce cry. It did not sound even remotely human. More like the howl of a night-hunting animal.

All around them the forest wall seemed to come alive.

Milo cringed back, terrified at what was happening as bizarre shapes erupted from the shadows.

"Oakenayl—now!" cried Evangelyne. "For all the forests they've burned, rend and tear them!"

As one Stinger raced forward, the leaves and branches of the trees seemed to reach out for it. Branches curled like long fingers around the mutant's forelegs, tripping it. Creeper vines tore loose from tree trunks and whipped around the hind legs. Thick branches came out of the shadows and wrapped around the barrel of the scorpion dog's chest. At first Milo couldn't understand what was happening. Then the truth forced itself through his shock. It was not the forest that attacked the dog. It was a single *thing* whose body was like a tree trunk, and all of the many branches turned and bent like arms; all of the smaller branches and twigs combined to form a dozen clutching hands. Framed by leaves and moss was a face that could have been the carved face of a teenage boy, except this was no piece of art. The face grimaced with effort and anger as it engulfed the struggling Stinger and bore it forcibly to the forest floor.

Milo understood now who—or *what*—had grabbed him yesterday. Not a group of people, but one impossible figure. A boy made from tree. Or one who somehow *was* a tree.

He mouthed the name.

Oakenayl.

The Stinger howled in pain as the forest creature fought to crush the unnatural life from it.

"Halflight—*now!*" cried Evangelyne, and Milo turned to look. "For seas boiled and meadows turned to ash, burn them!"

Something flew past him so close he could feel the cool air of its passage. For a moment he saw nothing more remarkable than a brightly colored hummingbird.

Except that there was something mounted *on* the hummingbird. A tiny figure of silver and gold that rode the bird like a warrior riding to battle on a warhorse. It was a girl no larger than his little finger, with hair that seemed to be composed of a cloud of bright orange fire. She raised her little arms, and suddenly the air exploded with fireworks of every color. Brilliant balls of flame that burst into view with sharp cracks and showered two Stingers with multicolored sparks. The Stingers tried to stop, to twist away, but the sparks fell like rain, and wherever they touched, the creatures' armor began to smoke and sizzle and then burn.

"Mook, for mountains torn down and valleys cracked open, smash them *now, now, now!*"

Evangelyne pointed to a pair of Stingers who raced toward her from either side of the crippled red ship. Huge beasts whose mouths trailed saliva and whose eyes burned with red flame. They separated to pass on either side of a pile of mossy rocks, but then the rocks *reached out for them.*

Milo cried out as the pile of rocks rose from the ground, leaping up and colliding to form, piece by piece, a towering figure that was, in shape only, human. Arms made from schist and granite spread wide; fists made of marble and iron ore swung through the darkening air. One fist struck a Stinger full on the face, and the sound of breaking bone rose even higher than the screams of the burning Stinger. The other hand caught the throat of the other scorpion dog and lifted it into the air.

"Mook!" cried a voice that was dusty and hard, and Milo realized that this thing, this boy of stone, had called out its own name. "*Mook!*" it shouted again, and with a grunt of titanic effort, hurled a Stinger across the clearing directly at the Huntsman.

That should have been the end of the Huntsman. Two hundred pounds of muscle and insect armor, tail slashing the air as it flew toward its target, should have smashed him down and dead. However, the Huntsman, with a sound like a man annoyed at a buzzing gnat, bashed it out of the air with the burned stump of his left arm. The Stinger twisted and fell badly to lie quivering.

I'm going nuts, he thought. *This isn't happening, so I'm really going nuts.*

"Now, Iskiel!" called the girl. "For a billion hearts stilled, turn theirs to ash."

And a huge salamander dropped from a tree onto the Huntsman. It was enormous—bigger than an iguana, with smooth gray-green skin through which intense red fire blazed, revealing the inferno *inside* the creature.

A fire salamander! Milo had read about one in an old book of fantasy stories. Yet here it was, real and hissing like a snake as it landed on the Huntsman's back. It instantly coiled its long tail around the alien's throat and dug into his flesh with the claws on four slender feet. The Huntsman dropped his whip and gagged as he dug his fingers in to find purchase.

Then, to confuse things even more, the girl raised her hands and called out in some strange language that Milo had never heard. It didn't sound like human speech, but rather the mingled calls of a dozen different birds.

There was a responding call from the woods. From everywhere in the woods. High-pitched cries that struck Milo's ears like ice picks, and then the whole clearing was filled with movement. Milo reeled as thousands upon thousands of small black shapes came pouring out of the trees to create whirlwinds of sound and movement.

Bats.

Thousands of them.

Tens of thousands of them.

They covered a half dozen of the Stingers, burying them under flapping leathery wings, tearing at them with needle-sharp teeth.

Not just bats.

Vampire bats.

A voice spoke to Milo. The witch, speaking not in dreams or while floating as a spirit, but here and now in the physical world. An impossible voice speaking to him in an impossible moment.

Now is your chance, child of the sun, she commanded. *Run for your life.*

"W-what?" he stammered, rooted to the ground with shock.

Run while you can. The Orphan Army cannot win this fight.

All around him these creatures were locked in deadly combat with the Stingers and the Huntsman.

"Looks like they're doing okay to me," said Milo. His comment caused the girl to glance at him, and Milo realized that only he heard the witch speaking.

That's 'cause I'm going nuts, he told himself.

"Mook!" cried the rock boy as he smashed and smashed.

"Die!" bellowed the tree spirit as he crushed and tore.

The salamander hissed and the little sprite shattered the air with fiery explosions while Evangelyne urged them on.

Then, as fast as the attack happened, it fell apart.

The Huntsman secured his grip at last, and with a grunt of effort, he tore the salamander's tail from around his neck. He raised it up and then slammed it down against the ground. Once, twice, until the creature simply exploded. The resulting fireball and concussion knocked the Huntsman back a dozen paces, but the towering mutant did not go down. He leaned into the shock wave and endured it, grinning at it as if proving to the world that nothing could defeat him.

From the woods came responding howls of at least a dozen more Stingers.

The shocktroopers drew pulse pistols and began firing at the swarms of bats, and immediately the air was filled with the stink of burning fur. Hundreds of bodies fell like cinders, and the others scattered into the trees.

Milo dug into his satchel for another grenade, but he

didn't know what to do with it. Everyone was too close.

That's the wrong magic, boy, whispered the voice. *There is a time to fight—and bless the shadows in your heart for wanting to—but there is also a time to run.*

Four Stingers erupted from the woods and hurtled toward Evangelyne.

"No!" yelled Milo, running to put himself between them and the girl. He dug out a grenade, twisted the arming cap, snugged it into the pouch of his slingshot, raised it, fired, sending the bomb over the heads of the Stingers. It exploded as it fell behind them, and the blast tore two of the monsters to rags.

The other two, undaunted, came on, teeth bared, barbed tails raised.

Run! implored the witch.

Milo held his ground between them and the girl as he fumbled for another grenade. He knew without doubt that he now stood well within the blast radius.

"What are you doing, boy?" growled the girl.

"Stop calling me 'boy'—and *run!*" he yelled to the girl. "I'll hold them here."

To his right there was a sound like nails being pried from green lumber, and he turned to see three Stingers tearing at the tree spirit. For a moment Oakenayl fought back, his many hands punching and tearing, but then all life seemed to vanish from the living wood and the Stingers tore him to splinters.

"No!" Milo felt totally helpless.

Suddenly, a bolt of blue fire punched down from above and the rock boy—Mook—exploded, spraying everything with smoking chips of stone. Above them a drop-ship came spinning down from the darkened sky, and a moment later shocktroopers leaped from it, riding steel cables down to the ground.

"NO!" Milo yelled again.

The Stingers were nearly upon him.

There was nowhere left to run.

Run, demanded the voice in his mind.

The Huntsman laughed and retrieved his whip.

Milo reached for the arming cap of another grenade. Better to go out in a blaze of glory, he realized, than let these monsters take him.

Maybe he'd see Shark and Barnaby and Lizabeth again.

Maybe Dad would be waiting for him on the other side. Not in some Bug collection, but on the other side of life. Somewhere else. Someplace where there was no invasion, no Swarm. No war. A place where Dad would be like he used to be. Happy. Playing his guitar. Singing old songs.

Maybe, Milo thought, if there were such a place, then all of his fear and doubt would be done with.

"I love you, Mom," he said as he took hold of the cap.

Then someone shoved him and he was falling. The

grenade, unarmed, rolled out of his reach, and he twisted on the ground to see someone leap over him.

It was the girl.

She jumped with incredible speed and grace and then dropped to the ground on the other side between Milo and the Stingers.

She landed on all fours.

Not on feet and hands.

She landed on four feet.

Four.

Four feet that ended in sharp black claws, and when she looked up at him, he did not see a girl.

Or a wolf. He understood that now.

Evangelyne was a *werewolf*.

Chapter 43

A werewolf.

His inner mind had been trying to tell him this since the first fight with the Stinger during the patrol. Maybe earlier. Barnaby's warnings of a *rougarou* had given fuel to the thought, but Milo's conscious mind had not wanted to hear it. Not wanted to accept it.

Werewolf.

Werewolf.

Werewolf?

Werewolves don't exist.

Neither do tree spirits or sprites, fire salamanders and boys made of rock, he told himself.

Neither do witches that step from dreams into the waking world.

None of that is true. None of that exists.

Except when it does.

Milo staggered to his feet and backed away. From the Stingers, from the Huntsman, from the shocktroopers.

From the girl.

He retreated from all of it.

"No," he breathed. He was panting like a winded horse.

But the moment said, *Yes.*

The scorpion dogs slowed and stood wavering, uncertain and confused. Even the shocktroopers seemed stunned. They had all seen the transformation.

All of them had.

Only the Huntsman seemed to understand what was happening. He stood with his back to the rim of his damaged ship and slowly raised the seared stump of his left arm. Perhaps it was a salute, perhaps a challenge. However, the expression on his face showed a kind of eerie joy, as if seeing the werewolf revealed something wonderful to him. Or proved some important theory.

Milo thought he knew what it was. He had been inside that dark mind.

The Huntsman, the evil man who had become a monster, *believed* in magic, but like most people, he could not prove it existed. He had stolen the Heart of Darkness to try to find that proof.

Now, here, in front of him and all around him, was proof. Spirits and sprites. And a werewolf.

The Huntsman nodded to himself.

"The black jewel is mine," he said, touching a pouch on one of the straps crossing over his massive chest. "And I will use it to hunt you all through forever. A billion-billion worlds will open to the Swarm. This world will fall, and then the worlds of shadow will fall. Look upon your doom, daughter of the wolf, and despair."

The werewolf wrinkled its muzzle and showed its teeth in brave defiance. Milo fumbled in his pouch for one more grenade.

At which point Milo did something that changed the world forever.

Not just his world. But *all* worlds.

Sometimes it isn't the action of presidents or kings; it isn't what soldiers or statesmen do that changes the course of history. Sometimes a single person, one who is not a hero in any conventional way, can do or say a thing that starts a chain reaction. This is how the universe turns.

Milo looked the monster in the eye and said, "No."

Chapter 44

The Huntsman ignored him.

So did everyone else.

Which was not surprising. Milo Silk was eleven years old. Sixty-seven pounds. Short and skinny and nobody's idea of a hero. Certainly not his own.

Not even at the moment when he became one.

"Yo, freakface!" he yelled, stepping closer to the master of the Stingers.

This time the Huntsman did look at him. It was a look of disinterest and annoyance. Like Milo—his life and everything he was—did not matter to this creature.

Milo held out the grenade.

The Huntsman looked at that, too. Everyone did, and for a moment the entire field of battle was silent. The werewolf turned and gaped at him, surprise written in its pale eyes. The sprite on her hummingbird mount hovered in the air, her body twisted sideways as she, too, stared.

"I won't let you," said Milo in a voice that quavered and cracked. Shivers rippled along every limb; sweat beaded his face and ran down inside his clothes.

The only part of him that didn't tremble was the hand holding the grenade.

The Huntsman looked from Milo to the grenade and back again. "Kill me and kill yourself, boy."

Milo swallowed what felt like a mouthful of dust. "I know. I get that. And right now I pretty much don't care."

"Yes, you do. You were inside my mind, but I was also inside *yours*. I can smell your fear. You are nothing and you know it. You can't do this thing."

Milo gripped the arming cap between his fingers. He really wanted to say something cool. Something Shark would appreciate.

All he could manage was, "Yeah . . . well, bite me."

He twisted the cap and threw the grenade.

Chapter 45

Several things happened at the same time. All of them were part of the wheel of destiny that Milo's action had started turning.

A Stinger leaped into the air to try to catch the hand grenade.

The werewolf jumped at Milo and knocked him sideways.

The shocktroopers dove for cover.

And the scattered rocks and stones that were all that was left of the rock boy—flew up from the ground and slammed together into a humanoid shape. Mook. He spread his arms wide and stood between Milo and the blast.

The blast was horrific.

It was a big fist of fire and noise that seemed to punch the whole world. The ground jumped and rocked. The shock wave scattered everyone.

The leaping Stinger was blown to bits.

The rock boy—for the second time in five minutes—was smashed to gravel and strewn across the clearing.

The werewolf and Milo hit the ground and rolled away from the blast. Dazed and cut in a dozen places by flying splinters of stone—but alive.

The Huntsman and three of the shocktroopers lay sprawled on the ground.

Milo could not hear or see, and he could barely breathe. He felt like his head was inside a metal drum and some maniac was hammering at it with a big metal spoon.

Well, he thought, *that was stupid.*

It was a little late to remember that the heroes in a lot of the books he read died saving the world.

Ah, well.

The sky was unnaturally bright for nighttime.

And then it was all really, really dark.

FROM MILO'S DREAM DIARY

How come in my dreams I'm never a hero?
I don't have superpowers.
I don't know how to do karate or kung fu.
I don't know guns.
I can't pilot a jet fighter.
I can't do any of that in real life, but I thought in
    dreams you were supposed to do anything.
Not me.
I'm always just me in my dreams.

Part
Three

Six Years from Next Wednesday . . .

"A hero is no braver than an ordinary man,
but he is braver five minutes longer."
—RALPH WALDO EMERSON

Chapter 46

When Milo opened his eyes, his first thought was, *I'm dead. Again.*

He waited for the moment when his consciousness would float free of his body again. He wondered what he'd see this time.

He waited.

And waited.

Nothing happened.

He realized that he was looking at something, and it took his fuzzy mind a few seconds to sort it out.

Rocks.

A rocky ceiling.

A cave?

In Louisiana?

A cave in bayou country?

Milo was sure that wasn't possible. If there were caves here, the Earth Alliance would have been using them for protection, building labs, housing refugees.

The rocky ceiling did, however, look very cavelike.

Milo turned his head. That hurt. A lot.

He saw a rocky wall, too. It was lit by candlelight, and he had to work up the nerve to turn his head in the other direction to see the candle.

It was there. A crude silver candelabra with five tapers on it from which wax ran down and made a white landscape on the table.

Table?

His mind was clearing slowly, but, yes, there was a table. Heavy, ornate wood. Very old. Like tables he'd seen in abandoned mansions and museums. Several matching chairs, too.

In a cave.

He tried to speak. Croaked. Licked his lips and tried it again.

"Wh-where . . . ?"

And his creaking voice continued that question and turned it into a different word entirely.

"Werewolf."

His brain replayed that word over and over again.

Werewolf . . . werewolf . . . werewolf . . .

He thought, *Well, Lizabeth would really love this*.

It was so silly a thought that a crooked little laugh bubbled out of his mouth.

Keep it together, he warned himself even though it was all totally crazy. *Keep it together*.

Werewolf.

Rock boy.

Tree boy.

Fire salamander.

Exploding color sprite.

"Oh, yeah," he said to the empty room. "I'm nuts."

And a voice replied, "No, you're not."

Milo turned way too fast, craned his neck too far up, and yelped in both pain and shock when he saw a group of people standing there. He jerked upward from the floor and turned as he scuttled backward on hands and heels.

Evangelyne stood there. She was human again. Her arms were folded, and she wore an expression of concern and consternation.

To her left stood a pile of rocks. To her right was what looked like a small tree with a face. Seated on a branch of the tree was a hummingbird, and standing next to the hummingbird was a little girl who was less than three inches tall.

Oakenayl.

Mook.

Halflight.

Milo said, "Yeep!"

Or something like it. Even he wasn't sure.

The tree said, "He's not dead after all. Pity."

The little sprite said, "He looks like he is about to faint."

The rock said, "Mook."

And the girl said, "We need to have a long talk, boy."

Chapter 47

Milo sat on one side of the table and the others were across from him. Evangelyne produced a plate of fruit from a small cupboard Milo had not noticed before, and she pushed it across to him. Mook poured water into a tin cup and set it down so hard it sloshed.

"Mook," he said, leaving any interpretation of that to Milo.

They all studied one another across the table as the candlelight flickered and threw bizarre shadows onto the walls.

"Well," said Halflight in a voice that was so high and small it was almost a musical note, "somebody should start talking."

Milo shook his head. "Sorry . . . I got nothing."

No one smiled. No one else spoke.

Milo pointed at Oakenayl. "I saw you die."

Oakenayl scowled. "You don't understand anything, do you?"

Milo ignored that statement as being too obvious. He pointed at Mook. "And I saw you die like . . . twice, I think."

"Mook," said Mook, as if that explained everything.

"So," concluded Milo, "like I said . . . I got nothing. I'm so freaked out I don't even know how to talk about this."

"Well, then, let's start with you answering some questions," said Evangelyne in the same imperious tone she'd used when they first met. "Like . . . how do you know my name, boy?"

Milo started to say something, stopped, and smiled.

"What—?" she asked.

"Funny, I almost said 'you wouldn't believe me,' but, you know, that would be stupid."

No one smiled.

"He's not going to tell us," said Oakenayl. His face was covered with tree bark in places, but where it was smooth, there was a complex pattern of wood grain. "Give me a few minutes alone with him and he'll beg to tell us everything he knows."

Milo shrank back because it was very clear the tree spirit was not joking. Oakenayl's face was stern.

"No. Stay your hand," said Halflight quickly. "We cannot do that."

"No, we can't," agreed Milo.

Halflight glared at Oakenayl. "Please. Let us *try* to be civilized about this."

"I'm *not* civilized," insisted the tree sprite.

"Then pretend it for now," snapped the tiny sprite.

"This human was willing to sacrifice his life to save ours. Show him some courtesy or go sit outside."

Her tone was stern, which sounded funny coming from a finger-sized person with fiery hair. Even so, the tree boy grunted and flapped a branch at her.

"Fine, fine," he muttered. "Have it your own way."

Milo smiled at Halflight. "Thanks."

Evangelyne interrupted. "Don't thank her yet. If you don't tell us what we want to know, then I'll be happy to let Oakenayl make you talk."

"Hey, I didn't say I wouldn't talk," Milo said with heat. "Give me a second, will you? Five minutes ago I thought I was dead. Now I'm having a conversation with a bunch of people I'm pretty sure can't be real. Let me catch my breath."

Oakenayl snorted, but Evangelyne nodded. "Fine. Take a breath, boy. Then talk."

"Are you really going to keep calling me 'boy'? We're the same freaking age."

Evangelyne colored and made a small, meaningless noise. Milo saw that Halflight smiled and turned away, and Oakenayl seemed to suddenly find the wood grain of the table very interesting. Milo guessed that the wolf girl's attempt to always sound like the adult in the room wasn't something directed just at him.

"Okay," he said after a moment. "You want to know how I know your name? Well, pretty much *you* told me."

"What?" she said. "No, I didn't."

"Yes, you did. It was in a dream. You told me your name was Evangelyne Winter."

They all gasped, except for Mook, who said, "Mook."

"That's impossible," protested Evangelyne. Her composure was shaken, but she firmed it up and in that fake adult voice began, "I would never—"

"Don't worry," interrupted Milo with a half smile. "I won't conjure with it."

"Wait," cut in Halflight. "What kind of dream was this? Was it a prophecy? Were you in a trance?"

"No," said Milo. "I was in my hammock."

There was no reaction to that other than blank expressions.

"No?" asked Milo, looking for some trace of humor in the group. "Nothing? Oh well."

So he explained. He told them about his dreams and how sometimes the things he dreamed about came true. He told them about his dream diary—which he realized was probably nothing but ashes now at the ruins of the camp. He told them about the nightmares of the hive ship invasion.

Then he told them about the Witch of the World.

That, he realized, was the equivalent of throwing another hand grenade right onto the table.

Chapter 48

You know the witch?" gasped Evangelyne, her eyes bugging wide. "How? I mean, you're only a boy. How's that even possible?"

"It's not like I *know* her," said Milo awkwardly. "We don't hang out. It's just that I sometimes, um, *dream* about her."

Oakenayl made a low, unpleasant noise. "He's a sorcerer, Evangelyne. You were right the first time. We should bury him in the dirt with an iron spike through his heart."

"Hey!" yelped Milo. "How about you go and—"

"Enough!" snapped Halflight. "We need to understand this, not fight about it. Oakenayl, behave yourself. And—Milo, is it? You mind your manners as well."

The two of them shut up, and Milo felt his cheeks burning. The oak boy's wood-grain face seemed to darken as well.

Evangelyne chewed her lip and looked uncertain.

"No, he is not a sorcerer," said Halflight in her tiny voice. "There is magic around him, though. I can see it, but it is not *in* him."

"What's that even mean?" asked Milo.

The sprite pointed at him. "If you were a sorcerer, you would glow a different color."

Milo held his hands up to inspect them. "Glow?"

"You cannot see it," said Sprite. "And that is even more proof. A sorcerer could see his own aura. No, Oakenayl; no, Evangelyne. This is just an ordinary boy, a child of the sun."

"That's what *she* calls me," insisted Milo. "That's what the Witch of the World calls me in my dreams."

Everyone looked at Milo, each of them reevaluating him. Oakenayl still wore his hostility like a cloak, though. It hung from him like Spanish moss.

Mook broke the silence to say, with no uncertainty, "Mook."

Halflight nodded as if that made sense, which to Milo it did not.

"You see magic around him, Halflight?" asked Evangelyne.

"Oh yes," the sprite assured her. She hopped onto her hummingbird and flitted around in front of Milo. "It is all around him."

"How?" asked Milo. "How could I have anything like that on my whatchamacallit?"

"'Aura,'" supplied Halflight.

"Right. Aura. How?"

Halflight looked at Oakenayl, who stared at Evangelyne.

"The witch," they said at the same time.

Milo looked at each of them and said, "Huh?"

Evangelyne was nodding to herself. "The witch you dreamed about was no fantasy."

"Yeah, I pretty much figured that," said Milo, who was no longer as surprised as he would have been a few hours ago. "What is she, though? Some kind of telepath or something?"

"No," snorted Oakenayl. "Telepaths require a physical body."

"What?"

"The Witch of the World was never alive," said Halflight. "She is not even a person. Not the way you are. Not even the way we are. She exists within the shadows; she drifts in thoughts and comes to us in dreams."

"Is she a ghost?"

The orphans exchanged another few moments of silent looks. Finally Evangelyne shrugged. "We . . . don't actually know what she is."

"Well, great," said Milo. "That's a big help."

"It is what it is," said Oakenayl.

"Mook," agreed Mook.

"No," said Milo loudly, "stop all that. You guys keep talking crazy stuff. It's not fair. Tell me what is going on."

"He is right," said Halflight after a moment. "We have the advantage over him, and we are being unkind. This must all be a little strange to him."

"A little strange? Really?" said Milo. "You think 'a little' covers it?"

"Okay," said Evangelyne, holding up a hand. "You're right, Halflight. This isn't fair. Boy . . ."

"Milo," he corrected.

"*Milo*, we'll explain what we can, but we don't have much time."

"Sure, but if you'd just come out and said it before, we'd have had time for the long version and a nap."

It took a moment, but a small smile bloomed on her lips. "You're a weird boy."

"You're a werewolf," replied Milo. "You outweird me by miles."

There was a creaking sound from Mook that might have been a laugh. He said, "Mook."

"Maybe. But the world is always stranger than even we think it is." She took a breath and began her story. "This world is old, Milo. Very old. Our people were here first. We call ourselves the Nightsiders. Not because we can't come out during the day—we can—but we like the darkness. We like shadows."

"Mook," agreed the stone boy, nodding.

"Our world is bigger, too. Bigger than the things you can see and touch."

Halflight murmured, "There are worlds within worlds within worlds."

Evangelyne nodded. "Life among the Nightsiders

takes a lot of different forms. I'm a lycanthrope—a werewolf—but there are other shape-shifters. Were-tigers and were-foxes and were-just-about-anything-you-can-name. There are the realms of faerie and there are as many kinds of sidhe as there are stars in the sky. There are cave trolls and bridge trolls and rock spirits like Mook."

"Mook."

"And natural spirits, like Oakenayl, who is a wood spirit."

Oakenayl said nothing, but he did summon enough manners to give a tiny bow of acknowledgment.

"There are the monsters you've probably read about in books," continued Evangelyne. "Vampires and ghosts and demons. There are imps and redcaps and will-o'-the-wisps and sprites like dear Halflight."

"Dragons?" asked Milo hopefully. "Are there drag-ons?"

Evangelyne looked at him like he was crazy. "Drag-ons? Dragons aren't real. Don't be silly."

He said, "Oh."

"Our ancestors learned how to move between those worlds. Not just between different versions of Earth, but into stranger places. There are kingdoms in the morning mist. There are the realms of faerie and the ghost worlds. There are worlds that hide at the bottom of wells and inside thoughts and behind doorways in dreams. I know that must sound like mystical nonsense to you, but it is the world as we have always known it. It's what's real to us. Do you understand?"

Milo nodded. "Kind of," he said.

"Some of us learned to move between those worlds," continued the wolf girl, "and for a long, long time our world was the infinite lands of darkness. Our greatest sorcerers and witches, the elves and faerie folk, built doorways that connected the many realms."

All Milo could say was, "Wow."

"The world you know came later. Your cities and nations sprang up so fast, though, and you grew in such numbers that soon this world"—and here she tapped the hard reality of the table—"became crowded."

"Too crowded to share," said Oakenayl bitterly.

"Why?" asked Milo.

"Because your kind don't *want* to share it," replied the oak boy. "You never did. As soon as you discovered fire, you began to burn us. When you forged iron and bronze and steel, you cut us down. When you invented guns, you hunted us."

"That's not—" began Milo, but he couldn't finish his protest because he knew that there was some truth in this. He'd read books about the witch trials and vampire hunters; about silver bullets and stakes and garlic.

Evangelyne nodded. "Because we're who we are, your kind thought we were evil. To us the word 'monster' means the same as 'different' or 'individual.' To you it stands for something to fear. Something to hate. Something evil."

Milo could not meet her eyes. This was hard to take.

"Be fair, Evangelyne," cautioned Halflight. "The people of the sun did not invent evil."

"No, but they treated us as if we were evil. They were evil *to* us." Evangelyne paused, head tilted as if listening to her own words. "But you're right. I'm not being fair. Evil isn't something that belongs to one species. There are evil ones among us too. Killers and haters."

"They started this war," growled Oakenayl. "They began hunting us long before we turned to hunt them." He made a fist that was all knots of wood, and as he clenched it, the wood squealed like a voice screaming. "You even cut down the living trees to make your spears and stakes. You built pyres from young trees to burn us."

Milo felt his face grow hot. He wanted to say that it was all lies, that it wasn't how things were, but Milo could not sit here with these creatures and lie. He could not.

"I . . . I'm sorry," he said, his voice thick with emotion, his heart heavy with shame and grief.

"Sorry?" began Oakenayl as if he was offended by the word. Instead Evangelyne touched his shoulder and he fell silent.

"This is what your people have done, Milo," she said. "We are not saying that *you* have done it."

"No," Milo said, "but none of 'my people' are here. No one else is going to say it, so maybe I should. I'm sorry. All of that was wrong. We shouldn't have done it. It was bad. It was . . . evil."

Halflight came to his defense with a smile and a shake of her fiery hair. "Not all of it was done out of malice, Milo. Much of it was done from fear. Your kind hate what you fear, and you attack what you hate. It's a mark of the people of the sun. Maybe that's how you survived those days when you huddled in caves and were hunted by tigers and bears. Maybe hate is your weapon. It seems to be."

Milo put his face in his palms. "That's the worst thing anyone's ever said to me."

A sob broke in his chest.

They waited in silence.

Finally, little Halflight spoke. "He weeps for us."

No one spoke.

"Has any of them ever wept for us before?" she asked the others.

Still no one spoke. After a moment, someone placed a finger under Milo's chin and raised his head. At first he thought it was Evangelyne. It wasn't. Nor was it Mook.

Instead Oakenayl looked him in the eye. He looked at the tears on Milo's face, and there was conflict in his eyes. Though Milo found it hard to read the expression of a face whose skin was bark and wood grain, he thought he saw regret there.

"Not in my lifetime," he said. "Not one tear."

Chapter 49

Milo sniffed and wiped his eyes.

"I lost people I care about too," he said. "My dad a couple of years ago. My friends today. Shark and Liza-beth and Barnaby. Bunch of others. I can't even process it yet."

Halflight flitted near him and sniffed at the wet places on his cheeks. "Tell him the rest, Evangelyne."

"Sure. Waste more time talking. Then we need to *stop* talking and *do* something," said Oakenayl, slapping a woody palm down on the table.

"Mook!"

"Hush, then, and let me speak." Evangelyne took a breath. "Because your kind wanted us to be monsters, Milo, that's what we became. Feral and strange. Vicious, at times. As you hunted us, some of us hunted you. It became very bad, and it stayed bad for a long time. Over time, as Oakenayl said, we turned and began to hunt you. We were very good at it too. Some of us became as bad, as vicious, as you humans. They became so frightening that now they are all that you know of. Because of them, we became the reason your people are afraid of the dark. They are the reason you fear the shadows. They are the things that go bump in the night."

Milo felt the room grow quiet and cold around him. It wasn't fear. Or, it wasn't *only* fear. The room was actually colder. As the strange girl spoke, her breath plumed between them as if each separate word revealed a ghost. Milo kept waiting—wishing, hoping—that she would burst out laughing the way Barnaby had done. The way Shark would after a practical joke ran its course. The moment stretched. It became excruciating as he sat there waiting for none of this to be true. There were already enough monsters in the world. The dark was already dark enough.

"Are you afraid of us now?" she asked calmly. The candlelight constantly shifted the shadows on her face, changing her expression, giving her a hundred different faces, none of them truly human.

"Yes," Milo managed to say. "Of course I'm afraid. I'm so scared I want to run and hide. Is that what you want? Are you happy now?"

Her icy gaze held for a moment longer; then she looked away. "There used to be whole villages of werewolves. Castles filled with vampires. Forests where elves and sprites and faeries lived. Caves where trolls and ogres made their homes. But even before the Swarm came, those villages had become only memories. The castles are in ruins; the graveyards are filled with silent bones; the caves belong to bats; and nothing but fish swim in the lakes. Except for those who escaped to other worlds and the few left here, the rest are gone. The world has fewer shadows in it than it had before. Do you understand?"

Milo said that he did, but asked, "Why didn't you escape?"

"This is our world too, Milo Silk," said Halflight. "Even when humans crowded us out, we still loved this world. We loved it first and we will always love it. Some of us do not want to leave it."

"Even now, when it is being torn apart," said Oakenayl, nodding.

"Even now, *because* it is being torn apart," corrected Evangelyne. "It would be like betraying a friend who needs you. It would be like leaving our mother to die alone because we did not care enough to protect her."

They all looked sad and weary. Mook clanked his rocky fists together.

"Mook," he said glumly.

"Besides," said the wolf girl, "now, even if we wanted to, we can't."

"Why not?" asked Milo gently.

"There was a time when all doors were open to those who knew how to find them. We had keepers—door wardens—who guarded those doors," explained Evangelyne. "They knew the secrets of moving between worlds. Your people destroyed many of those keepers."

"How?"

"Maybe they didn't know that's what they were doing. Doorways are hidden, and the wardens aren't exactly like sentries standing guard. Not in the way you think. A keeper might have been a certain tree planted from a magical seed. Or a waterfall whose waters were snow pure. Or a circle of twigs that the wind could not blow away. Each was placed there using great magicks."

"Old magicks," said Halflight. "Magicks the like of which have mostly faded from the world. The faerie folk knew some of them. So did we sprites and water witches and dryads. Each of our kind had their own special magic, and there were magicks known only to the oldest and wisest of us."

"What happened?"

Oakenayl ground his teeth. "Forests were cleared to build cities. Mountains were leveled to make roads. Waterways became polluted, and the spirits within them sickened and died. That's what happened."

"Oh," said Milo, deeply sorry that he'd asked.

"Our elders—parents and others who tended to the youngest of us," said Evangelyne, "tried their best to push back. Some even lived among you, blending in, trying to influence you to be kinder to the world in which we all lived. Sometimes they succeeded. Many times they failed. With each new failure, they became more disillusioned and sent more and more of us away into shadow worlds."

"Not all of us left," said Halflight.

"Some of us didn't want to go," said Oakenayl. "Some of us wanted to stay here and fight back."

"Against the aliens?" asked Milo.

"Against you."

"Oh."

Evangelyne said, "My mother and aunts stayed to fight the Bugs. So did Oakenayl's father and Mook's whole family. We're here because they stayed."

"The Nightsiders fought against the aliens?"

Evangelyne paused. "We started to, but then the Huntsman came."

Milo swallowed hard.

"We believe he was created to hunt us down," said Halflight. "That was part of a prophecy."

"From the witch?"

"Yes. Evangelyne's mother had a dream a few months ago. A dark dream filled with horrors. The Huntsman and his pack came the very next day, and with them legions of shocktroopers."

"What happened?"

"Whole forests burned," said Evangelyne. "Mountains were torn down to find the Nightsiders. The Huntsman set traps, and he threw the full weight of the Swarm against us."

There was a dreadful silence.

"I never saw my mother again," said the wolf girl. "I never saw another of my kind again."

"Nor I," said Oakenayl.

"Mook."

"I . . . I'm so sorry," said Milo.

They sat together in wretched silence.

Into the silence, Evangelyne spoke. She raised her head and in that moment truly did look older, more majestic. More powerful and far more dangerous.

"The orphans of that slaughter found one another," she said. "We formed an army. We are going to fight back. Today we tried to lay a trap for the Huntsman. To get back the Heart of Darkness and to claim revenge for what that *monster* has done."

Her eyes faltered and fell away.

"But we failed. The Huntsman lives . . . and the Heart of Darkness is lost."

A horrible thought blossomed in Milo's mind. "Wait. Today . . . you tricked the Huntsman into coming down and chasing you?"

She nodded. "We tried. We let ourselves be seen. We know he's trying to find Nightsiders for capture and study. To use us to unlock the secrets of the Heart."

"Yeah, I get that," said Milo sharply, "but did you deliberately set your trap near our camp?"

Evangelyne said nothing, but her eyes grew wide as the implications sank in. Mook looked down at his rocky fists; even Oakenayl turned away as if ashamed.

"We thought the Huntsman would come down with a

few shocktroopers," said Evangelyne, barely able to look at him. "We never—*ever*—thought the Swarm would send an entire assault force. We . . . did not know they would attack your camp."

"Didn't know or didn't care?" asked Milo bitterly.

No one answered him.

He sniffed and wiped tears from his eyes. "Everyone I know is probably dead," he said softly. "All of my friends. Everyone. Maybe even my mom, if she came back while the Bugs were still there."

He buried his face in his hands and wept.

Chapter 50

He cried for a long time. Grief was like a knife stuck deep in his chest. Halflight came and sat on his shoulder. After a while Mook placed a heavy hand on Milo's back.

"Mook," he said sadly.

Evangelyne touched the tears on Milo's cheeks and then stared at the wetness on her own fingers. There were tears in her eyes too.

Finally Milo pulled himself back from his pain. He knew that he would have to plunge into that icy water again, but not now. Not now. There was too much to do. He wiped his face on his sleeve and blinked his eyes clear.

"You're trapped here now?" asked Milo thickly. "On this world?"

"Yes."

"And all your parents are gone?"

"Yes."

"Like mine."

Evangelyne gazed at him with her pale eyes. "Yes."

"Look . . . I need to tell you guys something, but I have a couple questions first, okay?"

"We didn't bring you here to interrogate us," said Oakenayl.

Milo looked him straight in the eye. "Who cares? You guys are in trouble, and so am I. You guys lost everyone you loved, and so did I. You guys have some powers and some knowledge . . . *so do I.* Maybe we should, I don't know, work together? Am I the only one who doesn't think that's a bad idea?"

Oakenayl snapped his mouth shut and glared.

That was fine with Milo. He could deal with glares.

Halflight and Evangelyne exchanged a brief look.

"What are your questions?" asked the sprite.

Milo took a breath. "That pyramid—what was it? Was that one of those doorway things?"

"It was a door warden," corrected Halflight. "It protected the last known door to the worlds of shadows. As long as it remained, all that was required was for us to unlock the spells that would open it."

"Could you?"

"Yes. We all know the spell of opening."

"Good, then all we need to do is rebuild the pyramid, right? I mean, you guys seem like you can do magic, right?"

The tree boy almost smiled. "Can you build a kite?"

"Sure. Everyone knows how to—"

"Can you build a spaceship?"

"Um . . . no."

"It's like that," explained Evangelyne.

"Oh. Ouch."

"If it were that easy, we would be doing it already," said Halflight. "The door warden was constructed with magicks. Very old and immensely complicated. It took some of the most powerful Nightsiders a year, from winter solstice to winter solstice, to complete the ritual of making."

"Oh."

"There is one slight hope, though," said the sprite. "All great spells are recorded in case there is ever a disaster. In case the magic needs to be redone."

"Great! Where's that stuff kept?"

Evangelyne sighed. "The secrets were recorded in the Heart of Darkness," she said.

Milo bent forward and banged his forehead on the table. Twice.

"We have some magic," explained Halflight, "but like all things, there are levels and levels of it. I can do some simple spells, a few glamours, cast a few brief illusions."

"Illusions?"

"Yes," said a very tall, exceptionally beautiful red-haired woman who appeared out of absolutely nowhere. Milo jumped out of his chair. The woman turned into a silver-maned unicorn, who winked and then vanished. In its place was the little sprite on her hovering humming-bird. "They are illusions. You see them, but there is nothing actually there."

"How long do they last?"

"A few minutes at most. I am getting better at it, but so far . . . they are fleeting phantoms. And they require much of me," she said wearily. "Mostly I can create fireworks. My mother, though, she was very old and very powerful. She could transform dust into living creatures. She could take a handful of straw, throw it into the air, and turn it into an eagle. *That's* magic."

Milo grunted. The demonstration of Halflight's powers had planted a tiny seed of an idea in his mind. "What else can you guys do?"

"None of us are as powerful as our elders," said Evangelyne. "I become a wolf, but that wolf is only a wolf. It's not stronger than a regular wolf except that I heal faster and my senses are a little sharper. Lycanthropy doesn't come with any other special powers."

Milo looked at Oakenayl. "How about you? I saw you torn apart and now you're all together. That's got to be serious magic."

"I'm a wood spirit," said the oak boy. "Even this body is not who I really am. I can inhabit some growing plants. If they're destroyed, then I abandon the debris."

"So you can't die?" When the oak boy didn't answer, Milo looked at Halflight. "Can he?"

"Don't answer—" began Oakenayl, but the sprite ignored him.

"Yes, he can," said Halflight. "Fire will destroy any of us except Iskiel."

"Wait . . . Iskiel. That's what you called the big sala-mander," Milo said to Evangelyne. "What happened to him? He's not dead, is he?"

"No, but he was hurt. His body was destroyed, so he let it burn. He's like a phoenix in a way. It'll take him a few hours to make a new one."

"Wow. Can he be killed at all?"

"Why are you telling this boy our secrets?" demanded Oakenayl. "He's the enemy. He's of the sun."

Evangelyne stiffened with anger and turned on the oak boy. "Because, Oakenayl, son of Ghillie Dhu, this boy stood with us in battle. He risked his life for us."

The wood spirit made a disgusted noise and turned half away.

"And," said Halflight, buzzing over to land on his shoulder, "because the Witch of the World has clearly put her mark on him. I can see it in his aura. She speaks to him in his dreams. And in one of those dreams, Evange-lyne revealed her true name. How are those things the signs of an enemy?"

Oakenayl glanced at her, and Milo could see the doubt in his eyes.

In the ensuing silence, Milo asked, "The Heart of Darkness . . . what does it look like? I mean . . . is it a small black jewel?"

They stared at him, mouths opened.

"Cut like a diamond with a bunch of facets?"

They gaped.

He held his fingers two inches apart. "About this big?"

Oakenayl moved like lightning and grabbed him by the front of the shirt. Mook rose and cocked a rocky fist. Even Halflight seemed to glow brighter, as if ready to blast him.

Evangelyne was the only one who spoke. Her voice was low and threatening and far more wolflike than ever.

"How do you know what the Heart looks like?"

Despite the scowls and obvious threats around him, Milo managed to paste on a smile.

"Because I've seen it," he said. "I know where it is."

Chapter 51

I saw it when I was inside the Huntsman's head," explained Milo once Oakenayl released his grip. "I saw some of his memories, remember? I saw him take the Heart from the pyramid."

At first none of them could speak; then they all tried to speak at the same time. Oakenayl yelled, Evangelyne demanded details, Halflight tried to mitigate, and Mook banged his fists together and yelled, "Mook."

When he could finally get a word in sideways, Milo told them what happened. About being attacked by the Huntsman, about being dead—or near enough—for a few seconds. About floating above his own corpse. About falling into the mind of the Huntsman and seeing his memories and those of the hive.

He told them every detail he could remember, though he admitted that this was far from having lived it. "He has a little pouch on a strap across his chest. That's where he keeps the thing he stole."

Evangelyne turned sharply to Oakenayl. "See? I *told* you he had it. Back in the clearing, before the grenade, that's what he meant. He touched a pouch like he had something of great value there. The Heart is in there. I'm sure of it."

"It is," confirmed Milo. "And you heard what he said, right? About what he plans to do *with* the Heart?"

"I did not," said Halflight. "There was too much going on."

"I didn't hear him say anything," Oakenayl agreed. "I think I was out of it by then."

"I was pretty dazed," said Evangelyne. "So much of it is a blur."

"Well, I remember every word that freak said," Milo told them. "And, believe me, we have to get that stone back from him."

"'We'?" asked Evangelyne. "Why do you care if my friends and I recover the Heart of Darkness?"

"Because this war just got bigger than *us* and *them,* or even my people and the Nightsiders. This war just got bigger than everything else ever."

Oakenayl leaned forward, a frown of concern chipped into his features. "How?"

"Because," said Milo, "the Swarm know about you. They know you're supernatural. They know you can do magic."

"So what? They've known that for years."

Milo shook his head. "Not really. They fought you guys, but they didn't know what they were fighting. Remember, I saw their memories, too. The Swarm's.

When they came to Earth, they fought everyone. We're all from here." He pointed to the ground beneath them. "From Earth. But then two things happened."

"What?" asked Evangelyne.

"First, they created the Huntsman. They already knew about evil. As a concept, I mean. They're not evil—they're more like a virus. They destroy, but it's not personal. They encountered evil on different worlds."

"Evil exists everywhere," said Halflight. "So what?"

"Their science can't grow. It's . . . I'm not sure how to explain it. . . . It's kind of hit a wall. Their minds can't grow anymore. They're stuck. Maybe it's because they're insects, but they can't become more powerful than they already are. And it takes them thousands of years to go from one world to another."

"Space is big," said Oakenayl. "So?"

"So, they went looking for evil and they found this guy who was totally whacked out. A serial killer. A psycho. They found a really, seriously evil guy and they made him one of them."

"The Huntsman," murmured Evangelyne.

"The Huntsman. They used their science to *bond* with him. With his mind. They made him part of the Swarm so they could understand what power comes from evil. Does that make sense?"

"Too much sense," said Halflight, and she shivered at the thought.

"It gets worse. When they bonded with him, some of him went into the Swarm. They became like him more than they wanted. Understand, this guy is a total freakjob."

"That doesn't give them the secret of magic," said Evangelyne.

"No, but it made them aware of it. The guy they made into the Huntsman . . . he believed in magic. He really did. He thought what he was doing—all those killings he did—would somehow transform him into something else. Into someone who could do magic."

"That's happened before," said Evangelyne. "Even among us there are tales of madmen and madwomen who think that the pathway to power is through destruction."

"It is one of the many forms of evil," said the sprite.

"The problem is, the Swarm didn't know about magic before. They were hoping for more power, to use evil to jump to the next level. But now they know that there's something else out there. Something a whole lot more powerful than good or evil, something maybe more powerful than science."

"Magic," whispered Evangelyne. "Goddess of shadows . . ."

"Magic," said Milo. "That's what the Huntsman has been searching for. He went hunting and found the Heart of Darkness. Now the Swarm wants to figure out how it works. How its *magic* works."

"It will take them a thousand years to understand even the first secrets of the Heart," said Halflight.

"So what? They *have* a thousand years. They've been out there for millions of years. They've been stuck for a million years. Now they have the Heart of Darkness. They want to use it to do three things."

Evangelyne looked frightened to ask her question. "What?"

"They want to figure out how to use magic," said Milo.

They nodded with grave solemnity.

"I think," continued Milo, "they want to use the Heart to open the doorways to the worlds of shadow."

They stared at him in abject horror.

"And," said Milo softly, "they want to conquer the whole universe. All of it. Everywhere. Every dimension. Every world, even your shadow worlds. All of time and space. That's what the Bugs want to do."

Chapter 52

Four sets of eyes stared at him with equal measures of horror and fear.

Milo imagined the same emotions were there in his own eyes. He sure as heck felt that way.

At the same time, though, he felt different. Something was happening inside of him, and he wished he had time to stop and think about it. The process had started when he found the pyramid; he knew that much. That was the point at which the world, as he knew it, began to shift, to lose the sharpness around the edges. To become somehow less real. Or . . . to become real in a way he didn't yet understand.

The process of change had accelerated during the fight with the Stinger.

Milo had fought an alien mutant monster. He'd done that.

He'd survived it, too.

Then the rock boy had killed the Stinger, and any chance the world had to go back to something he recognized was shot to pieces. From there it all had a dreamlike quality, and for someone like him, someone who lived as much in dreams as he did in the real world, that was jarring.

Throwing the grenades had blasted big holes in the world too.

Being inside the Huntsman's head.

Seeing Evangelyne become a werewolf.

Then Milo himself defying the Huntsman. Making his stand, which is what the witch had said he needed to do. That was an action Milo still couldn't understand. If anyone else had done that, even Shark, Milo would have said it was what a hero would do. A noble sacrifice and all that stuff.

Except this wasn't Shark or Barnaby. They were dead or lost.

This wasn't his mom.

For a moment, Milo's heart felt ready to crack as he wondered where she was. There was no camp to go back to; nor was it safe to go to the ruins and wait for her. He didn't know what to do about contacting her.

What would she have thought about what he'd done? Risking his life? Prepared to throw it away to try to save the lives of people he didn't even know. To save the lives of monsters.

What would Mom make of that?

What did *he* make of it? Who was he? Certainly not a character from one of his books. Not a Bilbo or a Caspian or anyone he'd ever read about.

This was him. Milo Silk.

So . . . what did his actions make him?

He certainly didn't consider himself to be in any way heroic. He'd simply done the only thing that he could have done in that moment, even though he could have died. If Mook hadn't saved him, he *would* have died.

Throwing that grenade had saved Evangelyne, and maybe all of the orphans.

It still didn't feel heroic, though.

He wondered if that was the thing about heroes. Did any hero ever feel like he or she was a hero in the moment? Was taking action that much more important than being the hero who is expected to act?

That was a puzzle he didn't have time to sort out right then.

What mattered was the Huntsman.

They all sat there, staring at one another and into the middle distance. No one said a word.

Until Milo Silk had a very bad idea.

Chapter 53

Look," he said, laying his palms flat on the table, "I'm pretty sure I messed up the Huntsman's ship, right?"

Oakenayl gave a grudging nod. "You damaged two of the landing legs."

"Is there any way to find out if he fixed it yet? 'Cause if not, then maybe the Huntsman's still here."

"Oh, he is here," said Halflight.

"How do you know?"

"The bats told me," she said. "How else?"

Milo didn't have anything in his brain that was an appropriate answer to that, so he left it there. Bats. Right.

"If he's still here," he continued, "then the Heart of Darkness is still here. Still on Earth. That gives us a chance."

"How?" asked Oakenayl. "He has a hundred Stingers and countless Bug shocktroopers. We could never hope to take it by force. After all . . . we tried that and failed."

He cut a sharp look at Evangelyne, who colored again.

"Hey," said Milo, "you tried, right?"

"Tried and *failed*," Oakenayl repeated. He shot the

wolf girl a withering look. "I didn't like your plan from the start."

"Oakenayl . . . ," murmured Evangelyne.

"Why don't you lay off her?" asked Milo sternly. "At least she had a plan, didn't she? And you guys did some serious damage, right? You took out a whole bunch of Stingers and shocktroopers. And none of you actually died, so stop whining."

The oak boy looked absolutely furious, but Halflight turned away to hide a smile and Mook made a sound that might have been a chuckle.

Evangelyne, however, looked embarrassed and angry. "I don't need you to defend me, boy."

"I'm not, *girl*," said Milo sharply. "I'm trying to tell you an idea I have that might get the Heart back and save— let me count—I don't know . . . *everybody*."

That shut everyone up.

For one full second.

Then they were all jabbering for him to tell them his plan.

When he could stick a word in edgewise, he did.

They gaped at him.

Evangelyne looked horrified.

Oakenayl said he was nuts, that it would never work.

Halflight looked deeply uncertain and very scared.

Only Mook showed no expression because his face was incapable of it. However, he pounded a stony fist on the table so hard the candles jumped and threw wild shadows around the cave.

"Mook!" he cried.

Milo sat back. He was sweating because he was scared out of his mind by the plan he'd just outlined. His heart was hammering and his breath was coming as fast as if he'd run a mile uphill. But Milo managed to force a smile onto his face.

"Mook," he said.

Chapter 54

There was no time to talk it through. Night was passing, and Halflight's bat spies said that the red ship was nearly operational.

"We need to go now," said Milo, and he realized that he was pitching his voice to sound like an adult, a grown-up soldier. It was no different from what Evangelyne always did.

It turned out that the cave in which they hid was near the bayou. Milo didn't ask how there could be a rocky cave in an area that was so marshy. He figured the word "magic" was going to be part of any explanation, so he left it for later.

They emerged from between the tangled roots of an old cypress tree, and when Milo turned back to look for the door, there was none to be seen.

Cool.

The night was lit by starlight, and when they passed under the canopy of overlapping tree limbs, Halflight popped small fireworks in the air to light their way.

This is a dream, thought Milo.

No, child of the sun, this is the world.

It was the voice of the witch, and when Milo tried to get her to say more, there was nothing else. Even those words seemed to come from farther away than before, as if she was somehow fading back into his dream life.

Would have been pretty freaking useful for you to hang around longer, he thought. *Just saying.*

All he heard in his head—or thought he heard—was a faint whisper that might have been the echo of an echo of a laugh.

Their path took them half a mile from the camp where Milo had lived for the last several months. Even now, hours later, fires burned sluggishly, painting the curling towers of smoke in shades of Halloween orange and brick red. Milo slowed to a stop and stood for a moment, feeling the weight of all that he'd lost. The others, realizing he wasn't following, stopped too. Halflight buzzed over and landed her hummingbird on Milo's left shoulder. Evangelyne touched his right arm.

"I hung around your camp all day yesterday," she said, "watching to see if you really had stolen the Heart. And I followed your hike into the woods. I saw you with your friends. I . . . I'm sorry that you lost them."

Milo wiped tears from his eyes and said nothing.

"Was your mother there too?" asked the wolf girl.

Milo cleared his throat and explained about the patrol.

"Then there's still a chance that she's safe," said Halflight.

"Yeah. I guess. But how am I going to find her?"

No one had an answer for that.

"We have to go," said Evangelyne. He was happy she didn't call him "boy" again. He was already feeling very young and lost.

They moved quickly through the woods for another half hour before Milo realized that it was just Evangelyne and Halflight traveling with him.

"Hey—where's Mook and Oakenayl?"

"They transitioned from their constructs," said the sprite.

"They whatted from their whats?"

"I told you before," said Evangelyne. "Their bodies are only for convenience. They make new ones when they need them. The stones and wood they used back in the cave have been dropped, and they'll make new bodies when they need them. As long as some part of their constructs remain in contact with the earth, they can make a new body."

"That is right there between very cool and freak me out."

He caught a hint of a smile.

They hurried on.

There was a whispery sound in the air, and suddenly they were surrounded by a flock of bats fluttering in hysterical directions. Evangelyne and Halflight paused as if listening.

"Oh no!" gasped the little sprite.

"What's wrong?" Milo asked.

"The Huntsman's ship is powering up," she said. "He is about to take off. We can't let him take the Heart to the Swarm. All will be lost!"

There was no further conversation needed. They ran. Evangelyne moved like the night wind—silent and without effort, never tripping over a shadowy root, never walking into a darkened branch.

Milo, less so.

Eventually, he stopped trying to run next to her and fell into line behind her. Even then he tripped and collided a few times, but far less often. Halflight buzzed ahead, her hummingbird tireless and clearly able to navigate at high speeds in the dark.

For a while the task of running was enough to fill Milo's whole attention, but every once in a while he realized what he was running toward and who he was running with. At those times he was far more likely to run into a tree or fall flat on his face.

This is nuts, he thought. *This is totally off the chain. Running with a werewolf to fight an alien and save the world. Yeah. Like I ever saw* this *coming. Jeez.*

Then Evangelyne suddenly stopped, and before Milo could go smashing through the night, she grabbed his sleeve and pulled him down behind a bush.

"We're here," she whispered.

They slid onto their bellies and wormed their way forward under the shrubs. Beyond the branches, past the overlapping leaves, there was a faint glow. Milo gently parted the foliage and peered out.

There it was.

The red craft was still there, ringed by yellow and white lights. The eight metal legs all looked sturdy now, and the loading ramp was down. Bizarre figures moved in and out of the ship, carrying bundles and supplies. They were repellent five-foot-tall insects, their glistening shells the color of rust, the emerald lifelights burning on their chests.

As if sensing his question, Evangelyne leaned close and whispered, "Drones. They're like a slave race. Not sure if they even have their own personalities. They do the manual labor for the Bugs. I saw them once before, when my aunt Clara took me to one of the strip mines. There were thousands of them."

"Eww . . . They're like big cockroaches."

"What's wrong with cockroaches?" asked Evangelyne.

"Um . . . they're disgusting?"

She shook her head. "You people are weird."

He tried to figure a good way to respond to that but came up short and let it go.

Then Milo stiffened when he realized that some of the bundles being moved onto the Huntsman's ship were boxed supplies taken from his own camp. Crates of goods, cases of weapons, big jugs of water. Everything that could be salvaged after the attack had apparently been looted by the Bugs. It made Milo so angry.

"They take *everything*," he growled quietly.

"It is worse than that!" whispered Halflight in a shrill little voice. She hovered between them and pointed. Milo followed the angle of her finger and saw something that hit him like a punch to the face.

In a makeshift pen between two of the landing struts were dozens of figures. Not drones or shocktroopers. Not Stingers, ether. These were humans. Every prisoner had a thin metal collar clamped around his neck, and each collar had a ring set in front and another in the back. The Bugs had threaded these rings with tough cable that connected them all in a long line, one to the other.

Milo recognized every single one of them. Survivors of the camp. Milo counted them. Thirty-eight. Mostly children and older camp followers. No soldiers.

They were ragged, soot-stained, frightened, and desperate.

And among them, unmistakably, was one diminutive figure with pale hair, one tall, gaunt figure with wild brown hair, and one short, chubby figure.

Lizabeth.

Barnaby.

And Shark.

They were alive!

Then his heart sank. They were alive for now.

His friends were penned and bound. Waiting to be taken aboard the Huntsman's ship.

As what?

Slaves?

Or food?

Milo felt his blood turn to icy slush. But deep in his chest, a small and angry fire began to burn.

"Change of plan," he said grimly.

Chapter 55

Milo stood up and walked right into the clearing.

He didn't try to hide. He didn't have his slingshot in his hand. No grenades, either. He walked slowly from the night-dark woods to the ramp that stretched like a black tongue from the mouth of the Huntsman's red ship. He paused only for a moment as he approached the steady line of cockroachlike drones. They passed him by without so much as a quiver of their antennae. Milo waited for a break in the line, passed through, and crossed to the pen where the captives were kept. The guard was distracted, looking at a bunch of fireflies that had dropped from the trees and swirled around him. While his head was turned, Milo walked past and entered the pen.

The captives were huddled down and didn't notice anyone or anything. It was as if he were completely invisible to them.

Milo found a place to sit and lowered himself to the ground.

As the cluster of fireflies broke apart, the shock-trooper spotted a trio of drones who were clustered by the edge of the woods. The 'trooper made a series of loud and irritable clicking noises at these drones and pointed to the pile of boxes. The drones hurried over, picked up bundles, and joined the line of shuffling insects.

Satisfied, the shocktrooper glanced at the pen of prisoners and saw nothing out of the ordinary. It adjusted its grip on the batonlike shock rod it held and went on guarding the captives the way it had for hours.

It took another ten minutes for the cockroach drones to finish loading the stolen goods. Then the guard was joined by three other 'troopers. They each held a shock rod before them as they opened the gate to the pen.

One of the prisoners, a tall, gawky teenager with wild brown hair, spread his arms protectively in front of the others.

"Y'all stay back," he warned, speaking both to the 'troopers and his fellow prisoners.

A 'trooper scuttled forward on four legs and gestured to the ramp. Once, twice. The movements jerky and terse.

"I don't tink so, me," growled the teenager in a thick Cajun accent. "I wasn't born to be Sunday roast for a bunch of overgrown head lice."

Then, out of the side of his mouth, in a tight whisper, he said, "When I rush him, make a break for it. Head to da closest bolt-hole and—"

Before the teenager could even finish, the shocktrooper jabbed him in the chest. There was a huge *snapping* sound as the electric charge shot through the Cajun's body. The air was suddenly filled with the smell of ozone and the sound of screams. The teenager dropped to his knees, his face going slack, eyes rolling white. Other guards reached out to try to shock him again, and they would have succeeded if not for a short, chubby kid who caught the Cajun and dragged him backward out of reach.

"Leave him alone!" shouted the fat kid.

The 'troopers stood their ground, each of them making loud clicking noises. They showed the business ends of their shock rods to the rest of the prisoners. They pointed to the ramp. The Dissosterin couldn't speak English, but they made their point with perfect clarity.

The prisoners shivered and wailed, frightened to the point of despair. However, they began shuffling forward, each of them tethered by the collars and steel cable. The fat kid wrapped the Cajun's arm over his shoulder and lifted him to his feet with a grunt of effort. Together they shambled out of the pen toward the ship. Soon all thirty-nine captives moved up the ramp and vanished inside.

Then the Huntsman himself came and mounted the ramp. The ramp retracted, the door slid shut, the engines throbbed with energy, and the big craft rose away from the Louisiana swamps. The air beneath it shimmered and swirled.

Within moments, the red craft was gone, soaring through the night sky.

Chapter 56

Shark wrapped his arm around Lizabeth and held her close. The little girl was weeping uncontrollably. Barnaby lay with his head in her lap, his face tight with pain.

"It'll be okay," murmured Shark over and over again. However, the haunted look in his eyes told what he truly felt about their chances. There were dried tear tracks on his grimy cheeks.

"We're going to die," said Lizabeth in a tiny voice. "They're going to eat us."

"No, they won't," soothed Shark. "That's not what they do. Don't worry. Aunt Jenny and Milo's mom will find us. They're still out there. They'll come find us."

He went on and on like that, telling lies that were built on the thinnest framework of hope. Gradually, Lizabeth's sobs slowed, but they did not stop.

The prisoners were crammed into a small chamber that stank of engine oil and insect droppings. Shark stroked the girl's hair and looked around, nodding to some of the other refugees.

"He's right, Lizabeth," said a voice. "They're not going to eat you."

Every head in the group whipped around to stare at a figure that sat alone in one corner. A person none of them had even seen until that moment. They stared in shocked silence as Milo Silk stood up.

"Hey, guys," he said.

Shark's mouth opened and closed like a trout.

Lizabeth stared in mute silence for two seconds.

Then she burst into fresh tears.

"Oh no!" she wailed. "*Milo!* They got you, too!"

Shark and Barnaby and Lizabeth and a dozen other refugees all reached for Milo at once and pulled him into a cluster hug that nearly crushed the air from his lungs.

"I didn't see you in the pen!" said Shark, hugging him. "Don't know how I missed you. I'm so sorry to see you, dude."

Milo pushed his friends gently back. As he did, Barnaby reached out a weak hand and touched Milo's neck. "Hey . . . you don't got no collar, you. How'd you cut yourself loose? Dey took all our knives."

"Never had a collar," said Milo, "because I'm not a prisoner. I never was."

"Den how—?"

Milo didn't have the time to explain how Halflight had used her glamour powers to make Milo look like a 'trooper guard, or how she'd distracted the real guard with a firefly illusion while Milo slipped into the slave pen. Or even how she'd used a much smaller spell to create the illusion that Milo wore a prisoner's collar. Those explanations could wait for later. If there *was* a later.

Instead he said, "Long story."

He fished his Swiss Army knife out of his pocket, opened the tiny wire cutters, and handed it to Shark. Then he removed a wire handsaw from his scavenger microtool kit and gave it to Lizabeth. "Cut everyone free and stay ready."

"Ready? Ready for *what*? They destroyed the camp. They got us. We're done."

"No, we're not," said Milo. "We're going to get everyone out."

"'We'?" asked Lizabeth. "Who's 'we'?"

Milo grinned. "I didn't come alone."

"What?" asked Shark, totally confused. "Did Aunt Jenny and your mom get back? Are there soldiers here?"

"Not exactly."

"Then—"

"Trust me," said Milo. "We have a plan."

"Are you nuts?" demanded Shark. "Did you see that *thing* who's in charge?"

"The Huntsman. Sure. I saw him."

"And did you see all dem shocktroopers?" asked Barnaby.

"Saw 'em."

"Den how you going to get us out of a moving spaceship with all of dese monsters out there, you?"

Behind Milo, the door to the prison compartment

slid open. Shark and the others stared with mute incomprehension at the figures that stood in a cluster. A wolf with eyes the color of a winter moon. A boy who looked like a living tree. Another who seemed to be made completely of rocks, who had a huge salamander resting on his shoulders, and a tiny figure with fiery hair who sat astride a hummingbird.

"Because," said Milo, "I brought a few monsters of my own."

Chapter 57

Before the prisoners could ask the ten thousand questions that rose to their lips, Milo shushed them and backed out of the chamber.

"Be ready," he said quickly. "If this works, we're going to need to move fast."

The door slid shut, hiding them all. Milo caught a last glimpse of Shark staring at him with wide, wild eyes.

Then he was alone in a steel corridor with the Orphan Army. Milo slumped back against the wall, his air of cool confidence sliding off of him like melting slush.

"What if your plan *doesn't* work?" asked Oakenayl.

Milo sighed. "Then I guess none of them will ever know."

They shared a long, knowing look. Evangelyne morphed back into her human form—a sight that still gave Milo a serious jolt.

"Everything went smoothly," she said. "Halflight's glamour held. They thought we were drones carrying supplies. Mook carried Iskiel."

"Mook," said the rock boy. The fire salamander hissed

faintly. Small puffs of smoke curled from its nostrils. It made Milo wonder if Evangelyne was being facetious with her comment about dragons only being a myth.

"I don't like being here," said Oakenayl. "If my construct is destroyed up here, I'll die too. The same with Mook."

The rock boy shrugged. "Mook."

Milo grinned. "Then I guess you better not die."

It took a moment, but Oakenayl managed a smile too. "You're out of your mind."

"Yeah, looks that way."

Oakenayl looked up and down the corridor. "Big ship."

The Huntsman's ship was at least two hundred feet across. Inside, the lights were low and set to a weird color scheme—yellows and greens. He wondered if that was the part of the spectrum best suited to alien eyes. He personally found it difficult, and it ignited a small headache behind his eyes.

The tree spirit turned to Milo. "What's next?"

It felt weird to be asked, as if he knew how to do this. Sure, it was his plan, but that's all it was. A plan. Something he'd made up on the spot. It's not like he'd ever done this before.

On the other hand, neither had the orphans.

They expect me to figure it out, thought Milo. *What if I can't?*

The answer to that was obvious. It was the answer to virtually every question from here on out.

If he got it wrong—if any of them got any of it wrong—then they'd all die.

It was as simple and as ugly and as certain as that.

Milo bent close to Halflight. "Can you scout the ship? See if you can find out where the Huntsman is, and also where the command center is. Don't get seen, though. If anyone's around, use a glamour thingy, okay?"

"I will," said the sprite, "but glamours are difficult. I do not know how many more I can do without resting."

"How much rest are we talking?"

The sprite paused. "If I exhaust myself? Days. Maybe a week."

That was like a punch in the face to Milo. "Um . . . then I guess it'd be better just to not be seen. Stay out of sight."

She put on a brave smile. "I will do my best."

With that, the hummingbird zoomed off down the corridor. While they waited, Milo and the others found the compartment where equipment was stored. There were no guards, so they slipped inside.

It was an odd thing, but there didn't seem to be many guards anywhere. Once the ship was in the air, the drones and the shocktroopers seemed to all vanish. Milo wondered—and worried—about that.

While they waited, he explained to the others about how the Dissosterin ships were piloted.

"The EA techs said that a five-year-old could fly one of these ships," he said. "There's something called a control sphere. It's like a hologram. You guys know what that is?"

Evangelyne nodded. "It's like a glamour but made with science instead of magic."

"Kind of," agreed Milo. "Well, Bug ships have this thing that creates a 3-D hologram of whatever craft you're on. You stick your hand inside and then do whatever. If you want to go up, you raise your hand. Down is down. Whatever your hand does, the ship does."

Oakenayl frowned. "Why make it so simple?"

"Why make it hard?" asked Milo. "Let's face it: The Bugs aren't smart. Sure, some of them are, but not most of them. The shocktroopers are scary and tough, but not really brilliant. The drones are dumb as barrels of hair."

"They conquered Earth," said the oak boy.

"A virus could have wiped people out too," said Milo. "That doesn't make it smart."

"He's right," said Evangelyne. "Besides, he saw how the Swarm works when he was inside the Huntsman's memories. It's a hive mind. The real brainpower is in the queens. Everything else is like ants in an anthill. They do their jobs and that's it. Why wouldn't they make their tech easy to use? The easier it is, the more of the Swarm that can use it."

"So what?" insisted Oakenayl. "What does it matter if they can all use it?"

"Because," said Milo, "if any of them can fly this ship, then any of *us* can do it too."

Even Mook understood that. He nodded and said, "Mook."

There was the faintest scratching at the door—quick and with a detectable pattern.

"It's Halflight," said Evangelyne, rushing to open the door.

The hummingbird flew in and hovered in the dim air between them as they huddled around.

"There is good news, good news, bad news, and bad news," she said quickly.

"Give it to us good, bad, good, bad," said Oakenayl. "We need to know where we stand."

The sprite pointed to the closed door. "I found where the drones and shocktroopers are. As soon as the ship took off, they all climbed into holes in the walls."

"Like bees in a hive," murmured Evangelyne.

"Creepy," said Milo. "That's good news, right? 'Cause they're all asleep?"

"Yes, except one 'trooper who is piloting the ship. Oh, and I found the command center. The bridge, I suppose, because it is where the pilot sits. The bad news is that the Huntsman is not asleep."

"Figured that," said Milo. He touched the bag of grenades. He had three left. Not that they wanted to use one on the ship while it was in flight. However, it was nice to know that they had some real firepower.

"What's the other good news?" asked the wolf girl.

"The Huntsman still has the Heart of Darkness with him. I saw him holding it and staring at it. Trying to understand it. I could *feel* the anger rolling off of him. The frustration. And the desire. He wants to unlock the Heart more than I think anyone has ever wanted anything."

Oakenayl asked, "Halflight . . . what was the other bad thing?"

The sprite looked nervous. "Milo's plan—to surprise the Huntsman, overpower him, grab the Heart, and pilot this ship to safety? That is not going to work."

"Why not?" they all asked.

"If the drones and 'troopers are all asleep, then it should be easy," said Evangelyne.

"He's already hurt," said Milo. "I think we can take him."

"None of that matters because—" began Halflight, but before she could finish, there was a heavy *clang* of metal that vibrated through the entire ship. The sound of the engine changed too. It began winding down.

As if it was shutting itself off.

"What . . . ?" began Oakenayl, but he let it trail off.

"The ship is much faster than we thought," said Halflight. "I saw where we are heading, and we are already out of time."

The engine whine stopped.

The ship was no longer moving.

Milo understood what that last bad thing was in Half-light's report.

The red ship had already reached its destination.

"Oh no . . . ," breathed Evangelyne.

"We have just landed on the hive ship," said the sprite.

Chapter 58

The sprite landed her hummingbird and stepped off, then bent to the metal decking. A tiny fire ignited on the tip of one finger, and with it she drew a rough diagram of the ship on the floor.

"Here is where we left the prisoners," she said. "And here is the bridge. The cargo holds are here, here, and here. We are in the fourth of four holds. The one closest to the exit."

They discussed the best way to go and assigned tasks.

Evangelyne went to the door, opened it, and sniffed the air. "No Bugs close. We should go now while we have the chance."

They followed her out into the corridor, which was empty in both directions.

Around the far side of the left-hand curve, they heard noises. Evangelyne morphed into a wolf and ran quickly and silently to see what was going on. She returned just as fast and became a girl again. Milo wondered how many times he would have to see that before it stopped being amazing. Or creepy. He wanted to ask her what happened to her dress when she became a wolf but didn't think this was the right moment for that.

"The Bugs are already crawling out of their holes," she said. "They're off-loading supplies. The prisoners are still in the locked compartment. Perhaps they'll take them out last."

"Could you see if Shark managed to cut the cables? Is everyone free?"

She shook her head. "Only a few are. It is taking time to cut those cables."

"Rats," said Milo. "Shark will do it, though. He never gives up."

"He's the fat one? The one who was with you when you fought the Stinger?"

"He's not fat," said Milo defensively. "He's big-boned. And . . . yes. He's my best friend."

"A friend is sometimes more important than family," said Halflight. The other orphans nodded. She climbed back onto her hummingbird and buzzed near Milo's nose. "We will try to help you save your friends."

"They're not *my* friends," said Oakenayl. Mook looked at him for a moment, then punched him in the chest. Not hard, but hard enough.

Point made.

"Sorry," muttered the oak boy, though it was clear he didn't mean it. Milo wondered how much fun it would be to run Oakenayl through a wood chipper. Then something occurred to Milo. "What do we do if we get the Heart back but can't get off the ship?"

Evangelyne answered that. "We know how to destroy the Heart," she said. "If we have to."

"Destroy it? But . . . but . . ."

"Better that than let the Swarm gain possession of it," said Halflight. "Better for us to destroy the last link to magic than have it turned against us all."

What she didn't say—what none of them seemed willing to say—was that if things got so hopeless that they had to destroy the Heart, then it meant there was probably no chance of escaping.

Milo's great plan had morphed into what was almost certainly a suicide mission.

They all knew it.

He pasted on his best game face and stuck out a finger so the hummingbird could land.

"Halflight," said Milo, "I hate to ask, but—"

The sprite gave him a weary nod. "I can manage a few more glamours. But they won't last. And when they're gone . . ."

She didn't need to finish it.

They looked at one another, all of them knowing that this moment was the cliff they all had to jump off.

"For our mother, Earth," said Halflight. "May we acquit ourselves with honor."

"For Earth," said Oakenayl.

Milo said, "For the Nightsiders."

They stared at him. Then Evangelyne kissed his cheek. "For the children of the sun," she said.

Iskiel hissed.

"Mook," said Mook.

They left the storage compartment, and as each of them passed through the doorway, they changed.

Instead of a girl, an oak boy, a stone boy, a fire salamander, and a human boy, they were a line of rust-colored five-foot-high cockroaches. Only Halflight remained in her true form. Her face was gray and haggard, and even her fiery hair seemed to be nothing more than tangles of sparks. She slumped in her saddle and let the hummingbird carry her into the hall.

Chapter 59

The next few minutes were a strange blur for Milo.

He and the orphans hurried along the curved corridor until they found the place where the drones were climbing out of rows of slots in the metal walls. A knot of shocktroopers seemed to be directing their actions by shouting orders that sounded to Milo like clicks and pops. The drones turned around, formed a line outside of one of the storerooms, and began the orderly process of off-loading all of the supplies stolen from the destroyed camp. Milo joined the line and when he entered the storeroom, he tried to hurry over and pick up a crate of rifles, but a shocktrooper shoved him back into line. The 'trooper had his shock rod out, and there were more of the Bug soldiers climbing out of holes in the walls.

Milo shuffled back into the line, picked up the box the nearest 'trooper indicated—which contained nothing more important than cans of corned beef—and followed the rest of the drones outside.

He lamented his previous plan. If it had worked, not only would the orphans have recovered the Heart of Darkness, but he'd have stolen a working Dissosterin ship. If he could deliver it to the EA—or use it to find his mother—then the resistance would acquire a powerful weapon. Maybe a game changer.

Now that looked a lot less likely.

The drones moved down the ramp and into a vast chamber. Milo almost dropped his bundle when he recognized it. They were inside a great dark shell of metal whose curved walls were so massive that they were nearly lost in shadows. The air was so humid that clouds hung in the air *inside* the hive ship. There was a titanic column in the center of the ship, and it rose through the clouds and shadows. Hanging from it, or perhaps growing out of it, were hundreds of thousands of leathery sacs of various sizes. Some were as small as duffel bags while others were big enough to cover an attack helicopter. Each sac twitched and throbbed as things moved within them. Drones and shocktroopers and other creatures. Hundreds of different subspecies, jostling with others for space, for food, for air. Long strands of gleaming metal webs crisscrossed the immense chamber, connecting the sacs to feeding machines and other equipment so obscure that even having seen them from inside the Huntsman's mind, Milo couldn't understand them.

However, Milo realized now that the robot hunter-killers were not modeled after Earth insects, but were instead smaller automatons based on all of the dozens of living insect forms up here. And here, above and around him, he saw the true shapes of the aliens. The many, many shapes. Ten-foot-long wasps. Fiery-red ants the size of German shepherds. Ticks that were nearly as big as cars. Stick bugs as long as telephone poles.

And there were smaller ones, too. Smaller than the giants, but much larger than any insects on Milo's world. Teeming lice the size of mice; flies that there bigger than pigeons. Foot-long worms the color of old paste. Red-shelled beetles in their thousands, each of them larger than Milo's hand.

Centipedes with bodies as long as school buses writhed and crawled between all the sacs. Other creatures, like slow spiders of enormous size, climbed over the sacs, monitoring them, adjusting them, and killing any of the Swarm that showed even the slightest sign of imperfection.

The walls were encrusted with countless bays and landings, with ships magnetically clamped to the hull, with smaller hives of a thousand kinds.

There had to be a million creatures up there.

No, tens of millions. He could see countless green lifelights pulsing in the gloom.

This hive was a world unto itself.

And there are seven of them, thought Milo. Not an invading army. It was an invading population. In those seven ships was the whole of the Dissosterin race, and he was looking at one-seventh of them.

The chamber was as hot as an oven and so humid that Milo found it hard to breathe. He'd read once that insects grow largest in the hottest climates, and the hive ship seemed to take that concept and magnify it thousands of times. Beneath the false drone skin of his glamour, Milo was pouring sweat, and he stopped to try to catch his breath.

A series of angry clicks made him turn. A 'trooper was glaring at him, his shock rod raised. Milo did his best to scuttle forward the way the other drones did. He could feel the 'trooper watching him.

There was no chance to break the line for nearly fifteen minutes, as the procession of drones made several loops back into the red ship for more of the supplies. Milo began to worry that the glamour was going to fade. He kept looking around to see if Mook, Oakenayl, or Evangelyne was suddenly there with boxes in their hands.

They were not. For now the sprite's magic was holding.

At one point, on his fifth trip into the ship, another drone brushed against him.

"We need to get out of here," it said in Evangelyne's whisper. "We're never going to find the Heart doing this."

"I'm open to suggestions," he whispered back. He wanted to find the captives as well, but that seemed equally as unlikely.

They picked up boxes and followed the line outside

and, as if the universe wanted to finally cut them a little slack, a loud buzzer suddenly sounded from overhead. It shook the whole place, and Milo nearly dropped his bundle. Everyone—every drone and shocktrooper, and all of the insectoid creatures in the massive chamber, looked toward the gigantic central tower. One of the larger sacs was tearing open, and a creature was emerging. It was huge. The legs alone were thirty feet long and this had to be an infant.

A newborn monster.

As they watched, the creature shredded the leathery sac and clawed its way out. Its body was longer than a shocktrooper, but it had the same six-legged structure. However, its thorax was much bigger and banded with rings of bright scarlet and yellow. The monster crawled up the column, shedding the tattered remnants of the sac as it went. Once clear, it seemed to vibrate for a moment, and then its shell split apart and a huge pair of wings swept upward and out, the membrane glistening with moisture.

All around the chamber, the drones suddenly dropped their bundles and boxes, and the shocktroopers flung down their weapons as, in a mass, they bent and bowed to the ground. A chorus of clicking sounds—the language of the Bugs—filled the chamber like thunder.

It took Milo a moment to realize what he was seeing. This creature and the reaction of the Swarm.

This wasn't simply a new Bug hatching.

They had just witnessed the birth of a new queen.

Only four drones stood amid the sea of prostrate bodies. And far across the chamber, standing like a colossus in a sea of insects, stood the Huntsman. He was framed in the entrance of a side tunnel, and he stood looking up at the newborn queen. Milo couldn't see the monster's face, but there was something about the Huntsman's body language that spoke of an emotion other than blind adoration.

The Huntsman turned away and vanished in the tunnel while the masses still knelt in worship.

Had Milo been able to see the monster's face, he was sure he would have seen emotions the Huntsman wouldn't want the queen or her minions to observe.

After all, he'd been inside the mutant's mind. In his memories. And though he couldn't possibly remember everything in detail, Milo came away from the experience with the certain knowledge that the Huntsman did not care to bow to anyone. Or anything.

It was he who wanted the world to bow to him.

Did that mean he wanted the secret of magic for the Swarm or for some personal agenda?

Either possibility offered unending harm. Neither could be allowed.

Milo turned to the others and pointed to the tunnel where the Huntsman had vanished.

Suddenly, a voice spoke in Milo's mind. A voice he had not heard in hours.

I have whispered a horror into life, said the Witch of the World. *I have helped birth a monster so that you may have a chance. Do not waste it!*

Milo gaped at the exultant queen.

I cannot offer more help than this. Time is burning, and if you don't act soon, the world itself will burn. Now is your time, Milo Silk. Now.

Now.

And once more. *Now.* But that was like a fading echo in his mind.

"Come on," Milo whispered to the orphans. "We have to go—now!"

Chapter 60

They moved as quickly as they could through the hordes of insects, being careful not to speak and not to bump against any of them. The ritual of bowing to the queen seemed to be overriding all other actions.

Milo prayed that their luck would hold.

Just a little longer.

A little longer.

Once they reached the interior wall of the hive, the party cut left and began hurrying along it toward their destination. The crowd was facing away from them, which allowed them to run instead of shuffle. Evangelyne threw herself forward, and although to Milo's eyes it was a drone running on all fours, the speed and fluidity told him that the girl had once more become the wolf.

So weird, he told himself.

He was the second fastest of their group, with Oakenayl and Mook falling behind with every step. Milo wasn't sure if Iskiel was still draped over the rock boy's shoulder or if he was slithering along in some other guise. The salamander seemed able to blend into the background of any location so as not to be noticed, and Milo realized that he actually had to work at noticing the creature at times.

Magic, he mused, and stopped trying to figure it out for now.

They reached the corridor and ducked inside just as the first of the drones were beginning to rise and the worshipful clicking changed in tone.

Was that lucky timing or more of the witch's intervention? No way to know. Another mystery for later.

As they left the big chamber, the glamour vanished with the speed of a light switch being flipped. Evangelyne was a wolf again, and when he looked down at his hands and body, he was a boy once more.

The corridor was empty, and now they raced along it at full speed. Evangelyne was far ahead and the two elementals far behind. The Huntsman was nowhere in sight, but several times he saw the wolf stop to sniff the ground and raise its head, ears swiveling, to hear things that Milo could not detect. Each time, the wolf leaped forward again, racing to follow the Huntsman's scent. Surely even on this ship—this hive of a thousand different life forms—there could not be two like the psychotic mutant.

The corridor ended at a T-junction, and Evangelyne took the left-hand turn without a pause and then another junction going right. A left, two rights, another left. So many that Milo lost all track of their path. He paused for breath and glanced back but saw no trace at all of the elemental boys or the salamander. When he looked forward again, his heart lurched in his chest.

Evangelyne was not there.

The corridor stretched on and on before him and it was totally empty.

He strained to hear the sound of sharp nails on metal deck plating.

And heard absolutely nothing.

Nor did he hear the stomping footfalls of the rock boy.

With sinking horror, Milo realized that he was lost.

And alone.

On a *hive ship*.

Milo knew that he could not go back. If it was a matter of him having taken a wrong turn, then going back would only confuse things. If it was simply that he'd fallen behind Evangelyne, then his only chance would be to keep going forward in hopes of finding her.

"No, no, no, no, no . . . ," he muttered as he ran, alternating that with, "Come on. Come on. Come on . . ."

He reached a juncture of four corridors and stopped. All four were empty.

He tried to sniff the air the way the wolf had done.

Nothing. Of course nothing.

He closed his eyes and listened.

The hive ship had very quiet engines that made a soft hum so subtle he really had to strain to hear it.

Nothing.

Nothing.

Then . . .

Something.

For just a moment he thought he heard a voice murmur his name. It came from the right-hand tunnel, one that was shrouded in shadows.

Was it Evangelyne?

No.

No, definitely not. He strained to hear.

Was it the witch?

Milo couldn't tell. He took a step into the tunnel and immediately winced as a wave of stink came rolling at him and struck his senses like a punch. He winced and recoiled from a stench like rotting fish and old sewage.

Milo.

That time he definitely heard it.

Or . . .

He was so confused he wasn't sure if he could trust his ears or his mind. Everything was a crazy jumble.

Did he *really* hear the witch call his name?

He didn't wait for an answer he knew wouldn't come. He forced himself to take a step. And another. Moving into the almost palpable wall of rotten air.

Milo plucked the slingshot from his belt, fished out a stone, and socketed it into the leather pad. It wasn't much, but it was better than facing the unknown with nothing but nervous tension in his hands.

He kept moving forward, leaving the pale corridor lights behind and entering a space of total darkness. It felt like walking into the mouth of a waiting dragon. It felt like being swallowed whole.

Chapter 61

It was even hotter in the corridor than in the rest of the tunnel system, and Milo felt like he was drowning in humidity. There was no light at all, and he had to feel his way along the walls. He was afraid to use his flashlight for fear of being seen.

The walls were metallic and slick with a greasy substance. Milo didn't want to know what it was.

Sounds suddenly came rolling through the darkness. Milo froze to listen, but they were far away down that long, black corridor.

He heard . . .

There it was again.

It was not the clicking sounds of the Bugs. Not the howl of a Stinger, either.

Though it was, indeed, a howl.

It was a wolf.

Howling in agony.

Milo had no choice but to dig out his flashlight. The beam stabbed through the darkness to reveal a tunnel that sloped downward and out of sight. Water dripped from the ceiling and ran crookedly down the walls. Tendrils of mist writhed like the tentacles of some hidden monster.

And the stink was even worse down there.

Milo held the light before him as if instead of alerting the enemy, it could somehow shield him from whatever might be waiting. He could feel his heartbeat in the veins of his neck and head. His labored breaths sounded too loud.

He began moving forward, though.

Into the tunnel.

Toward . . . *what?*

What new horrors did the Swarm have for him?

The wolf howled again. Louder.

Milo moved more quickly, his sneakers skidding on the slick floor.

"I'm coming," he said under his breath. "I'm coming. . . ."

He passed a row of doors that were shut and locked. Then another whose door was wide open. Milo skidded to a stop and listened.

No more howls.

But . . .

From inside the chamber, he could hear grunts and growls and the skitter of hard nails on damp metal.

Milo had received a lot of training over the last few years, and it had intensified as he got older. When Barnaby took over the pod, the young Cajun had taught them all a lot of crafty tricks. Milo used one of those tricks now.

Instead of rashly charging into an unknown situation, he knelt quickly beside the doorframe and then reached inside and sent his flashlight rolling across the floor to the left. Then he darted in and cut right, bringing up his slingshot.

The flashlight beam painted the room in pale light, revealing a scene of horror.

There were two shocktroopers crouched in combat stances, their shock rods raised to strike but frozen in a moment of surprise as they turned toward the light. A third 'trooper lay sprawled on the ground, his throat torn out. Huddled between the Bugs was a gray mass of fur and fangs.

Evangelyne!

She stood quivering, her eyes blazing but head hanging low.

She and the 'troopers all stared at the rolling light.

Milo understood the scene at once.

Evangelyne had either come into this chamber or was chased. She'd taken down one of the Bugs, but the others had struck her with their shock rods. The wolf was not bleeding, but Milo had seen the effect of those weapons on the sturdy Barnaby. The fact that the wolf was even able to stand was a testament to her supernatural power.

Or, Milo thought, her fierce will to save her people and her world.

The tableau held for two seconds.

Then the Bugs swiveled their insect heads toward where Milo crouched.

He fired his stone. He'd had more than enough time to aim a perfect shot.

Milo knew from the attack on the camp that the life-lights were too well protected to be an easy Achilles' heel. So he shot for the head. These 'troopers had body armor but not helmets. They wouldn't, here on their home ship.

The stone hit one 'trooper in the right eye, snapping its head back, blowing apart the multifaceted lens, staggering the alien killer. He wailed in a series of alarmed clicks as he toppled over.

In the instant that followed, Evangelyne, dazed and hurt as she was, leaped at the second 'trooper. Milo saw a flash of white fangs, and then the crunch of chitinous shell filled the room.

Milo had a second stone out, and he fired at the first 'trooper's other eye, scoring a solid hit. Then he was up and moving. He kicked the shock rod out of the Bug's hand, dipped down, snatched it up, whirled, and rammed the tip into the 'trooper's chest. Once, twice. On the third jab, the shock rod bent and snapped, shooting sparks into the air.

The Bug collapsed back and did not move.

Milo spun around to help Evangelyne, but the fangs of the wolf had already done their work. The lifelight flickered weakly and then went dark.

That fast it was over.

Milo felt like he was inside one of his dreams. He let the broken shock rod fall from his hands, stunned by what had just happened. He had defeated a shocktrooper in single combat.

Him.

Milo Silk.

Sure, the 'trooper was not in full combat rig and wasn't firing a pulse rifle. But still.

He'd taken out a shocktrooper.

The knowledge that it was possible, that *he* could do it, seemed to change something within him. He felt stronger. Not physically, but in some indefinable way.

He knelt beside the wolf, who was still quivering and panting.

"Evangelyne, are you okay?"

She morphed from wolf to girl, but the process was much slower than before. She wobbled and fell, but Milo caught her and helped her sit down.

"I—I'll be okay," she said. But she sat for a minute with her head down between her knees, making small gagging sounds. Milo, not knowing what else to do, rubbed her back the way his mom did when he was feeling sick.

The flashlight had stopped rolling by one wall, and the reflected light allowed him to see some of the room. There were tall banks of machines that he figured were Dissosterin computers. They hummed quietly, and Milo wished he had a hammer so he could smash them. He thought about the bag of grenades he had but didn't know if this would be the best use for them. What if these machines only regulated sewage or processed foods? Probably only crippling the engines would matter.

He said as much to Evangelyne.

"I don't know computers at all," she said. "My mother had one when I was little, but after the invasion, there was no use for it. No Internet. No power unless we wanted to use portable generators."

"We need to get out of here and find the Huntsman," said Milo. "Did you see where he went?"

She wiped sweat from her eyes and nodded. "Help me up." When she was on her feet, she picked up his flashlight and walked carefully over to the far wall. The beam revealed a doorway with a hatch like an airlock. "I followed him in here and saw him pull this door closed as he went inside. The Bugs must have seen me come in here and they attacked before I could open this door."

"Did the Huntsman see you?"

She ran one hand over the edges of the door. "No." Then she turned and looked at the door through which Milo had come. "Where are the others?"

"We got separated in the tunnels. This place is a maze."

Evangelyne bumped her small fist against the heavy steel of the door. "I'm not even sure Mook could get through this."

"Maybe I can," said Milo as he bent and studied the lock.

"How?"

He removed his scavenger tool kit. "The Bugs are dangerous, but they're not paranoid."

"Huh?"

Milo tapped the lock. "Shark and me and the others . . . we're scavengers. That's what we train to do. That's why we were at the crash site yesterday. We find stuff and we take it apart so we can salvage whatever's useful. The Bugs' entire tech is designed so all of them can use it. So it's all pretty simple. We've always been able to take apart their stuff. It's just that their ships are so hard to shoot down that there isn't much left of them. That's why we haven't built any for us to use against them. It's why I wanted to steal the Huntsman's ship."

She nodded.

"Up here, they have guards," Milo said as he began fiddling with the lock, "but from what I can see, they don't care much about good locks."

"Would there be much need for that with them?" asked Evangelyne. "Could there be crime in a society with a hive mind?"

Milo shook his head. "Probably not. This lock is so lame it's like they put it here to keep accidents from happening rather than for real security."

"How lame is it?"

Milo smiled at her and tugged on the door. There was a single sharp click and it swung open.

"Pretty lame."

They grinned at each other for a moment. Two conspirators whispering in the dark.

"Milo," Evangelyne said quietly, "I'm sorry for the way I treated you."

"It's cool."

"No," she said, "it's not. I . . . I've never been around human kids before. Not ever. I spent my whole life with the Nightsiders, and even then it was mostly with my mother, my grandmother, and my aunts, and some of them are—*were*—very old. Kids like Oakenayl and Mook spend even more time alone than me. Oakenayl sometimes spends a whole year standing in a forest."

"Like Treebeard?"

"Who?"

"From *The Lord of the Rings*. He's a big tree guy."

"I suppose, though I don't know that book. I've only read a few books written by the people of the sun. Most of what I read are grimoires and ancient tomes. Even some scrolls. Histories of the Nightsiders. Magic. Lore about the lycanthropes and other shape-shifters." She sighed. "I don't know how to be a kid."

"Yeah, well, sometimes it's overrated."

"No," she said. "I don't think so. I saw you with your friend Shark when I was watching the camp the other night.

You were being young together, not trying to be grown-ups."

"I guess."

"I . . . don't know how to do that."

Milo laughed. "Stick with me. I'm pretty sure I'm going to be immature my whole life." He paused. "However long that is."

She touched his arm. "If we get out of this . . . maybe we can be friends?"

"Aren't we friends now?" he asked.

The question seemed to startle her. "I don't . . . know."

"Well, I think we are, and I swear on a stack of Bibles that I will never, ever try to conjure with your name."

"You're not going to let me forget that, are you?"

"Probably not."

She punched him on the arm.

"Ow," he said.

Then Evangelyne stiffened. She sniffed the air, and a look of mingled fear and anger twisted her features. She gripped Milo's wrist.

"He's close," she said.

"How close?" asked Milo, reaching for his slingshot.

And a deep and ugly voice said, "Too close."

They looked up.

The Huntsman stood there, just inside the door, massive, powerful, and infinitely dangerous.

With a smile that twisted his face into a mask of hideous joy, he reached for them.

Chapter 62

Milo and Evangelyne both tried to shove each other out of the way as the Huntsman grabbed for them. The resulting double shove knocked them both aside and the grabbing hand missed.

The Huntsman laughed.

Somehow that made it worse for Milo. It reminded him how twisted this killer was. In the past, when he was a human serial killer, the Huntsman had enjoyed the chase as much as the actual murder. It meant that the victim had more time to be afraid. More time to despair. It was a strange and appalling way for a person's mind to turn rancid.

Milo fell onto his back and kicked up with both feet, knocking the grasping hand aside. Evangelyne rolled sideways and midroll stopped being a girl and became the wolf again. She snarled and scrambled to four feet, then lunged up at the Huntsman.

Her attack was lightning fast, and it knocked the man a full step back into the adjoining room; the Huntsman clubbed at the wolf with the stump of his left wrist. Evangelyne yelped and crashed to the floor. The mutant raised his good fist to smash down on her. Milo got to his knees and fired his slingshot. The stone hit the Huntsman on the shoulder of the raised arm. It did no real harm except that it spoiled the blow, and the Huntsman's fist struck the floor instead.

That hurt. He hissed in pain and kicked at Milo, missing only because Milo flung himself flat on his back, then twisted into a sideways roll as he fished out more stones. He came up to a kneeling position, fired two stones and hit the Huntsman both times. Once in the chest and once on the cheek.

Green and red blood flowed from the wound, and for some reason, the two colors would not blend, as if somehow the alien and human blood refused to accept that they flowed through the same veins.

Evangelyne came at the Huntsman again, nipping at his legs, trying to damage a tendon in order to drop him, but he kicked out and knocked her back.

Even so, the werewolf's attack drove him back into the other room. Milo raced forward and dove inside, finding himself in a chamber that was forty feet across and twice as high. The walls were lined with exotic machines that were much more sophisticated than anything Milo had so far seen. Central to the room was a device that was the size of a troop truck. It had a bucket-shaped body and a big glass dome to which all manner of pipes, wires, and hoses were attached. The glass was opaque with condensation, but a pale blue-white light emanated from inside. The smell in this room was incredibly bad; it was worse, if that was possible, than anything he'd smelled so far. Milo gagged as he stepped inside.

The Huntsman was fighting with Evangelyne near the glass-domed machine. Milo fired another stone and another and another; then he fished for one more and came up with his lucky black stone. He grinned. This one had always found its mark. Every single time.

He fitted it, aimed, fired.

The stone flew like a black blur toward the Huntsman's right eye.

And the mutant *caught it*.

He snatched it out of the air like it was a slow line drive by a weak batter. The Huntsman glanced at the stone, snorted, and tossed it away.

"You'll have to be a lot better than that, boy," said the Huntsman.

"Let me try," snapped Milo as he dug into his pouch again. His scrabbling fingers found nothing.

Not so much as a pebble.

"I'm out!" he yelled to Evangelyne, but she was already in motion. The wolf snarled as she leaped past Milo to try for the Huntsman's throat.

The powerful mutant stepped into the lunge and clamped his hand around Evangelyne's throat. The wolf yipped in pain and surprise and *hung* there, feet working, nails clawing at the creature's armored body.

The Huntsman pulled her close and studied her with great interest.

"I was right," he murmured as if speaking to himself. "A werewolf. An actual werewolf."

He laughed.

"Let her go," demanded Milo. "Don't hurt her."

"Hurt her? Now, why would I do something like that? This little pup is worth far more to me alive. She reeks of magic. I thought so when we fought at the bayou." He tapped Evangelyne on the snout with his stump. "It's worth even this to keep her alive for a long, long time."

Evangelyne slashed at him with her nails, trying to do enough damage to make him let her go. Milo dug his knife out of his pocket and flicked it open. It was a small utility lock-blade knife with a two-inch blade. It looked and felt pitifully small in his hand. Even so, he began circling the Huntsman, looking for an opening. The killer smiled and turned with Milo, keeping Evangelyne between them.

"How'd you do it? Stow away on my ship?"

Milo shrugged and didn't answer.

"Stowed away," said the Huntsman, nodding to himself. "You probably thought it was something brave. Why take the risk? You're from that camp we burned. Your people were squirrely and weak. A bunch of mice hiding from the big, bad cat."

He shook Evangelyne, making her yelp in pain. She kept clawing at him, at his clothes and weapons. A pistol tore loose from a shredded holster and clattered to the floor. The Huntsman didn't even bother to look at it. Other gear popped off, and he ignored it all.

"And this lot. The Nightsiders. Oh, don't look so surprised. I've known about the supernatural world since I was a boy. Why do you think I destroyed their shrine and took that stone? I've spent my life searching for proof that they existed. Now . . . now imagine how disappointed I am. We burned them, you know. Our ships found their covens and grottos, their caves and fens, and we *burned them*. That does it. Oh yes. Fire purifies."

He shook her again. She was getting weaker, though she kept trying to slash at him. Milo could tell that she wanted to slash open the pouch with the Heart of Darkness, but she was getting too weak. Her nails had ripped his gear to rags. For his part, the Huntsman didn't seem to care.

"Let her go!" begged Milo.

"No. Between you and me, boy, I expected the Nightsiders to be pretty fearsome. I wanted them to be, you know? Vampires and werewolves? I wanted them to be like gods. Instead . . . Ah well." He shook his head sadly. "But . . . even though they disappoint me, what they represent does not. You see, they *prove* that magic is real. Their very existence is my key to the secrets of countless centuries of magical knowledge. It is *my* pathway to becoming a *god*."

Chapter 63

Y ou're freaking nuts," said Milo, gripping his knife in his fist. "You know that?"

The smile on the Huntsman's face grew wider. "Oh, I know that very well. I know the scope and dimension of my madness. Just as I know that madness and genius are two sides of the same coin. Did *you* know *that*? Madness is not a weakness, boy. It is proof that a mind is too vast for the organic cage in which it is trapped. It is proof that the mind has unlocked a treasure trove of vast potential. So . . . yes, I know that I'm insane. I embrace it. And I will use that power and marry it to the infinite power of magic."

The knife seemed so tiny, so useless. He let his arm fall to his side, the knife hanging in slack fingers. Milo wanted to run away and hide from this. He'd glimpsed enough of this creature's memories to know that the Huntsman truly believed what he was saying. That's how deep his insanity went.

Miles and miles deep into the black well of his soul. To a place into which no light has ever shone.

"The black jewel is the key to my immortality," continued the Huntsman. "When the Swarm took me, I was already becoming something more than human. They thought they were making me into their weapon, but . . ." He paused to chuckle. "You've been in my head, boy, so I think we both know how that turned out. They shared their secrets with me, thinking that I would be another mindless part of the hive. If anyone ever needed proof as to why they've become a stagnant race, that's it. They made me into something that now they don't understand."

He looked intently at Milo.

"Do you know that before they merged with my mind, they had no true understanding of evil? It was only an abstract concept to them. They understand it now. And more than that, do you know that they have never once, not in their millions of years, experienced the emotion of fear? Amazing. Now . . . Oh, yes, Milo. They know what fear is."

He pulled Evangelyne so close that she could have bitten him if she wasn't drifting on the edge of unconsciousness.

"And they fear *me*!"

Milo saw his black stone on the floor. He began edging slowly toward it. If he could get off one more shot from this distance, maybe he could stun the monster. A shot to the eye, the temple . . .

"You see this machine?" said the Huntsman. "This is the heart of their ship. That's why I came here. This is a birthing processor. As the queens lay their eggs, they pass through this machine. Every single one of them. And as they do, they are exposed to something very special. Come look at it. No—leave that stone where it is, boy, and do as I say. Do it or I'll snap her neck right now."

Milo stopped moving toward the stone. He kept his knife, though, useless as it was.

"That's right, boy," said the Huntsman. "I'm actually glad you came here. It's fate. It's destiny. You, of all people, should witness this because you, of all people in the world, actually *know* me. You've been in my head and I've been in yours. You know what I am."

"N-no . . . ," said Milo.

"Yes. You know what I was, and you know what I've become. Now I want you to witness what I will be when my transformation is complete. Look into the chamber."

"I . . . don't want to."

The Huntsman shook Evangelyne again. "Do you *want* to be responsible for her death? Will you force me to punish her for your weakness?"

Milo felt tears burning in his eyes because he knew that he had no choice. They'd tried. And they'd failed. Of course they had. They were kids, and this was a monster who had an entire alien race behind him. Milo hated himself for his stupidity, for his weakness.

For believing that someone like him could ever become a hero.

It was ridiculous.

Defeated and small, he walked over to the machine. He had to stand on his toes to look in through the glass. The condensation clouded things, but up close he could see what was inside.

There were two conveyor belts that ran continually, both fed from pipes that ran from the floor and exited on the far side to other pipes in the ceiling. On each belt were eggs. Small, gray-green, and speckled. They were half the size of chicken eggs, but there were so many of them. The belts rolled on and on without pause. But Milo knew that wasn't what the Huntsman wanted him to see. Resting on a platform of solid gold was another, larger egg. This one was an inch and a half long, the size of a crow egg. It was not made of shell, though. This egg was made from the purest crystal, and a brilliant white light glowed from inside.

Milo gasped.

He recognized that egg.

He *knew* it.

He'd seen it in a dream. The Witch of the World had offered him a plateful of them.

"This is the heart of this whole ship, boy," said the Huntsman. "That egg contains the DNA of the queens, and it has a hundred thousand sequenced genomes stored in it. Every one of those eggs that pass by becomes imprinted with one of those codes. If the hive needs a thousand drones, then the crystal egg imprints a thousand eggs for exactly that. If they need a legion of shocktroopers, they can have them. The eggs are imprinted, and the troops are bred in birthing pens. Everything's there. Knowledge, training, the necessary skills. We can create any kind of army we want whenever we need it. All we need is the right molecular bulk materials. Minerals, water, and . . . oh yes, organic components. You don't think your friends from the camp were brought up here as slaves, do you? The Swarm doesn't use slaves. They *are* slaves, every one of them, bound to the will of the queen and the hive mind that is the combined brains of each queen on all seven ships. That's why you can't win, boy. That's why no one has ever beaten the Swarm. They don't conquer. They assimilate their enemies into the raw materials for the next wave of the Swarm."

The truth of it was so horrible that Milo staggered and fell to his knees.

"That's how the Swarm has dominated thousands of worlds," said the Huntsman. He pulled Evangelyne close and sniffed her. A long, deep lungful of her scent. "Can you smell that? The perfume of magic. She reeks of it. Imagine what will happen when I add her organic material to the mix. Imagine what will happen when I force her to give me the secrets of the black jewel so I can bond it to the crystal egg. Can you imagine it, boy? You must have seen the beauty of it in my mind."

"No . . . ," gasped Milo. "You can't do this."

The Huntsman gave Evangelyne a final shake, and she went slack in his hand. As she did so, her wolf form melted away to be replaced by a girl who hung as if dead.

The Huntsman dropped her unceremoniously to the deck.

"Trash," he said, dismissing her. He advanced on Milo and stood over him, ignoring the empty slingshot and the short-bladed knife. "But you, Milo Silk, you have promise."

Milo raised his head and looked up at him.

"W-what?"

"A god needs worshippers," said the Huntsman. "You have seen my majesty. You alone *know* what I will become. And, look . . . You are already on your knees. Worship me, *follow* me, and I will make you a prince of a new empire that will spread across time and space."

Milo turned his face away, unable to look at the monster.

"Boy," said the Huntsman, "don't forget that I've seen into your mind, into your heart. I know what you want."

Milo shook his head.

"Oh, yes, I do. You want your parents."

Milo shot him a nervous look.

"Your mother wasn't at the camp, was she?" asked the Huntsman, then answered his own question. "No. She might still be alive. With the resources of the Swarm, you could find her. You could keep her safe."

Milo didn't dare speak.

"And your father . . . You think he's dead. Or you think he's in some collection." The Huntsman snorted. "The Swarm doesn't *collect*, boy. The Swarm *uses*. If they took your father, it wasn't to keep him as a pet or hang him on a wall. No. He was probably taken by one of the science teams. He could still be alive. Do you know that? Do you believe it? Alive and waiting for you to come to him. To *rescue* him. Would you like to do that, Milo? Would you like to be the hero that rescues your father?" The Huntsman paused as if listening. "I can almost hear him singing. It's there inside your memories. Or . . . maybe I hear it for real. Out here, outside of dreams and memories. Or perhaps it's here in a hive ship. You never know, Milo. *I* don't know. Not yet. But if you join me, we could look for him together. And your mother. We could have a nice, happy family reunion."

His voice was oily and filled with mockery. But Milo also believed him. Believed that this insane offer was genuine.

Could the Huntsman find Dad? And Mom?

Doubt gnawed at him with hungry, hungry teeth.

His lucky stone was across the room, lying by the

door to the hall. It was achingly out of reach, sitting in a small pool of golden light. He looked at the knife he held. It was like bringing a peashooter to a fight with a tank.

"No one who's ever lived has been offered so much," continued the Huntsman. "Join me, and I'll even spare all your friends. What are their names? Shark? Yes. And Lizabeth? I remember them from when we shared one mind. I'll let you bring them with you. With us. I'm making this offer once. Now. Come with me. Be *like* me. Be *something*."

The Huntsman placed his hand on Milo's shoulder. Milo turned away and stared at the black stone. It was no longer bathed in light.

He frowned at that, trying to make sense of it.

"I know your secrets, Milo. You want to be a hero. That's noble. That's a goal. You should be proud of wanting that. You came here, to this ship, to fight the entire Swarm. To fight me. That says something. It shows you have grit. It shows you have something special. But there's no future in being a hero. Trust me. I had a chestful of medals. None of them made me a better man. None of them made me what I am now. A god waiting to be reborn."

The words hurt Milo. Tears rolled down Milo's cheeks. He looked away, not wanting to meet the creature's eyes. He saw the glass dome of the machine where the crystal egg did its endless job of building the Swarm's army. He saw the doorway that was too far away for him to run through. He saw the black stone, equally useless. He saw the slumped form of Evangelyne, her face bathed in light.

In a soft, golden light that seemed to come from nowhere. So strange.

So lovely in the midst of all this horror.

"All you have to do is drop that knife and stand with me," said the Huntsman. "That's it, Milo. Drop the knife. Show me that you are *with* me, and you'll be more powerful than any *hero* who ever lived."

Milo mumbled his answer. A broken whisper.

The Huntsman bent over him. "Speak up, boy. The powerful aren't afraid to be heard."

Milo raised his head and looked up into the face of the creature that was poised to conquer *everything*.

"Okay," he said.

The Huntsman smiled. "Get to your feet and speak to me like a man."

Milo struggled up. His body felt leaden and infinitely weary, but he slapped one sneakered foot against the deck and forced himself up.

"Now, say it again," said the Huntsman.

"Okay," repeated Milo.

"Okay—*what*? Come on, boy. This is a turning point in your life. Put some drama into it. Give it some importance."

Milo took a breath, coughed to clear his throat. Then

he looked up at the Huntsman. "Sure. You want drama, you big freak? How's this?"

He screamed as loud as he could, threw himself at the Huntsman, and stabbed the monster in the chest with the little knife.

Chapter 64

The blade punched through the stiff leather of a cross belt, hit the steel armor beneath, and snapped. The broken blade skittered sideways across the Huntsman's chest.

The Huntsman laughed and seized Milo with his powerful right hand. His fingers knotted in Milo's shirt and lifted the screaming, kicking, flailing boy into the air. Milo howled at him as loud as he could. He kicked him with both feet. He pounded on him with his fists.

With a bray of contemptuous mirth, the Huntsman flung Milo against the side of the birthing chamber. The resulting *carooom* bounced off the walls. Milo slumped down to his knees, his head filled with fireworks.

"Seriously, boy?" said the Huntsman. "Did you actually think you were going to sucker me with a toy knife? Did you actually think I'd let you this close if I thought you had any chance at all? How could you be inside my head and think I'm that stupid? Is that your idea of being a hero?"

Milo spat some blood onto the floor.

"No, you enormous whacko," he said. "I wasn't being a hero."

"Then what—?"

"He was being a distraction," said a voice.

The Huntsman spun around to see three figures behind him.

A teenager made of oak.

A sprite whose hair burned with soft golden light, sitting astride a hovering hummingbird.

And a pile of rocks in the shape of a boy.

"What—?" began the Huntsman.

"Mook," said Mook.

And he punched the Huntsman in the face with a fist made of twenty-two pounds of marble and iron ore.

Chapter 65

The Huntsman tried to evade it.

He tried to block it.

Instead he just got hit by it.

The punch smashed the Huntsman's jaw and sent him flying past Milo into the birthing chamber with such incredible force that the whole machine canted sideways. It hung there for a moment and then it fell. The glass dome exploded into a thousand gleaming fragments. Hundreds of eggs smashed onto the deck, and the conveyors kept running, kept sending more and more of them into the ruined chamber. The belts spat them out and they splatted to destruction. Milo had been leaning against the chamber, and as it fell, he dropped down into the mess. He was covered in green egg yolk dotted with glass and pieces of shell.

Instantly, an alarm began that shook the whole chamber. It was even louder and more insistent than the one that had signaled the birth of the new queen.

Halfflight flew immediately to Milo as Oakenayl hurried over to check on Evangelyne, who was stirring feebly.

"We need to hurry," called the oak boy. "This place will be swarming with Bugs any second. If he can't travel, then leave him."

The sprite hovered in front of Milo.

"Milo! You saw my light!" she said happily. "You gave us a chance to sneak in. That was so smart. That was so brave!"

"Brave? I don't think so." Milo spat alien egg out of his mouth. He sniffed away the last of his tears, grinned through the muck and the pain. "I guess if I can't be a hero, then being a nuisance is okay."

He jerked upright and immediately hurried past her to where the Huntsman lay. The monster was dazed and semiconscious, but alive. It amazed Milo that anyone could survive Mook's punch. It frightened him, also.

He fumbled at the pouch on the Huntsman's cross belt. Evangelyne had tried to tear it open but succeeded only in damaging it. Milo undid the snap, dug his fingers inside, and pulled out the stone.

The gleaming, multifaceted black diamond.

He heard Halflight gasp.

The Heart of Darkness.

It pulsed in his hand as if it were a real heart. He could feel its energy. Its power. He closed his eyes and held it to his chest.

He never understood why he did that.

It seemed to matter, though. Way deep down inside.

"Milo," murmured Evangelyne. He opened his eyes and saw her there, leaning on Oakenayl. Her throat was badly bruised and her legs wobbled. The oak boy, Mook, and Halflight looked at him, at the thing he held.

Milo opened his hand and stared deeply into the stone for a moment.

In that moment, he could understand why the Huntsman wanted it. Looking at it was like staring through a doorway into the entire universe. That kind of power was awesome to behold. To *hold.*

"That doesn't belong to you. Give that here," snapped Oakenayl, holding out his open hand. "Give it here and be quick about it."

"Mook," growled Mook, though it seemed to Milo that the stone boy's comment was directed at Oakenayl.

Milo ignored them both. He extended his hand to Evangelyne, fingers open, letting the golden glow from Halflight's fiery hair ignite tiny flames on each facet.

"I know this isn't mine," he said. "Here. This is yours."

Evangelyne hesitated as she reached for it, as if she wasn't sure even she should touch it. On the floor, the Huntsman groaned. She closed her fingers around the stone and did the same thing Milo had done—she pressed her fist to her chest over her heart.

The alarm kept blaring, and now there were sounds in the hall. Angry clicks and the scuttle of many feet.

"We're out of time," said Oakenayl.

"Then we fight our way out," said Evangelyne. She morphed into the wolf. Milo did not know where the stone went, but this was magic after all. If she had it, then it was safe.

"Mook!" said Mook as he clanked his fists together.

Milo turned to the little sprite. "Halflight, you know we'll never fight our way through the entire Bug army. Can you . . . ? I mean . . . is it possible?"

The sprite looked beyond weary. "A final glamour? Yes. I think I can do it."

He did not like the way she said "final."

"We have to try," he said. "I'm sorry."

Then he stopped and turned and looked at the fallen Huntsman.

"Wait . . . There's something else I have to do."

"We don't have time," insisted Evangelyne.

"You'll get us all killed," growled Oakenayl.

Milo ignored them as he approached the murderous monster who lay amid the debris of the conquering race.

Chapter 66

The shocktroopers burst through the door, pulse weapons ready, eyes blazing, pincers clicking, ready to kill.

They saw the overturned birthing chamber that still spewed eggs.

They saw a dead drone lying amid the debris.

They fanned out through the chamber, searching for the cause of this disaster.

They fell back to allow the Huntsman—tall and powerful—to brush past them with a small group of armed guards in his wake. Not one drone or 'trooper dared interfere with the Huntsman as he led his troops along the winding corridors, into the loading bay, and up the ramp into his crimson ship. None of this was irregular to their insect brains. The Huntsman went where he wanted to go.

The shocktroopers didn't even care about the destroyed birthing chamber.

Or the broken eggs.

Or even the conveyors that relentlessly dumped more unborn Bugs onto the ground.

No, their entire attention was locked onto a small golden pedestal that lay on its side.

Empty.

Seeing that, understanding what that meant, sent a ripple through them and then outward into the hive mind. Before encountering the man who would become the Huntsman, they had never experienced the emotion of fear.

Now they did.

And in that moment, staring at the empty golden pedestal, that fear blossomed hotter than the hottest flame. It was instantly shared by every drone and 'trooper, every subspecies, every queen—newborn or ancient—who dwelt in that massive hive ship. Forty million minds linked by a shared consciousness knew fear in that moment.

Great fear.

Fear so towering that it caused them all to throw back their heads and scream.

The crystal egg was gone.

Gone.

The heart of their ship.

The hope of their hive.

Gone.

They screamed and screamed and screamed.

Then the 'troopers closest to the birthing chamber saw something impossible happen. The drone who lay amid the debris groaned and sat up, shedding shell fragments and glass. It was a drone for only a moment longer, and then it wasn't.

It was the Huntsman.

The 'troopers turned toward the door where this same Huntsman had fled minutes ago. Then they turned back to this one. Bruised and bleeding, but irrefutably the Huntsman.

It was in that moment that for every Dissosterin, their fear transformed into another emotion. Another one that was new to them. An emotion planted like a seed in their shared consciousness by the evil mind of the Huntsman.

Hate.

Chapter 67

As the Huntsman's ship lifted off from the landing bay, the door remained open long enough for three small round green globes to come rolling out. They bounced onto the deck and wobbled to a stop in front of a knot of shocktroopers.

The shocktroopers had time to click a single warning to one another.

It was a second too late.

Sound and fury.

Chapter 68

The crimson ship dropped out of the clouds and kept descending until it was below the tree line, moving fast only a few feet above the rippling surface of Bayou Teche. Alligators watched it with their ancient eyes and seemed to grin with evil mouths.

The ship wobbled as it flew. It clipped a few trees. Twice it dipped too low and bounce-splashed atop the surface of the water. Then it corrected awkwardly, gradually straightened out, and finally came to rest beneath the shadows cast by a great canopy of oak trees. It stood on its eight metal legs, looking alien and ominous.

The engines whined for a moment and then died away into a ghostly silence.

After several long minutes, the hatch opened and the loading ramp stretched down to the marshy ground.

A figure emerged.

Skinny, short, disheveled, with clothes that were stained with blood and green goo. With him was a girl who had hair the color of ash and eyes the color of the moon. She had one hand clutched into a fist, and she kept it pressed against her heart.

Behind them came a fat brown boy who had his arm wrapped around the waist of a tall boy with wild hair that stuck up in all directions and a little blond girl with pale blue eyes. Others came down. Boys and girls. Older teens. And a few old people who leaned on one another.

"Milo!" called Shark, and the skinny boy and the fat boy gave each other a fierce hug. Like best friends do. Like brothers do. Lizabeth squirmed in between them, and then the Cajun joined them, not so much adding to the group hug as leaning on it.

"Dang, Milo . . . You is more dan *motier foux*, you," he mumbled. More than half crazy. There was a smile on his face and tears in his green eyes.

The last to emerge were two boys who stood at the top of the ramp. One made of wood, the other of stone. The huddled refugees stared up at them with glazed eyes, as if unsure if this was a dream.

A hummingbird stood on the oak boy's shoulder.

The rock boy held one hand out, palm upward, and in it was a tiny form who lay absolutely still. Milo Silk tore himself free from Shark and the others and ran back up the ramp, his heart leaping into his throat. He skidded to a stop and stood looking down at the sprite in the rock boy's hand.

"Oh no!" he cried.

"Mook," said the rock boy softly.

"Is she . . . ?" Milo's voice trailed off. He didn't want to finish that question.

Evangelyne bent and blew a kiss at the tiny form. "She used all of her magic," she said.

"All of it?" asked Milo, and there was a hitch in his voice.

Evangelyne looked up at him with eyes that were bright with tears. "Almost all. She's asleep."

"But . . . she's going to get better, right?"

The wolf girl placed the Heart of Darkness in Mook's palm and nudged it against the sprite. Halflight groaned softly and curled herself around it, hugging it as if it were the only thing that tethered her to life.

"There is still magic in the world," said Evangelyne. "Thanks to you, there is still magic in the world."

She kissed him on the cheek.

Milo wiped away his own tears. There was a rumble of thunder in the east. They looked up. There, partially hidden by the storm clouds, was the great bulk of the hive ship. It might be damaged. They might have stolen its crystal heart. They might have left it in confusion. But they had no illusions that it was no longer a threat. Maybe it would be a great threat. Time would tell.

Milo could feel the weight of the crystal egg in his pocket. Warm, alien, repellent.

He wondered if they should have killed the Huntsman while they had the chance. It would probably have been the smartest thing to do.

But Milo had not done it. He hadn't crossed that line.

The egg seemed to throb. Like an unspoken threat. Like a promise.

He looked away, and Shark and Lizabeth and Barnaby stared up at him like he was someone they didn't even know.

Maybe he wasn't.

Not anymore.

He touched Evangelyne's shoulder. "Come on," he said. "I want you meet my *other* friends."

She hesitated. "They've seen what I am. What we are. They won't want to—"

Milo turned to her. "They're orphans now too," he said. "We all are. This isn't about the Nightsiders and the children of the sun. C'mon, that's the old world." He removed the crystal egg from his pocket. "We just won the first major battle against the Bugs. We, Evangelyne. Not the Earth Alliance. Not the Nightsiders. We. Maybe it's time we stopped being scared of one another. This is our planet. *Ours.* All of ours. If we want it to survive, if we want us to survive, then we have to fight this war together."

Her eyes searched his for a long time. Then she took a deep breath and let it out slowly.

"Okay," she said. "Let's go meet your friends."

FROM MILO'S DREAM DIARY

Last night I dreamed I was sitting on the top of a
    mountain, which is funny because there aren't too
    many mountains in Louisiana. But it was a dream,
    and anything can happen in a dream.
In the dream I was watching a hive ship burn in the
    sky.
It was strange. I know I should have been happy to see
    it burn, but I wasn't.
It made me sad.
In the dream the Witch of the World came and sat
    down next to me. She was older than dirt. And I
    think that might actually be true.
She said that she was proud of me for what we did.
She said that it would help everyone to have the
    courage to fight back. The EA, the rogues, the
    Nightsiders. Everyone.
But she said that it came with a price. That's how she
    put it.

A price.

She said the crystal egg was more important than we
    thought. She said that the Bugs will do anything to
    get it back.

Anything.

The only thing we have going for us is that they can't
    just bomb us because they have to get it back
    undamaged.

That still leaves a lot they can do to us.

She said that the Huntsman would come after us. Not
    just for the crystal egg. He hungers for the Heart
    of Darkness.

Her word.

"Hungers."

She said, "He will burn the fields of the earth and
    topple mountains to find you and get back what
    you stole."

Harsh.

Scary, too, 'cause I know she's right.

Tomorrow we'll go back to looking for Mom and Aunt
    Jenny. And Killer. I hope they're all safe somewhere.
    I asked the witch about them, but she didn't answer.

Instead, the witch told me something else. Something
    that I hope was just dream stuff because it really
    scared me.

She said, "There are horrors more dreadful than the Huntsman, Milo Silk."

I asked her what she meant, but right about then I started to wake up.

I think I heard her say one last thing before I woke, and I don't know if it was an answer to my question or something else.

She said, "Your father lives."

That was it. I woke up.

AUTHOR'S NOTE
ON JOURNALS AND DREAM DIARIES

I began my first diary when I was in the second grade and kept writing one well into my thirties. I wrote in it nearly every day, and after a while the old diaries filled many feet of space on my bookshelves.

Writing in a diary is a great way of getting to know yourself, exploring different ideas, experimenting with different ways of thinking, and allowing your imagination to run wild. Imaginations—trust me—should always be encouraged to run wild.

Sometimes my diary entries were simple lists of things I did that day, or things to do, or things I wanted to put on a list. Favorite things. Least favorite things. Like that.

Other times my diary was me having a conversation with myself about the things that happened in my life. The death of my best friend when I was a kid. The first time I saw the ocean. The hurt I felt when I lost a friend after a bad argument. The happiness I experienced when I won my first martial arts trophy.

I also wrote a lot of ideas for stories in my diary. I

always wanted to be a writer, and sometimes the ideas I had as a kid have been given new life as a story now that I'm an adult. *The Orphan Army*, for example, came from a story idea I had when I was ten, called "The Shadow Boys." No idea is ever wasted. Every idea should be written down. Don't trust to memory. Keep a record. Even if you don't yet see the value in the idea, its day may come. Trust me.

But of all the things I wrote about, the most common entry was my attempt to recapture the previous night's dreams. I would record every detail of every dream I had. After a while I became better at recalling those details because the process of writing them down helped me remember more and more.

I learned a lot about myself from those dreams. I still do. Many of my dreams become the stuff of new short stories, comics, and novels.

Perhaps the most important thing I learned was the same thing that Milo discovered with his dream journal: When you have a nightmare and write it down, it loses its power to frighten you. When you frame it in words and lock it on the page, you've just succeeded in capturing and caging the things that scare you. Once caged, you can look at them, understand them, and over time discover that the more you understand something, the less frightening it is. And the more powerful you are.

TURN THE PAGE
FOR A SNEAK PEEK AT
VAULT OF SHADOWS

Milo Silk was trying very hard not to die, but the day was not cooperating.

It was that kind of day, in a week of days like that, and lately Milo seemed to have only those kinds of days and nothing else.

This one was a classic.

He ran through the thick foliage along the muddy banks of Bayou Sauvage, trying not to fall into the churning water, trying not to get eaten by alligators, and trying especially hard not to get shot by alien shocktroopers.

He wouldn't have bet a fried circuit board or a fused diode on his chances.

All around him the Louisiana swamplands seemed to be filled with lurching shadows, bizarre shapes, and the *clickety-click* sound of insect legs. Blue pulses of phased energy burned through the air all around him. One blast was so close that it set his hair on fire and he had to slap his head to put it out. It wasn't a big fire, but it was on his head, so it was big enough.

The stink of burned hair chased him through the swamp.

The hardest part, for Milo, was remembering that this was supposed to be an ambush.

Supposed to be.

It reminded him of an old saying his dad had said once when a bunch of things went wrong during a garage clean-out at their house: "When you're up to your armpits in alligators, it's easy to forget that you came here to drain the swamp."

Yeah. Milo hated that saying.

Because there were alligators all over the place.

And they wanted to kill him too.

This is the story of what happened when everything Milo tried to do went wrong.

And what happened after that.

"C'mon, c'mon, c'mon," muttered Milo as he ducked under the low arms of a dying pecan tree. He did it just in time, too, because less than a heartbeat later, another of the blue pulse blasts shot out of the dense shadows and blew the tree limb to splinters. Milo dove forward, rolled down a mossy slope, jammed his feet against the exposed roots of a bald cypress, came up running, and splashed through ankle-deep water until he reached a thick stand of slash pines. Then he squirmed into the tight cleft between two of the pines.

And froze.

Even though he was panting from the exertion, he forced his breath to go in and out of his mouth without noise. He tried very hard to become the bayou, to blend into it the way he'd been taught in survival classes.

To be one with the swamp. Or, as his backwoods Cajun pod leader, Barnaby Guidry, put it, "To be dere like you ain't dere, you."

To be there like you're not there.

Milo tried to not be there while he hid and watched the aliens come hunting.

When he saw them, his heart nearly turned to ice. Even though he'd seen them before, fought them, killed them, the fear was always there. He knew he'd been lucky—luckier than he had any right to expect, because fully trained adult soldiers couldn't beat the Dissosterin shocktroopers one-on-one. The alien invaders were seven feet tall and powerful, with armored insect bodies, heads like praying mantises', bulging red eyes, quivering antennae, and six limbs. Sometimes they stood on two legs so they could fire four pulse guns simultaneously; other times they scuttled on four legs faster than greyhounds and simply ran people down. They wore nearly impenetrable body armor and carried guns, grenades, knives, and shock rods.

As he watched, the wild sugarcane that choked the slope quivered and parted and a shocktrooper stepped cautiously out. A crystal had been implanted in the center of its chest and it pulsed a ghostly green. Every soldier, every hunter-killer, every creature belonging to the Swarm had an identical jewel, and these "lifelights" were tied to the actual life force of the Bugs and their mutant creations. Soldiers spent hours in camp working on their marksmanship, because if you blew out the lifelight, you killed a Bug.

The alien warrior made a soft chittering sound. Milo wasn't sure if it was talking to itself, communicating with other hunters via radio, or just making creepy noises. Whatever was going on, it skeeved him out.

The reeds crunched under its weight as it moved slowly

down the bank toward the edge of the muddy water. It bent low and peered at the clear print of a sneaker.

Milo's sneaker.

Then the shocktrooper turned in a half circle, scanning the bank to follow the natural path of whoever had made the print. Those multifaceted red eyes glared right at the copse of slash pines. The long, slender trunks of the trees offered little cover except down toward the ground, where they grew together in tight bunches. The canopy of needles interlaced with the ceiling of leaves from big live oaks and cast everything in near darkness. Only the shocktrooper, standing exposed on the bank, was visible to Milo, and he was certain he was invisible to it.

At least he hoped and prayed that he was.

The insect warrior gripped a gleaming pistol in one hand, and its segmented fingers held it rock-steady. The glowing blue focusing crystal on the end of the barrel was like an azure eye trying to penetrate the darkness.

Please, Milo thought, screaming the words inside his head. *Please, please, please.*

He was not begging the creature to go away.

He didn't want the shocktrooper to go away.

In fact, Milo needed him to be right where he was.

No, actually, he wanted him to be about five steps to the left. Closer to the water.

But the alien held his ground, clearly suspicious, searching for his elusive prey.

Finally Milo decided that the creature was not going

to move in the right direction and this plan was going to fail and end very badly for him. Like so many attempts before this.

So, to save his own life, Milo Silk stepped out from between the pines, raised his slingshot, and yelled at the alien.

"Yo! Roach-brain!"

He fired the slingshot in the same instant the shock-trooper spun to face him. The stone hit the creature on the side of the head, bounced high, and fell into the water without having made so much as a dent in the alien. Milo wished he had something to fire that could shatter the shielding around the lifelight. No stone would do that.

The shocktrooper instantly raised its pistol and rattled off a string of clicks and buzzes that Milo figured were probably very bad words in a language he was glad he didn't understand.

That's when three things happened in rapid succession.

The shocktrooper fired its pulse pistol, and the bolt seared past Milo's cheek and blew a six-inch burning hole through the trunk of one of the pine trees.

Milo dove for cover behind a fallen log.

And the thing in the water, disturbed by the noise, the movement, and the fall of Milo's stone, lunged up, jaws wide, and *attacked* the shocktrooper. It burst from the surface of the bayou like something tearing its way from a nightmare into the waking world. Massive, muscular, scaled, furious.

A bull alligator.

Old Chompy. Fierce and murderous and evil tempered.

Milo screamed and shimmied backward up the slope as nine hundred pounds of gator snapped his powerful jaws shut. Teeth like daggers crunched through the armor and shell as easily as Milo bit through a corn dog. And Old Chompy bit the Bug soldier clean in half.

It was a horrible sight, and even though this had been Milo's plan, it was gross and shocking and mind-numbing. The alien's chittering turned into a single piercing shriek of pain, and then dwindled to a gurgle as the fourteen-foot-long reptile dragged his unworldly meal down into the muddy depths.

Old Chompy was the undisputed terror of this part of the bayou. The ancient gator had dragged down wild pigs and even a ten-point buck unlucky enough to come to this section of the bank for a drink. Now he had claimed a fully armed and armored Dissosterin shocktrooper.

Milo stared in horror as green blood swirled around and around in the vortex of ripples. He saw the glow of the lifelight beneath the surface, but it quickly winked out and did not reappear. Milo knew it never would.

Old Chompy never gave back what he took.

A ball of tension that felt like a knot of hot barbed wire burst from his lungs and he sagged to the ground.

It was a terrible, stupid, insanely dangerous plan.

And it had worked.

THE ANSWERS TWINS NICK AND ERYN FIND COULD HAVE
REVERBERATIONS FAR BEYOND ONE FAMILY'S HAPPINESS . . .
TO THE FATE OF ALL HUMANITY.

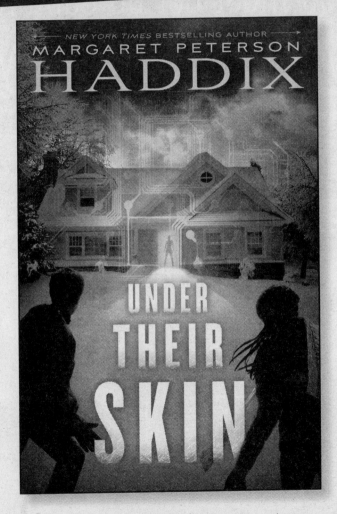

NEW YORK TIMES BESTSELLING AUTHOR

MARGARET PETERSON
HADDIX

UNDER
THEIR
SKIN

PRINT AND EBOOK EDITIONS AVAILABLE
FROM SIMON & SCHUSTER BOOKS FOR YOUNG READERS
SIMONANDSCHUSTER.COM/KIDS

For life on Earth to survive
you must not be captured
Everything depends on you
Prepare for earthfall.